DEEDS LEFT UNDONE

Also by Ellen Crosby

The Wine Country Mysteries

THE MERLOT MURDERS
THE CHARDONNAY CHARADE
THE BORDEAUX BETRAYAL
THE RIESLING RETRIBUTION
THE VIOGNIER VENDETTA
THE SAUVIGNON SECRET
THE CHAMPAGNE CONSPIRACY
THE VINEYARD VICTIMS
HARVEST OF SECRETS
THE ANGELS' SHARE
THE FRENCH PARADOX *
BITTER ROOTS *

The Sophie Medina Mysteries

MULTIPLE EXPOSURE *
GHOST IMAGE *
BLOW UP *
DODGE AND BURN *

Other Titles

MOSCOW NIGHTS

* *available from Severn House*

DEEDS LEFT UNDONE

Ellen Crosby

Severn
House

First world edition published in Great Britain and the USA in 2025
by Severn House, an imprint of Canongate Books Ltd,
14 High Street, Edinburgh EH1 1TE.

severnhouse.com

Cover and jacket design by Nick May at bluegecko22.com

British Library Cataloguing-in-Publication Data
A CIP catalogue record for this title is available from the British Library.

ISBN-13: 978-1-4483-1161-3 (cased)
ISBN-13: 978-1-4483-1162-0 (e-book)

All Severn House titles are printed on acid-free paper.

MIX
Paper | Supporting
responsible forestry
FSC
www.fsc.org   **FSC® C013056**

Typeset by Palimpsest Book Production Ltd.,
Falkirk, Stirlingshire, Scotland.
Printed and bound in Great Britain by
TJ Books, Padstow, Cornwall.

The manufacturer's authorised representative in the EU for product
safety is Authorised Rep Compliance Ltd, 71 Lower Baggot Street, Dublin D02
P593 Ireland (arccompliance.com)

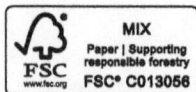

Praise for the Wine Country Mysteries

"The fully developed characters and the vividly depicted
vineyards and Virginia countryside make this
one hard to put down"
Publishers Weekly on *Bitter Roots*

"Character-driven . . . A good mystery"
Kirkus Reviews on *Bitter Roots*

"A treat"
Booklist on *Bitter Roots*

"Intriguing . . . Well-researched historical details bolster
the complex plot"
Publishers Weekly on *The French Paradox*

"This entry in the long-running cozy series, with its
sympathetic main character, will please fans"
Booklist on *The French Paradox*

"Imagined revelations about Jacqueline Kennedy's early
life provide a brilliant background for a tale of treachery
and deceit"
Kirkus Reviews on *The French Paradox*

About the author

Ellen Crosby is the author of the Mary Higgins Clark Award-nominated Wine Country mysteries, the Sophie Medina mysteries, and *Moscow Nights,* a standalone. Previously she was a freelance feature writer for *The Washington Post*, Moscow correspondent for ABC News Radio, and an economist at the US Senate. She lives in Virginia.

www.ellencrosby.com

For Dick and Phyllis Hermann,
Friends extraordinaire during the hardest year.

'The bitterest tears shed over graves are for words left unsaid and deeds left undone.'

— Harriet Beecher Stowe

'Grief is the price we pay for love.'

— Queen Elizabeth II
(Originally attributed to Dr Colin Murray Parkes, British psychiatrist and author of *Bereavement: Studies of Grief in Adult Life*)

ONE

I had begun calling it 'The Summer of MacGyvering' after the guy on the eponymous cult television show who could disable a missile with a paper clip, make tear gas out of kitchen spices and vinegar, or put together a defibrillator out of candlesticks, a rubber mat, and a microphone cord. Once he'd even used rosary beads to help launch a catapult.

For the last few months, almost every piece of equipment we relied on during the frantic, fraught months of harvest seemed to break or required parts that were unavailable or back-ordered for weeks since everyone who owned a vineyard apparently needed that same damn part. We got clever – because what are you going to do, right? – jerry-rigging whatever it was, putting it back together until it worked, just as MacGyver would have done. Duct tape, hair scrunchies, paper clips, playing cards, Q-tips, matches, an eyeliner pencil, and once, gummy bears, but the less said about them the better.

So when Antonio showed up in my office while I was doing paperwork and said, 'Lucie, I'm sorry, but . . .' I held up my hand because I did not want him to finish his sentence.

Anyway, he didn't need to. The look on his face said enough. Either it was going to be 'the pump is broken' or 'the chiller conked out again' or 'the destemmer just *stopped.*'

He threw me a look with enough reproach to make me feel guilty for snapping at him, even though all of us had been irritable and on edge these last few months.

'I'm sorry. I shouldn't have cut you off. What is it?' I stopped before I said *this time* but he was as weary of the relentless problems as I was.

Besides, Antonio takes these things personally, as if it's his fault because he's the vineyard manager at Montgomery Estate Vineyard and believes he's responsible for making everything run like clockwork even though he knows better. We may grow grapes and make wine, but the bottom line is that we're also farmers living at the whim and mercy of Mother Nature, who can be kind or churlish in the flash of an instant. And now that climate change has become part of our daily lives, she can also be moody and unpredictable in the 'never-have-I-ever' way. Antonio believes the least he can do is make sure the equipment – which he figures he *can* control – is working.

He shot me an unhappy look. 'It's not what you're thinking. It's not the equipment.'

'Then, what . . .?' The question died in my throat. Not what: *Who*. 'Antonio, is it one of the crew? Please, *no*,' I said as he nodded.

Our worst nightmare. What we did could be dangerous, though you might not think so because, after all, we make wine. But the process involves using equipment with long, lethal-looking blades and swiftly whirling parts, pruning knives so sharp they could slice off your finger in the blink of an eye, floors that could be slick and wet, rooms that could quickly fill with enough carbon monoxide to knock you unconscious if you weren't careful – or even kill you if no one found you fast enough. There are more accidents at vineyards – including a lot of fatalities – than any of us would like our clients to know about. Because, frankly, a lot of people figure what we do all day is toddle up and down rows of grape-laden vines, glass of crisp Chardonnay or an exceptional Cabernet Sauvignon in hand, beaming with pride as we admire God's handiwork. Let me tell you, it's *nothing* like that. That worn-out old joke about how to make a small fortune when you own your own business?

Especially true if it happens to be a vineyard: start with a large one.

Plus, the work is hard manual labor. During harvest the hours are insane.

'Who is it? What happened?' I asked.

The look on his face. This wasn't going to be good. Someone didn't just need stitches after nicking a finger on the blade of a pair of secateurs.

'It's Benny and I'm sorry, it's bad. He slipped on the crush pad and went down hard on his right knee,' he said. 'He can't walk at all – he collapses if he tries. Jesús practically had to carry him to his car. Nelia is driving him to the ER at Lansdowne

Hospital. He wouldn't let me call an ambulance, which is what we should have done, but you know Benny.' He touched his fingers to his forehead. 'Cabeza de vaca.'

Bull-headed. That was Benny, all right. He was also Antonio's loyal second and if he was out of commission because he couldn't walk, we were in trouble. Especially now when it was the beginning of October and harvest could stretch into the end of the month and even to the beginning of November, depending on how fast we worked. Not to mention the weather – which, up until now, had been practically a continuation of summer.

'Is Quinn still helping Toby?' Antonio asked.

After almost twenty years in the US, when he'd literally walked across the Mexican border into Texas at the age of twelve, Antonio's English was fluent. However, every time he pronounced Quinn's name it sounded like he was talking about royalty: *Queen*. Quinn Santori, winemaker at Montgomery Estate Vineyard, and, as of a few months ago, my husband. He'd gone over to help Toby Levine, our next-door neighbor, former Secretary of State, and owner of La Vigne Vineyard, with a tank of Merlot that had suddenly stopped fermenting, meaning it could potentially end up as very expensive vinegar. It's called 'stuck fermenting' and it's as bad as it sounds.

'He is,' I said. 'He's been gone a while.'

Antonio's dark brown eyes met mine, both of us in agreement. Quinn didn't know about Benny and the bad news could wait until he got back from helping Toby with his problem. No sense piling it on.

I stood up and reached for the cane I use after a nearly fatal car accident a dozen years ago almost ended my chances of ever walking again. Hopefully whatever had happened to Benny, he would recover and be back on his feet, no cane needed. Back to his old self.

'I should go to the hospital,' I said, even though it was the last place in the world I wanted to be. I'd been in too many emergency rooms, operating rooms, *hospital* rooms because of that accident, each visit seared into my brain like I'd been branded.

'Don't go, Lucita.' Antonio shook his head, a reprieve. 'Nelia said she'd call when they know something. He'll just be more upset if you show up. He was pretty mad that he fell, a stupid accident. Especially because he's the one who hosed down the floor.'

'OK, but you will let me know the minute you hear something?'

'Claro. Of course.' He hooked a thumb over his shoulder. 'I need to go. I want to check the pH and the Brix on the Cab Sauv again. I told Quinn this morning that we should pick the day after tomorrow at the latest. With that storm coming up from North Carolina, better a day too early than waterlogged grapes.'

Underripe and a bit green or waterlogged with the taste washed out? Decisions, decisions. Quinn and I referred to it as the Goldilocks Syndrome: would the grapes be overripe and spoiled, underripe and green, or – please God – just right if we rolled the dice and decided to wait a bit longer? Technically the decision when to pick is supposed to be based on science and math – a lot of math – but the reality is that it's basically a crapshoot. Cross your fingers and hope you called it right, mostly on account of the weather.

Too bad what we were picking wasn't Cabernet Franc. Those grapes were bulletproof. The rain wouldn't do them any damage. Cabernet Sauvignon, on the other hand, the noblest of the noble grapes, could throw a full-blown tantrum if things didn't go the right way. Too much rain and the skins would burst.

I spun the pen I'd been writing with around on my desk like the spinner on a roulette wheel. 'The last I heard, they weren't sure about the trajectory of that storm,' I said. 'If it goes out to sea we could wait.'

They, as in the National Weather Service, could also get it comprehensively wrong either way. Quinn always marveled that being a meteorologist was one of the few careers where you could be mistaken again and again and not get fired.

Antonio shrugged. 'Your guess is as good as mine. Probably better than the weather guys.'

We smiled at the little joke, but without our hearts in it, and he left. I went back to the work I'd been doing before he showed up – ordering fermentation supplies and chemicals for the vineyard, which always gives me a headache – and tried not to think about losing Benny for the rest of the season.

Twenty minutes later, I gave up and threw down my pen. How were we going to replace him? This late in the year it was nearly impossible to find someone new and bring them in. Everyone had already been spoken for months ago. We had a good crew that we kept on year-round, all of whom were related to each other, a sort of Mexican mafia. Either they had a connection to Antonio or his wife, Valeria. But unless someone could conjure up another cousin or an uncle we'd never heard of who might be looking for work, we were stranded.

I left the cool dampness of the office I shared with Quinn in the barrel room, the place where we made and stored wine, and stepped outside into the boiling cauldron of an unusually hot early October day.

When I walked into our tasting room five minutes later, Francesca Merchant, who ran the day-to-day operation of the winery – the business of selling our wine – was slotting wine glasses into overhead racks.

'We have staff to do that,' I said. 'You're the boss. What are you doing here?'

She flicked a quick glance at me and said, 'It needed doing, so I'm doing it.'

A lie.

Something was on her mind, and I didn't think it was Benny's accident. In fact I didn't think she even knew about Benny's accident, which is why I'd come to talk to her. See if we could maybe persuade one or two of the graduate oenology students from Northern Virginia University to help with picking grapes while Benny was out of commission. A couple of them poured wine here from time to time, especially during our busy season – and right now with Virginia's glorious autumn weather and harvest going on, we were busy. Frankie would know whom to ask.

'Hey,' I said. 'Come on, it's me. What is it?'

She'd begun working for us three years ago, starting on weekends as a sort of hobby after her two kids left for college and there were no more cookies to bake for chorale trip fundraisers, football game rallies to support, costumes to sew for school plays, or PTA committees to chair. It had taken one weekend of alphabetizing her spices and dusting her husband's power tools in the garage to realize she was bored out of her mind. After two weeks of working in the tasting room she'd quietly rearranged the place and suddenly everything ran so much more smoothly. I asked her then and there if she'd consider working full-time running the retail side of the business, even though I couldn't come close to matching her salary with the high-powered D.C. environmental law firm where she was a lobbyist. I did throw in that she was welcome to take home all the wine she and Paul wanted to drink. To my surprise, she said yes.

I pointed to the wine glass she'd just been polishing with a small towel. 'That glass is clean.'

She set the glass down and put the towel on the bar, folding it until the edges were perfectly aligned. 'OK,' she said, 'you're right. It's Paul. He had a meeting in Washington this afternoon with Nash Blake. *Another* meeting. He called me on the way home. He sounded upset. It didn't go well.'

Nash Blake was the CEO of Blake Construction, the umbrella corporation of a family-owned business that had a number of offshoots like Blake Design-Build, Blake Land Development, Blake Consultants, and a few others that I'm forgetting. The Blake family catered to clients throughout the country – and on two continents – who had a net worth of hundreds of millions of dollars, many in the billions. Nash was also a neighbor who lived on a gated two-hundred-acre estate in a mansion known as Connemara, named for their family's ancestral home in Ireland. It had been built in the late 1800s and was still remembered for the legendary over-the-top parties Nash's parents and grandparents used to throw – the most notorious being during Prohibition.

'Let me guess,' I said. 'Nash and Paul were meeting about paving the roads.'

She nodded.

'What happened?' I asked.

It's one of the political hot-button topics out here in Loudoun County, Virginia. In fact, it's so white-hot that touching it could give you a third-degree burn. Developers like Nash Blake insisting it was high time the dirt roads that wound through parts of the county were finally paved, no matter that they'd been this way since Loudoun was established in 1757. Sure, gravel and dirt roads were better for the horses, and, yes, our idyllic little enclave attracted tourists and cyclists, but unpaved roads weren't good for cars and they were the future.

Newcomers and even a few old-timers complained about rutted, bumpy tracks that could break an axle, flatten a tire, make a trip to the car wash a regular necessity, and, in heavy rain, wash out the roads so they became impassable. The Pro-Loudoun Progressives, as they called themselves – Nash Blake was their leader – claimed that preserving the unpaved roads was impractical, choking development and stalling progress.

Paul Merchant came down hard on the other side, heading the Don't Pave Paradise Coalition and claiming – justifiably – that suburban Washington was creeping further and further west into Virginia. Commuter traffic clogged highways, including Route 50, formerly known out here as Mosby's Highway for a famed local Confederate general, but now called Little River Turnpike as part of Virginia's collective purge of places named for Civil War heroes. The daily grind of bumper-to-bumper traffic had earned Washington, D.C. the sorry distinction of having the second-worst commute in the country after Los Angeles. The frenetically paced development of D.C. was rushing headlong into our picturesque rural enclave which had been defined by horses and farmland since colonial days.

Even though I am a business owner, I sided with Paul. So did Quinn. My family had lived on our land for over two hundred years, so for me it was a matter of preserving what was so beautiful about this region. Besides, every time I drove into Washington some new parcel of pristine land had suddenly sprouted signs touting future construction, the number of houses that would be built with price tags in the lofty hundreds of thousands, or even one or two million. They'd also pick some clever name for the new development that made you wonder if there really was a forest of old English oaks hiding on that land, or they'd pick horsey street names like Seabiscuit or

Affirmed since this was also horse and hunt country. That really ticked off horse farm owners and anyone who rode horses because, if you knew what you were talking about, you'd know this was steeplechase territory. Seabiscuit, Affirmed, and the others raced on flats. Either way, it was starting to seem inevitable that it wouldn't be long before bulldozers and earth movers would be creeping onto our doorstep, ready to start excavating our hard-packed Virginia clay soil until the rust-colored ground looked like so many bloody wounds.

Where did it stop?

The pave-versus-don't-pave debate had also brought together a web of unlikely alliances among people who normally didn't see eye to eye. The conservationists and the fox-hunting community, for example, who agreed on almost nothing else.

But the bitterness and anger were tearing friends and neighbors apart and it was heartbreaking.

'Paul met Nash in his office in town,' Frankie said to me now. 'He went alone, thinking it was just going to be the two of them. That they could sit down and have a talk about where this was going, a friendly chat. Maybe not cordial, but at least civil. I mean, they've played golf together in the past.'

'And?'

She fiddled with the edges of the towel again, an unhappy look on her face. Unusual for Frankie, who was always so calm and serene. The person everyone hoped would pour their glass of wine when they came to Montgomery Estate Vineyard because Frankie would always listen to whatever you had to say without judgment or criticism as you unburdened your heart or spilled out your problems. The joke among the staff was that she heard more confessions than the priests at St Michael the Archangel Church on Saturday mornings.

'Paul said Nash showed up with a lawyer and two beefy guys who looked like security or else extras from the set of *The Godfather*. He said he's sure Nash brought them to intimidate him.'

'How awful. What happened?'

She shrugged. 'He told Nash and the lawyer that he had no intention of backing down. Lucie, Nash had found out that Paul took over Violet Rossi's plan to map the unpaved roads around here and get them listed on the National Register of Historic Places. Paul said he was livid.'

It was a unique and unconventional solution – and incredibly creative. But in order to get the imprimatur so that the roads could be listed as historic sites – and therefore harder to pave – the Don't Pave Paradise Coalition needed to prove they *were* of historic interest. Six weeks ago Violet Rossi, who had been the architect of that idea, had been killed in a car accident – ironically on an unpaved road – and that had temporarily brought the project to a halt until Paul stepped in.

Loudoun County had one of the largest networks of unpaved roads in Virginia – which was surprising for a region that was only fifty miles from Washington, D.C. The earliest roads followed trails that had been laid out by Native Americans. A young George Washington traversed others as a surveyor. Still others were trade routes during colonial times, bringing grain from local mills to newly established ports like Georgetown and Alexandria on the Potomac River, and even as far away as Baltimore. Over the next two hundred years Quakers, Germans, and descendants of British colonists laid the foundations for a network of roads until it resembled a giant spiderweb – and these roads had history. Some had been the site of Civil War clashes between Union and Confederate armies. Slaves had built the low stacked-stone walls that lined many of them. And then there were the 'witness trees' – old oaks and other ancient trees that had provided shade for centuries, maybe even as long as the country had existed.

With such a big project, and one that needed to be done with some speed, especially after Violet's accident, Paul had taken over and quietly began asking for help. Quinn and I said we were in. My older brother Eli, who was an architect, promised to draw all the maps pro bono. My half-brother, David Phelps, who was a professional photographer, agreed to take all the photos that were needed, also pro bono.

'Nash and his musclemen – or whoever they were – can't stop Paul from mapping the roads. Or Quinn, Eli, David, and me and the others who have volunteered to help. It's a free country,' I said.

'I hope he can't,' she said, throwing me a worried look.

'What do you mean?'

'Nash's lawyer said they *would* stop him. Paul said the guy was stabbing his finger into his chest, as if he meant they were going to physically stop him.'

'What are they going to do? Slash his tires so he can't drive? That seems beneath someone like Nash Blake. The Blakes throw money around, not people. Make some backroom deal with whichever person or persons whose palms need greasing so they get what they want.'

She arched an eyebrow, still unconvinced. 'I hope you're right.'

'Look, go home and see Paul. Have a drink and talk it out with him. He has a lot of committed, determined people on his side. I think the Don't Pave Paradise Coalition has a good chance of getting the roads listed on the Register of Historic Places and it will be thanks to him. And Violet, of course.'

She glanced at her watch. 'It's only five. I've got a few more things to finish up here . . .'

'That can wait.' I waved her off. 'Family first. Go home to your husband.'

'Are you sure?'

'It's an order. I own the place.'

She cocked her head. 'All right, but when you came in here you looked like you had something on your mind. Now it's your turn. What is it?'

She was going to find out anyway. And she'd be furious that I hadn't told her.

'Benny fell in the barrel room and did something to his knee. Nelia took him to the ER at Lansdowne. It might be bad. I thought I'd stop by and see if you had any names of oenology students at NVU who we might be able to persuade to pick grapes while he's out of commission. Plus we've temporarily lost Nelia while she's taking care of Benny, so we're down two people.'

You really don't want to have inexperienced people picking your grapes because they're more trouble than they're worth. To begin with, they don't know what they're doing and the first thing they do is nick a finger with their secateurs and then it's a whole drama and a lot of blood. Oenology students, at least, would know not to cut the green or overripe grapes along with the good ones. They might be slow, but they'd know what to do.

'Benny?' Frankie sounded stunned. 'Oh my God, I hope he's OK. Maybe I should stop by the hospital on my way home.'

'Antonio told me I shouldn't go by because Nelia's taking care of everything. So, same for you. He said Benny would have a fit if any of us saw him in the ER. You know that macho pride of his.'

She nodded, giving in. 'OK, fair enough. And I do have a list of oenology students who might be interested in picking grapes, though they're in the middle of midterms right now, so I don't know if anyone's going to be available. Anyway, the list is in my office. I'll be right back.'

She was halfway across the room when her phone rang. She'd left it on the bar. I flipped it around and looked at the display.

'It says "Sonny",' I called to her.

Over her shoulder she replied, 'The pool guy. We're having some trouble with the automatic cleaner. I wonder why he's calling me if Paul's there.'

'Should I take it?'

'Yes, please.'

I answered the call and before I could say anything, a garbled torrent of English and Spanish spilled out. All I could make out was Señor Paul.

And muerto.

Dead.

TWO

'Wait. Slow down. *Please.*' I held up my palm as if he could see the gesture. 'Did you say Señor Paul . . . is *dead*? Are you sure?'

Frankie spun around, sprinting across the room, the look on her face alternating between shock and disbelief. Probably mirroring what was on mine.

'Yes, yes. I found him,' he said. 'Estaba en el fondo de la piscina. In the swimming pool. On the . . . floor.' His words kept tumbling out, still a jumble of two languages. 'I'm sure.'

At the bottom of the pool. *Drowned.*

Frankie reached my side and I gave her the phone. 'Sonny says he found Paul at the bottom of the pool,' I told her.

'I heard, I heard. Oh my God.' She clutched the phone to her chest with both hands as if she needed a moment to gather herself and then put it to her ear. 'Sonny, it's Frankie. Did you call 911? Did you get help? Is there anyone there with you?'

She listened for a moment, then looked at me and shook her head. 'Never mind. It's OK. I'll call – no, they *have* to come, the Sheriff's Office, too. Don't worry, you're not in trouble. Where is Paul? You're sure he's . . .?' Another pause. 'OK, just stay with him. Please, Sonny. Don't leave. I'll be right there.'

She disconnected and looked around the room, her eyes wild and confused. 'Sonny dove in and managed to get him onto the deck. I have to go to him . . . I have to go now. My purse. My keys. Where are they?'

I laid my hand on her arm. 'Probably in your office where you always keep them. Get your things while I call 911 and then I'll drive you home. You're not in any shape to get behind the wheel of a car.'

She nodded, the motion jerky and rigid, looking at me as if I were speaking in tongues. She didn't move and I gave her a gentle shove. 'Frankie. Your car keys. Go. You're faster than I am, so you get them. I'll meet you at your car.'

She left as I hit the red emergency button on my phone. By the time she came outside, I was standing next to her dark blue Audi sedan having just finished a brief, terse conversation with a dispatcher from 911 who didn't understand why I wasn't anywhere near the scene of the accident I was reporting and therefore couldn't absolutely guarantee the veracity of what I'd told her. But something in my voice must have persuaded her this wasn't a prank call because after a moment she promised someone would be on the way and I breathed a sigh of relief. I was texting Quinn and telling him to meet us at the Merchants' house – that it was urgent and he needed to hurry – as Frankie hit the unlock door button with her remote and we got in the car.

What happened? Quinn wrote back.

Pool guy found Paul Merchant at the bottom of his pool. 911 on the way.

A long pause and then three dancing dots. OMG.

I was lucky I didn't get pulled over for speeding on the trip to Frankie's house, which was just outside the village of Middleburg. Frankie, sitting next to me, her eyes now glassy with shock, repeating, 'I don't believe this . . . he's a good swimmer, a strong swimmer . . . something must have happened . . . a stroke or a heart attack? Except his heart is fine. *Was* fine.'

'We'll find out when we get there.' I wanted to reassure her, but whatever had happened, it didn't change the awful immutable reality of the news Sonny had just given her. 'We're almost at your house.'

The white Loudoun County Sheriff's Office cruiser with the tan and gold stripes and the Sheriff's Office badge stenciled on the door was already speeding up the Merchants' long dirt and gravel driveway when we turned onto it from Zulla Road. Before I'd even stopped to park behind the cruiser, Frankie opened the passenger door and jumped out, shouting directions at two deputies who had gotten out of their car.

'The swimming pool, in back. He's there.' She pointed to the house and took off running, following them, as if she still wasn't convinced and that maybe there was a chance – maybe Paul had somehow survived, and Sonny had been mistaken that he was dead, lying there on the bottom of the swimming pool.

I reached for my cane and climbed out of her car. Once upon a time I ran cross country in high school and college, and I was *good*. I won medals, almost made state champion my senior year of high school, got a full ride to undergrad school on an athletic scholarship. Now because of a limp and a deformed right foot, my running days are over. My inability to run or even sprint and the fear of being at the mercy of whatever emergency or crisis could befall me that I wouldn't be able to escape – a pursuer, a violent storm, a swiftly spreading fire, a spray of bullets – terrifies me and occasionally gives me nightmares.

At times like this, however, it just frustrates the hell out of me.

A fire truck and an ambulance going full lights and sirens screamed up the driveway and pulled up behind Frankie's car, the occupants scrambling out with their gear. One of them, a tall, good-looking guy with curly black hair and caramel skin, said to me, 'The 911 caller said a homeowner was found at the bottom of the swimming pool?'

'I was the caller,' I said. 'Yes. They're around back.'

Ten seconds later I was the only one standing there.

Quinn caught up with me as I reached the backyard and the eight-foot security fence that surrounded the pool and kept the deer out of the garden. Someone had propped the wrought-iron gate open, so we had a view of Frankie and two paramedics kneeling over Paul's body. They looked as if they were framed in a photograph or we were watching a movie without a soundtrack, even though what was happening was perfectly, devastatingly clear. One of the paramedics laid a hand on Frankie's shoulder, gentle and unhurried, any sense of urgency gone. She looked up at him, her face blotchy and tear-stained, then covered her eyes with her hands as her shoulders began to shake. I looked away, feeling like a voyeur who had accidentally stumbled on an intensely personal moment of the rawest grief. She and Paul had been college sweethearts, married even before they graduated and were oh, so young – happy and joyous. Thirty-five years later they were still crazy about each other. Still madly, passionately *in love*. Now he was gone. My heart ached for her until I thought it would split open.

Next to me I felt Quinn go tense. Frankie, always so calm and stoic, the one who held everything together for the rest of us, regardless of how bad or awful the situation, was falling apart and unraveling before our eyes. The world must be coming to an end.

'Damn,' he said, his voice harsh and low. 'How did this happen? Paul's an athlete. A runner. A strong swimmer.'

'I don't know. I should go to her.'

'Go ahead,' he said. 'I'll see if I can talk to the two deputies who are questioning her pool guy, offer to translate. I bet he'd rather answer questions in Spanish so he knows *exactly* what he's saying.'

'His name is Sonny.'

'Well, Sonny looks like he's scared out of his mind right now.'

Of course he did, and Quinn, who was bilingual thanks to a Spanish mother, could hopefully talk Sonny off a ledge, calm him down enough to realize he wasn't considered a suspect in a homicide – it appeared to be an accidental death, after all – and that it was OK to answer questions. Sonny's body language was all too familiar; I'd seen it with our guys who didn't have their Green Cards yet. They never wanted to be pulled over and stopped, much less questioned by anyone in law enforcement since one thing could lead to another and then another. Next thing you knew you could be on a bus with a one-way ticket back to some hellhole country where people wanted to kill you as soon as you set foot on your home soil.

I reached Frankie and the paramedic who had his arm around her. He looked up at me. 'You family?'

'I am.'

As good as.

He got up and I took his place, kneeling beside her. Someone had covered Paul with a beach towel featuring a cat with outstretched paws surfing on the huge curl of a massive wave. Already Paul's face – which was all that was visible, thank God – had the pale, waxy look of death as if his skin had receded into his bones.

'What can I do?' I asked Frankie.

She shook her head, confused and distraught. 'I don't know

what happened. He was going swimming after he got home, but he's still fully dressed. He couldn't have just fallen in the pool . . . that's not possible.' She looked up at the paramedic who had given me his place. Then she turned back to me and said, as though she still couldn't believe it, 'He says they have to take him away, but they'll wait until I'm ready.'

I tightened my arm around her shoulder. 'They need to find out what happened, sweetie. You know that. Win Turnbull will do the examination, he's the medical examiner. He'll tell you everything and he'll find out exactly what happened. You *know* that. He's good.'

Dr Winston Churchill Turnbull was a local doctor who also acted as a medical examiner. And he was a good friend. After he retired from his medical practice a number of years ago, he volunteered to serve overseas working in military hospitals in war zones – what he called his 'Peace Corps work.' Eventually he'd seen enough limbless children, maimed and wounded women, and dead, mutilated bodies that he decided to return home to Virginia where he thought his experience could be put to better use. He would tell Frankie what had happened to Paul. He would sit down with her, hold her hands in his, and look her in the eye.

Frankie nodded, swiping at her eyes with the palms of her hands. 'I know,' she said. 'You're right.'

'Can they take him now?' My voice, gentle. 'Or do you need more time?'

She seemed to steel herself. 'It's OK. I'm ready.'

I helped her stand up and nodded to the paramedics, who brought over what looked like a stretcher with a body bag covering it. They knelt in unison and set the stretcher alongside Paul, removing a black shroud from inside the body bag. Quietly and respectfully, they covered him – including his face, which made Frankie gasp. I tightened my arm around her shoulder again as they removed the beach towel, which one of them placed on a nearby lounge chair. More quiet, whispered words between them and then they transferred the body bag onto a gurney in one quick, smooth move, after which they performed a sleight-of-hand trick until the gurney rose to waist height so they could wheel Paul's body to the waiting ambulance.

I kept my arm firmly around Frankie's shoulder as we walked – slowly because of my cane and my limp – following the gurney to the ambulance. More whispered words from the two EMTs before they did a synchronized well-rehearsed maneuver, sliding the body bag from the gurney onto a small platform inside the ambulance.

One of them climbed in with Paul and the other slammed the doors, the noise reverberating in the thick, heavy silence like a gunshot, startling Frankie, Quinn, and me so that each of us flinched. A small sob escaped Frankie's lips but she quickly swallowed it. The other vehicles had already gone, including the pool company truck, so the ambulance was all that was left behind. The three of us watched as it drove slowly down the rutted dirt and gravel road, a dream-like scene in the filtered, viscous end-of-day light. I could feel Frankie struggling not to sob as the ambulance disappeared out of sight.

'Why don't we go inside?' I said. 'You look like you could do with a drink.'

'Only if you two will have something with me,' she said.

I caught Quinn's eye and he nodded. 'Of course we will.'

The Merchants had hosted numerous parties at their beautiful home over the years, my favorite being the tree-decorating party the Friday before Christmas in Middleburg Weekend, after Yale and Lily had gone back to college and it was just the two of them left to hang dozens and dozens of ornaments on a twelve-foot Fraser fir. Paul, wearing a Santa Claus hat Frankie had knitted for him, would climb the ladder to put the decorations on the upper branches and place the Moravian star on the very top. The house would echo with Christmas music and a lot of laughter on those nights. We drank homemade Glühwein – hot spiced wine made from Paul's Austrian grandmother's recipe – and everyone wore the requisite ugly sweater. After dinner – Frankie always did all the cooking, including five different kinds of homemade Christmas cookies – we sang carols around the piano while Paul played.

The semi-circular mahogany wet bar was in a corner of the Great Room next to where the Christmas tree always occupied center stage. I glanced at the spot where an enormous pot of persimmon-colored mums was now placed in the middle of a mother-of-pearl mosaic table they'd brought back from a trip to Morocco. A bottle of Beefeater dry gin sat on the bar. Next to it was a half-full bottle of tonic water, a wooden cutting board with a wedge of lime sitting on it, and a small sharp knife. An empty glass was next to the gin bottle.

Frankie walked over to pick up the glass and peered into it. 'That's strange. This glass is clean. I told Paul to have a drink when he got home and it looks as if he did, since the tonic is open and he cut up a lime.' She picked up the bottle of tonic. 'It's not cold any more. It's been out of the fridge for a while . . . probably since he went and got it.'

She set the bottle down and stared at Quinn and me with haunted eyes. 'What is this clean glass doing here? Why did he go out to the pool, and what happened so that he fell in and drowned?'

Quinn put his arm around her and hugged her to him. 'Win will find out,' he said. 'Let's wait and see what he has to say.'

She swiped at her eyes again and went behind the bar. 'I need something stronger than a G and T,' she said. 'Rémy Martin, anyone?'

She took the bottle off a glass shelf lined with bottles of alcohol, their reflections glinting in a smoky mirror behind them.

'I'll pour,' Quinn said and reached for the bottle.

'Thanks . . .' She got out snifters for the cognac as her eyes strayed to a shelf where sparkling glasses – wine glasses, high-ball glasses, tumblers – were lined up like rows of orderly soldiers. 'That's weird.'

'What?' I asked.

'There are only six of these tumblers on the shelf.' She picked up the clean one on the bar. 'This is the seventh but there are supposed to be eight. Where's the eighth glass?'

'In the kitchen?' Quinn gave her a quizzical look as he handed her a snifter. He passed one to me and took one for himself.

'I doubt it.' She shook her head. 'We have a sink here. And a small dishwasher. We wash all the barware here.'

'Maybe a glass broke?' I said.

'There's nothing in the trash. No broken glass.'

'What are you saying, Frankie?'

She frowned, as if she were thinking this through. 'I wonder if someone else was here with him?'

'And . . . took their glass with them?' Quinn asked.

'I know. It doesn't make sense, does it?'

'Especially because this glass is clean, so maybe Paul never got around to having the drink. Maybe he went out to check on something at the pool,' I said. 'And then . . .'

'And then he somehow fell into the pool and drowned? Sorry, it just doesn't make any sense. Plus now there's the missing glass.' She was still staring at it. 'Where is it?'

Quinn and I exchanged glances. She was overwrought. She'd just found her husband dead at the bottom of their swimming pool. She was obsessing over a glass that was probably broken. Or in another room. Maybe Paul had taken a gin and tonic upstairs to the bedroom for some reason and left it there. Maybe he decided not to go for a swim after all. She was right, though. It was odd.

I took one of her hands in both of mine. 'Do you want to come back to our house and stay with us tonight? I know you have a lot of calls to make, but you can have all the privacy you want – the library, the parlor, the veranda. Wherever you want, whatever you need. And you should eat something, too. I got a text from Persia earlier. She left a homemade chicken salad and her buttermilk biscuits for us. You know Persia. There'll be more than enough for three.'

Frankie covered my hands with her other hand. 'I need some time alone. I want to sleep in our bed tonight. Thank you anyway.' Her eyes filled with tears. 'Besides, I have a funeral to plan. I'll probably call Father Joe after you leave and talk to him. I need to be here.'

Of course she'd want to call Father Joe O'Malley. He was a regular dinner guest at the Merchants' home; he, Frankie, and Paul were the closest of friends. The funeral would be at St Michael the Archangel Catholic Church where he was the pastor. He would say the Mass, deliver the homily that would be intensely personal and from the heart.

'Are you sure you want to stay here?' I asked. 'By yourself?'

'Very. I need to call the kids. They're going to be devastated. They adored their dad.'

What would she say? It would be a complete and utter shock. Yale was twenty-one; Lily had just turned twenty. They were still kids. They wouldn't be expecting this only a few weeks after they had kissed their parents goodbye and driven back to their respective college campuses. There was no easy way to tell them, nothing that would make it any less harsh and final.

'We should finish our drinks and let you do that,' I said.

We drank, the brandy burning like fire down my throat. When we were done, Frankie walked us through the Great Room and into the light-filled two-story foyer. The only thing I could see through the large picture windows on the second floor was an ominous wall of gray clouds shifting and moving swiftly.

'I thought we weren't supposed to get that storm for two days, if at all,' I said.

Quinn and Frankie looked up. 'The trees are starting to sway,' Frankie said. 'I can hear the wind.'

'Something's coming,' Quinn said.

'You'd better go,' she said. 'It looks bad . . . Wait a minute.'

She walked across the foyer, swift purposeful steps. Then she stopped and looked around.

'Where is it?'

'Where is what?' I asked.

'Paul's briefcase. He always leaves it right here.' She pointed to an armchair upholstered in a rust-and-cream fabric. 'I know he would have brought it with him to the meeting with Nash today.'

'Maybe it's still in his car,' Quinn said.

'Or . . .' She opened one of the French doors to the hall closet. 'Here it is. I wonder why he left it here.' She picked up the briefcase, then walked back to Quinn and me and thrust it into my hands. 'Please. Take this. Paul kept all the notes he'd been making on mapping the unpaved roads in this briefcase, plus everything that was given to him after Violet died, all her notes as well. Eli said he'd draw the maps so Paul could submit them to the National Register of Historic Places. Eli's going to need what's in there. Paul was so passionate about this project, taking over the running of the Don't Pave Paradise Coalition after Violet's accident. I don't want anything to happen to what the two of them started now that they're both gone. I *want* this to succeed. It meant everything to Paul – and Violet.'

Her hands were shaking as I took the briefcase. 'Don't worry,' I said. 'It *will* succeed, and when it does, it will be because of Paul and Violet's passion and dedication to keeping a beautiful part of the county the way it's always been.'

The briefcase was heavier than it looked, heavier than I'd expected.

'Screw Nash Blake,' she said, her eyes flashing with anger, her voice edged with bitterness. 'If he thinks Paul's death – and Violet's – is going to make it easy for him and his damn bulldozers to come in and destroy where we live, he's wrong.'

She opened the front door as a gust of wind blew up a swirling pile of dry leaves and a distant clap of thunder sounded.

'Storm's coming,' Quinn said.

I looked at him. 'I know,' I said, and wondered if we both meant the same thing.

THREE

I told Quinn about Benny's accident on the trip home in the middle of a fierce, driving rainstorm. Paul's shocking death and Frankie's raw, unvarnished grief had chased my conversation with Antonio – was it only a few hours ago? – out of my head.

Quinn's reaction was the same as mine had been. 'Jesus. Not Benny!'

'I'm afraid so.'

'When's the last time you talked to Antonio? Have you heard from Nelia?'

'I haven't talked to Antonio since he told me the news in the barrel room. He might have texted while we were with Frankie.' I flicked through the messages on my phone. 'Yup. He did. Half an hour ago. Benny was admitted to Lansdowne Hospital. They're going to do emergency surgery on his knee tomorrow. He'll be out of commission for . . . *wow*. Maybe a couple of months. The surgeon said it was a bad break. Transverse. His kneecap was sheared in half. Apparently that's worse than a vertical break.'

'Damn. Maybe we should drive over to Lansdowne.'

'No, there's another text. Antonio says they gave Benny enough pain meds to tranquilize an elephant. Nelia is going to spend the night at the hospital and she'll be in touch after his surgery to let us know when it would be OK to come by. It might not even be until the day after tomorrow.'

The rain, which had been keeping up a steady drumbeat, turned up the volume and intensity, pummeling the roof of the Jeep until it sounded as if a thousand hammers were banging over our heads. I had to raise my voice so Quinn could hear me. 'Don't you want to pull over for a few minutes?'

'No. I want to get home and out of this storm. There's no place between here and there to wait it out, no underpass or anywhere to take shelter. Besides, after living here for five years,

I know these roads almost as well as you do. I can drive them blindfolded. I want to get us out of here before the usual low spots flood and then we *can't* get through.'

He wasn't kidding. *Turn around, don't drown* was dead serious advice around here. Some of the creeks and runs could overflow faster than you could blink an eye in a storm this intense, inundating roads and turning them into small rivers with raging currents that swept away whatever happened to be in the way. Even a car.

The accident that had left me disabled and needing a cane had been on a night exactly like this almost a dozen years ago, the rain lashing the windshield of the car my then-almost-ex-boyfriend had been driving so the wipers were useless. An ugly argument because I'd discovered he'd been cheating with a future sister-in-law – also now an ex – our voices raised in anger, both of us distracted. He'd taken the turn at the entrance to the vineyard much too fast, skidding and losing control of the car. We rammed into one of the stone pillars at the gate at full speed. You can still see the seam in the stone where Leland, my father, had it rebuilt – or at least I can. I never fail to notice it every time I drive by. My boyfriend was thrown from the car. A bit banged up, but he was fine. It took the Jaws of Life to extricate me. Months in the hospital. Multiple surgeries.

I took a deep breath as the rain continued beating on the roof. Quinn wanted to tough it out.

'OK,' I said so quietly I wasn't sure he heard me.

He slid a quick sideways glance my way, recognition dawning on his face so I knew he'd heard what I said and figured out exactly what I'd been thinking.

He reached over and squeezed my hand. Protective, reassuring. 'Don't worry, honey. I'll get us home safely. I can't drive fast in this rain anyway. I'm not going to speed. We'll be fine. I promise.'

I nodded and closed my eyes. I believed him. He was a good driver.

I just didn't like driving in rainstorms any more.

We were both drenched just from making the dash from the car to the front door, since it was still coming down in torrents with wind that blew the rain sideways, stinging our faces. What should have been the garage – an old carriage house that had been built in the mid-1800s, some sixty years after Highland House, the main house, had been built – was now my brother Eli's architecture studio on the ground floor with a small apartment for Persia Fleming, our housekeeper, on the second floor. So we always left the cars in the circular driveway.

'Guess we don't have to worry about whether the Cab Sauv will be waterlogged or not,' Quinn said. 'That decision's been made. We'd better pick tomorrow, regardless of what the pH and Brix are. I'll call Antonio. Then I'll call Nelia, tell her our workman's comp insurance will cover Benny's bills.'

'Are you going to tell both of them about Paul?'

'Antonio, yes,' he said. 'Nelia, maybe not. It can wait. She's got enough on her mind right now.'

I nodded. 'Then tell Antonio you decided not to tell Nelia. I'll call the winery staff and let them know.'

'Good luck with that. They worship Frankie. It's going to be rough.'

'I know. Plus there's the news about Benny. I don't think they know about him, either.'

'Jesus.' He shook his head.

'What?'

'Too bad we can't MacGyver what happened today like we've been doing with everything else around here lately. Fix what's broken.'

'I wish.' Benny's knee. Frankie's heart.

'Drink?'

'Yes, please.'

'Red, white, or hard stuff?'

'Hard stuff now. Wine with dinner.'

'Yup. That kind of night. Scotch?'

'Scotch.'

Quinn fixed our drinks and walked into the kitchen to call Antonio and Nelia. I chose the library, drawing the curtains across the two large leaded glass windows – by now the storm had nearly abated – and turning on the goose-neck lamp that sat on my father's antique partner's desk, now my desk, where I took care of the rest of the vineyard business I didn't get to in my office in the barrel room. Then I called Nikki Young, our event planner and Frankie's assistant. Actually, she was more like a daughter to Frankie, after she lost her own mother to breast cancer the year before last. Nikki would take the news the hardest of anyone.

After I told her, she was silent so long I wondered if the call had disconnected. When she spoke, her voice broke. 'Oh, Lucie, how awful. What can I do? What does she need? How can Paul be *gone* . . . just like that? It's not fair. It's not *right*.' She gulped back a sob.

'I know. I'm so sorry.'

'Tell me what to do.' She was pleading. 'I need to do something, but I don't know how to help.'

'Well . . .' My thoughts ran wild.

Hug her and let her cry her heart out until there were no more tears.

Put the winter cover on the swimming pool until she could finally bear to look at it without thinking of her husband lying at the bottom.

Be the buffer between her and the well-meaning relatives, friends, business associates, neighbors, and especially the curiosity seekers who would want to know the real *story behind Paul's sudden, startling death.*

Was it just a tragic accident? Was Paul drunk? Drugged? Were there money woes no one knew about? Was he having an affair? Could it have been suicide?

I took a breath and said to Nikki, 'Frankie said she was going to call Father Joe O'Malley this evening after she told Yale and Lily. She said she needed to start planning Paul's funeral.'

Nikki hiccupped another sob. 'She would do that.'

My family has lived in the village of Atoka, Virginia, population 221, for generations. My ancestor Hamish Montgomery was given our land for service to his country in the French and Indian War, so my roots are as deeply embedded in our red clay soil as the roots of our oldest vines. What I especially love about where I live is that we are a community that helps each other, takes cares of each other. *Shows up* for each other. Most days we leave our front doors unlocked because how else would someone get inside – after yelling 'yoo-hoo, anyone home?'

when they opened the front door – to return a borrowed platter or leave a bag of zucchini and tomatoes because they had more of both of those vegetables growing in their garden than grains of sand on the beach? We're that kind of town, those kind of people. Brought up on the Four Sacraments of the South: kinship, civility, hospitality, tradition.

That didn't mean people wouldn't talk. I mean, *small towns.* There would absolutely be a conversation about Paul's death tomorrow morning around the coffee pot in the General Store. And everyone would have a theory to go with their crullers and croissants and jelly donuts, starting with Thelma Johnson, the sassy octogenarian owner who kept her finger on the pulse of everything that happened in three counties. It would also include the Romeos, Thelma's acolytes and partners in crime whose name stood for Retired Old Men Eating Out, and whose mission in life, other than providing steady business for local restaurants and watering holes, was to ferret out every bit of news in our little corner of Virginia, which they then brought back to the mothership for further dissemination.

'There'll be a Mass for Paul at St Mike's, of course,' I continued. 'I imagine it will be in the morning. I'm sure Frankie is going to want to have a reception or, more likely knowing her, a sit-down lunch afterwards. I think we should have it here, take care of everything for her, take that off her plate. She'll plan the funeral down to the last detail, you know that. We can organize the luncheon.'

'Of course we will,' Nikki said.

'Will you start making arrangements?' I asked. 'I'll tell Frankie tomorrow. I'm not going to bother her tonight.'

'Absolutely.' She had brightened up now that she had a mission, a purpose. 'Does Dominique know?'

'Not yet. Or, at least I think she doesn't. I don't know how fast the news has gone around. I'll call her,' I said. 'About Paul *and* the reception.'

My cousin, Dominique Gosselin, owns the Goose Creek Inn, consistently voted most romantic place to dine in the Mid-Atlantic region and, most recently, the recipient of a Michelin star. The inn also owns Goose Creek Catering and we use them for all our events. The family relationship cemented that, of course, along with our newest joint venture: the enormous vegetable and flower garden we'd planted last spring at the vineyard. What produce and flowers the inn couldn't use for their daily menus and table settings, we sold at a farm stand painted barn red that Eli had designed and built. Mia, my baby sister and the family artist, hand-painted all the signs, drawing whimsical pictures of dancing cantaloupes, jitterbugging tomatoes, big-eyed eggplants, and mustached zucchini in top hats.

When Dominique heard about Paul, I knew she'd personally take over supervising the menu and catering. As a business owner, she'd been on the side of the Pro-Loudoun Progressives who believed it was time to pave more of our roads. But she'd respected Paul and Violet immensely for what they'd been doing to get them designated as historic landmarks.

'Lucie,' Nikki said, her voice soft and thoughtful. 'Let me call the rest of the staff and tell them. You've had a hell of a day. It's almost nine o'clock. I bet you and Quinn haven't even had dinner yet.'

'I feel like I should be the one to do it.'

'You haven't eaten, have you?'

'Well . . . no.'

'If we're going to pick the Cab Sauv tomorrow, you know as well as I do it's going to be an early day and we're already short-staffed without Frankie. I'll call the others.'

'All right, but I'm afraid there's something else.'

'Good God, what?'

I told her about Benny and she groaned as if I'd just landed a hard punch. 'Oh my God, this is awful. So we've lost Benny and Nelia as well. Look, I'll make those calls. You go find your husband and hug him tight.' She paused, adding as almost an afterthought, 'Because you never know, do you?'

'No,' I said. 'You don't.'

She hung up.

When I walked into the kitchen a few minutes later Quinn had already set the table and gotten out the chicken salad and homemade buttermilk biscuits Persia had left for our dinner. He'd also opened a bottle of chilled Sancerre and was filling our wine glasses. We ate by candlelight every night – it was our rule – so I lit the two honey-colored tapers that were in my mother's favorite brass candleholders and turned down the lights.

I hugged him and he wrapped his arms around me, resting his chin on the top of my head. Then he pulled back and tucked his finger under my chin, tipping up my face for a kiss that went on for a very long time.

'What was that for?' he said, when we'd finally caught our breath.

'Paul. And Benny. Because I have you and you're whole and healthy. And because I love you so much.'

'I love you so much, too.'

We sat down and Quinn said, 'Antonio said he'd put out the word that we need help tomorrow.'

'Good,' I said with some relief. 'I forgot to get Frankie's list of kids from NVU who might be able to come pick for us.'

Though in fact I hadn't forgotten. Sonny's phone call had overtaken everything else as Frankie and I had raced to her house.

'I'd rather have someone Antonio knows than one of the kids,' Quinn was saying as he broke open a biscuit and slabbed butter on it. 'They'll have more experience.'

'True.'

'How'd it go with your calls? You were gone a while.'

I told him. 'We're going to have the funeral lunch here – I'm sure Frankie's going to want something for everyone attending the Mass. Nikki and I already started planning it. After dinner I need to call Dominique and talk about the catering and a menu. We should probably call Persia as well. She'll want to know. Also, Eli and Sasha. And Mia. And Kit . . . though Bobby probably already knows. And . . .'

'Lucie.' He held up his hand. *Stop.* 'Sweetheart, there'll be plenty of time to make those calls in the morning. It's late. Sometimes it's better to give folks an extra night of sleep not knowing the sadness that's waiting for them.'

I nodded and thought of Frankie, alone tonight for the first time, and wondered how she would bear it, knowing Paul was gone forever. Wondered how I'd feel if it were me and I had lost Quinn.

Then the tears I'd been holding back came.

FOUR

I slept poorly, dreaming about Frankie and Paul and Benny jumbled together in a confusing story that made no sense. At one point they were underwater – in a swimming pool – carrying on a conversation as if it were the most normal thing in the world. I watched them, a spectator peering through a glass wall into an aquarium tank until they became obscured by a red mist that I realized with a shock was blood. Next to me Quinn tossed and turned, wrestling with the sheets and blankets as if he were fighting something. Or some*one*. We both woke before the alarm went off, neither of us rested or feeling as if we'd slept well. Not a good start to the day.

Antonio was already at the winery when we got there with to-go coffee mugs from the pot Quinn had made at home which, true to form, could also double as tar to fill potholes. Antonio looked like a couple of miles of bad road, but who was I to talk? I'd scraped my hair into a ponytail, yanked on a Nationals baseball cap, and pulled down the brim. A burgundy tee-shirt with our logo on it, since red grape stains don't show as much, old jeans, and sneakers. Voilà, my harvest wardrobe. Hopefully the hat helped so no one noticed the deep circles under my eyes.

Antonio had already driven the bright yellow plastic lugs the pickers would fill with grapes out to the field and dropped them at the ends of the rows of Cabernet Sauvignon vines. Later he, or sometimes Quinn, would go back with the tractor, making passes up and down the rows to load the full lugs onto the trailer bed and bring them back to the crush pad where they'd immediately be put on pallets into the refrigerator truck we always rented at this time of year.

'Any word on Benny?' I asked him.

'Nelia texted me a little while ago. His surgery is scheduled for nine o'clock so they're getting him ready now. She said he had a rough night because he was in a lot of pain, but the drugs were helping. She'll call after he's back in his room.'

'Poor Benny. I hope it goes all right.'

'Me too. After this they're sending him to a rehab hospital for a week, maybe ten days. Another hospital is gonna drive him nuts.'

'I know, but at least our workman's comp insurance will pay his bills. He and Nelia won't owe a dime for anything.'

He nodded. 'Nelia said that's the only good thing about what happened, that they won't go broke paying for it.'

'Did you find anybody to help out today?' Quinn asked him.

'I did. Chiara.' Antonio flicked a piece of dirt from under a fingernail.

'Chiara Rossi?' Quinn's voice rose in disbelief. 'Seriously?'

Antonio shot Quinn a look and I could feel the temperature of the conversation start to go up. 'She's worked on her family's farm all her life. Now that Violet's gone, she'll take over when Marco steps down. It was generous of her to offer to help us out. She knows what she's doing.' He sounded defensive.

'It's a *cattle* farm.'

'Did *you* try to find anybody? Look, she heard about Paul. It hit her pretty hard since he's the one who took over that "don't pave the roads" group from her mother after she died,' Antonio said. 'Frankie and Paul were both checking in on her, so they were tight. Chiara called Nikki after she found out about Paul and they got talking. Nikki told her about Benny and said we were short on pickers today, so Chiara called me and said she could get away to help out if I needed her, since Carlo runs the farm now that her mom is gone. I didn't have anyone else so I said yes.'

'I thought you were going to find a cousin or someone who knew what they were doing.' Quinn left out: *'Because Chiara doesn't.'*

'I told you. There *wasn't* anyone, OK? The grapes aren't going to pick themselves. Look, Quinn, it's Cab Sauv. If we don't bring it in today, it won't matter if we have a hundred pickers tomorrow because the fruit is going to start to rot after all the rain we had yesterday.' Antonio folded his arms across his chest and gave Quinn a combative look. 'If you don't want her, *you* tell her we don't need her. But we do, and you know it.'

The two of them snapping at each other and the day hadn't started. I dug my elbow into my husband's ribs. *Stop.*

'I know what we're picking.' Quinn still sounded irked. 'Put her next to Orlando. He'll keep an eye on her.'

'Already done,' Antonio said in a short, tight voice before he turned on his heel and walked away.

'That certainly went well,' I said after he left. 'You and Antonio.'

'Lucie—'

'Quinn. We don't need this. Come *on*. At least we've got someone to help out, thanks to Antonio.'

'I know we do,' he said, and now he was irritated with me. 'But she never picked a goddam grape in her life. The sorting's already going to take more time because we've got so much damn MOG.'

MOG. Material other than grapes. If the grapes weren't clean – and we already knew these wouldn't be – there'd be plenty of stuff to get rid of and weed out once we started sorting. Animal damage, rain damage, uneven ripeness, plus the usual sticks and other debris that got mixed in when the grapes were picked. That meant that it was going to take forever and a day to clean out the junk as the grapes moved along the sorting table conveyor belt after they came through the destemmer. A couple of monotonous hours of staring at bunches and bunches of grapes passing endlessly by could give even an experienced person a bad case of vertigo. When that happened and Quinn realized the sorters were missing green grapes or letting stems go by without removing them, he'd slow down the speed of the conveyor and then it took even longer to get the job done.

I didn't want to put any more pressure on him. I already knew he'd been sleeping badly because the biggest decision any winemaker makes in the vineyard is *when*. When to pick. And Cabernet Sauvignon? It's the grape that makes our most expensive wine, the jewel in our crown, and it's also the hardest grape to get to ripen.

Though I wanted our wine to be made from grapes grown only on our land – *our* terroir – I finally relented when Quinn said we needed to start buying grapes from other growers, though I insisted they had to be grapes from Virginia growers. And they couldn't make up so much of the wine that we would be required to call it Virginia wine instead of Montgomery Estate Vineyard wine.

So he found two growers with a couple of acres of grapes, suppliers we knew and trusted would send only good-quality fruit. But they, too, had been bugging Quinn because while a winemaker wants the grapes to hang on the vine as long as possible in order to get the most flavor, which in turn makes better wine, a grower wants just the opposite. The sooner the grapes are picked, the sooner he gets his money and the less he has to spend on labor and chemicals needed to maintain the fruit, keep it healthy, and keep it from rotting while it was still hanging on the vine. I knew Quinn had been having some blunt conversations with both growers – including a heated one last night – so his temper was already frayed.

'Let's just try to get through today without anybody jumping down anyone's throat,' I said to him.

'Fine,' he said. 'As long as everyone does their job. The reefer truck just got here. I'm going to go check on it.'

I bit back a sharp retort and watched him walk away. Jesus, we were all melting down.

The refrigerator truck, also known as the reefer truck, had been our salvation these last years once we started shelling out the money for it. Now, once we picked the grapes, we could store them and keep them cold until we were ready to process them, even if it meant waiting another day because we didn't finish picking today.

The crew started trickling in. Jesús, who was Benny's best friend; Valeria, who was Antonio's wife; Orlando, who was Valeria's brother, and Dante, who was Antonio's cousin. Like I said: a Mexican mafia of friends and relatives; a tight, close-knit group. They worked well together but today everyone was unusually quiet and I knew they were rattled and unsettled. Benny in the hospital, Nelia by his side for what was serious surgery. And Frankie's husband Paul – whom they all knew and liked – dead, drowned in his own swimming pool.

Chiara Rossi showed up after everyone else had already gone out to the field. Pretty, slender, long dark hair, dark, expressive eyes, olive skin – a beauty. Violet had raised Chiara by herself, never breathing a word about her father or who he was. She had even kept her maiden name, Rossi, passing it on to Chiara.

'Sorry I'm late,' she said. 'I was taking care of Nonno Marco. Carlo had to leave early to get over to the office. The fall cattle sale is coming up. It's our biggest one every year.'

Nonno Marco was Marco Rossi, Chiara's eighty-four-year-old grandfather. Carlo was the farm manager who had worked with the Rossi family for more than thirty years, becoming a son to Marco and an uncle to Chiara. Now that Violet was gone and Serenità Farm would be Chiara's to run someday when Marco finally stepped down, Carlo was going to stay on but Marco had stated that Carlo would also have part ownership in Serenità. He had earned it.

'Don't worry about being late. We're just glad you came,' I told her, grateful Quinn wasn't around to hear me say that. 'Thanks for helping out.'

'You're welcome. I know I don't have any experience picking grapes, but I used to help my mom in the garden at Serenità when I was growing up. I hated it – all that weeding and pruning – but now I'm glad I did it. It's a memory of times the two of us spent together. And I know pruning roses isn't like picking grapes, but at least grapes don't have thorns. Plus I can handle a pair of secateurs, so I won't slice off a finger.'

Smart girl. She'd zeroed in on Quinn's number-one worry. Blood.

'That's good to know. I'll be sure to tell Quinn,' I said and she grinned. 'I used to help my mother in our garden when she was alive and I hated it, too. Now that she's gone those are some of my happiest memories of being with her. Come on, I'll drive you out to the vineyard.'

We climbed into the ATV, which was parked next to the crush pad. Quinn was somewhere inside, in the barrel room or our office. Antonio had disappeared so it was just Chiara and me. I turned the vehicle around and we headed out to the Cabernet Sauvignon block. The greens of summer had faded and the colors were now the shades of autumn – gold, rust, burnt orange, russet, and the brilliant red of the maples.

'How's Marco?' I asked. 'How is he doing?'

'He hasn't been the same since Mom died,' she said. 'I worry about him.'

'I'm sure he worries about you, too,' I said. 'You have a lot of responsibility on your shoulders now, managing the farm.'

Two thousand acres of land that the Rossi family owned and leased. Twelve hundred head of Angus cattle, making Serenità Farm one of the largest breeding suppliers in the US. People came from all over the country for their fall and spring cattle sales.

'I have Carlo, thank God. He really runs the place, and he'll take on more responsibility after Nonno Marco retires, although I don't think my nonno will retire until the day he dies,' she said. 'Now that Mom is gone, there's only me and I can't manage everything on my own. It's grown too much, and a lot of that is thanks to Carlo. As for Nonno Marco, I haven't told him about Paul Merchant yet. He'll just get upset all over again.'

'What do you mean?'

We were almost at the Cab Sauv block. I could see flashes of yellow between the rows of vines – the lugs in the field – and hear the faint tinny sound of a boombox that I knew would be blasting loud Spanish music when we got closer.

'He never believed Mom's accident was an accident,' she said in a flat, hard voice.

I slowed the ATV down and said, surprised, 'Do you agree?'

'I do.' Emphatic. Certain.

I chose my words with care. Because if it wasn't an accident, it was intentional. Someone had wanted Violet Rossi dead. 'What do you and your grandfather think happened?'

She threw my question right back at me. 'What do *you* think? The obvious, of course. That someone was responsible for her car going off the road the way it did.'

I pulled up in front of the Peace rose bush my French mother had planted years ago. In French vineyards it was a custom to plant roses next to the vines, because they acted as a sort of canary in the coal mine. If the roses started to look as if they were struggling or begin to show signs of disease, it was a harbinger that the vines were suffering as well. And my mother also loved their beauty.

'Chiara, the investigators didn't find anything. There were

no other cars on that road when it happened. It was ruled as driver error. She was speeding. The car went off the road and ended up in Goose Creek.' I tried to keep my words and my tone gentle because she was still clearly hurting. And angry.

She snorted. 'My mother was an excellent driver. She knew those roads so well she could have driven them blindfolded. You can't make me believe she missed that turn, which was why they say her car ended up in the creek.'

I didn't want to keep pushing, but Violet had removed the doors from her Jeep so it had been more like a dune buggy than a car, offering no protection when she crashed. That was fact number one. Fact number two was that she'd been speeding on a winding dirt road at twilight after it had rained that morning and had to slalom around the water-filled ruts in the road. Fact number three – and the most damning of all – was that she'd been driving on Crenshaw Road as it followed Goose Creek and when she'd lost control, the Jeep had gone off the road and careened into the creek, landing on its side. It had been impossible to determine whether the impact of the crash had killed her or she'd drowned first because she'd passed out. Either way, she'd been found in the driver's seat with her seatbelt firmly attached. She hadn't even tried to escape.

'Then how did it happen?' I asked. 'There was no evidence of anyone else at the scene. Sweetie, it was ruled driver error. I know it's hard . . .'

'I'm telling you it *wasn't* an accident.' Her bitterness bled into her words. 'And now Paul Merchant is dead. Six weeks after Mom. The two people who were behind the campaign not to pave the roads.'

'So you think – what? That they're related?'

'Come on, Lucie. There's money in asphalt. For a lot of people. If those roads don't get paved, there are people who stand to lose money. A *lot* of money.'

'Chiara,' I said. 'If that's true then you're talking about murder.'

FIVE

'That's right,' Chiara said. 'I am. *Murder.*'

I stopped the ATV and turned off the engine so abruptly that the vehicle lurched to a stop and jolted the two of us forward. Chiara put her hand on the dashboard to steady herself.

'Sorry,' I said, and then added in a sharp, disbelieving voice, 'Really? That's a hell of an accusation with no evidence to back it up. Do you *know* something? Do you have any proof it wasn't an accident?'

'No,' she said. 'I don't.'

'Then what makes you think you're right? *Two* people who supposedly died in tragic accidents? As far as I know, Win Turnbull hasn't even done the autopsy on Paul Merchant, but it looks like he had a heart attack or a stroke, something that caused him to tumble into the swimming pool where he drowned because no one was with him when it happened. I was there yesterday, at the Merchants' house, when the EMTs arrived.'

'And when Win does that autopsy, he probably won't find anything that leads him to believe Paul's death was anything other than an accident, like you said. Just like Mom.' She folded her arms across her chest as if she were hugging herself. Her dark eyes had turned the color of obsidian. Flat and fathomless.

'Win's pretty thorough,' I said.

'I dated a guy once who was studying to be a doctor,' she said. 'He told me that one of the first things they teach you in medical school is that if you hear hoofbeats, think horses, not zebras.'

I wrinkled my forehead. 'Meaning?'

'Meaning that if you examine a patient and they've got symptoms of an upper respiratory infection, you should consider something sinus-related or, worst case, maybe pneumonia. But it's not likely to be bubonic plague.'

'OK, I get that. But I still think if there's anything suspicious about Paul's death, Win would know about it. He'd figure it out. He's pretty sharp.'

'I guess we'll find out,' she said, 'won't we?'

She had been chewing on this, thinking it through for a while.

'Do you suspect anyone?' I asked. Because it half-sounded as if she might have someone in mind.

'There are plenty of people who didn't want my mom going through with her plan to map the unpaved roads around here and get them listed on the National Register of Historic Places.'

Plenty of people. Right now, I could narrow that list down to a few specific individuals.

'Are you talking about the Blakes?'

Frankie's statement that Paul had told her Nash Blake had practically physically threatened her husband – or his lawyer had – at their meeting in Washington yesterday had been swirling around in my head. *We will stop you.* Except that Nash, owner of Blake Construction and all its subsidiary companies, might be a shrewd businessman who expected to get his way and occasionally played hardball, but the idea of him committing *murder*?

Twice?

The Blakes were philanthropists, generous benefactors who contributed to many local charities such as the food bank, endowing a state-of-the art cancer wing for the hospital, and funding full tuition scholarships for underprivileged kids at Northern Virginia University. The list went on.

They had also recently become involved in a restoration project for the old Hollywood Theatre in Middleburg, which had burned to the ground in 1941. Eleanor Blake, Nash's grandmother, a wealthy heiress in her own right, had owned the theater and died tragically in the fire. Her husband, Redmond Blake, had never gotten over her death and never remarried. Wyatt, Nash's father, was his only child. Eleanor had had the theater built next door to the Red Fox Inn, Middleburg's most famous and oldest establishment, and then financed the movies that were shown there, convinced people needed a distraction from the aftermath of the1929 stock market crash and the years of the Great Depression. Not only did she believe that the movies being made during the Golden Age of Hollywood were just what the doctor ordered, she also personally knew Clark Gable, Will Rogers, Fred Astaire, Katherine Hepburn, Bette Davis, Vivien Leigh, and Spencer Tracy, to name just a few of the era's most luminary movie stars. So, whenever Clark's or Fred's or Vivien's movie was playing at the Hollywood, she would invite him or her to come east for lavish, over-the-top Gatsbyesque parties at Connemara and, of course, to attend a showing of their film at the theater. Hollywood East, Middleburg was called. Local folks loved the glamour and glitter Eleanor brought to our charming, pretty little village, which was also just starting to become known as the center of Virginia horse and hunt country.

To my surprise, Chiara echoed my thoughts. 'No, *not* the Blakes. They're not involved,' she said, and she was adamant.

'You seem pretty certain about that.'

Her cheeks turned pink, but all she said was, 'If I'm going to pick grapes for you today, I'd better get started, don't you think? Looks like everyone else is already here. Where do I go?'

'See that guy at the end of the row?' I pointed to Orlando, who had stopped what he was doing and had been watching us. I waved and he waved back. 'He's going to help you today. His name is Orlando. Go see him and he'll get you sorted out. And thanks again for doing this.'

'It's OK,' she said. 'It's what neighbors do. We help each other out.'

I watched her walk down the grassy middles between two rows of leafy Cabernet Sauvignon vines that were still heavy with dark purple grapes, her slim body swaying gracefully as she moved. Orlando hadn't taken his eyes off her and I didn't blame him. She was lovely.

Chiara didn't want to believe that her mother's death was an accident, that Violet had been speeding on a road she knew so well she could practically drive it with her eyes closed and had lost control of her Jeep. Because that was the thing about these unpaved country roads: one of the reasons for keeping them that way was that it discouraged speeding. You *couldn't* drive fast unless you wanted to break an axle or destroy your shocks.

There were plenty of locals who complained bitterly that after they paved Limekiln Road in Middleburg it had changed from being a sweet country lane into the Indianapolis 500 Speedway.

So if Chiara didn't suspect the Blakes – especially because Nash was the president of the Pro-Loudoun Progressives and his lawyer had verbally threatened Paul yesterday – then *who*?

The other thing I didn't know, or even understand, was *why*.

By four o'clock it was clear we weren't going to get all the Cab Sauv grapes picked, and we'd have to do this all over again tomorrow. That was the bad news. The good news, relatively speaking, was that there weren't many grapes left to pick and, besides, the reefer truck bought us extra time and today's grapes could chill nicely overnight before we started processing everything tomorrow.

I found Quinn on the crush pad as he was finishing loading a pallet of lugs into the back of the truck, the overwhelmingly pungent smell of just-picked ripe fruit perfuming the entire crush pad like a vapor cloud. I told him I wanted to check on Frankie who, uncharacteristically, hadn't responded to either of the text messages I'd sent her. Nelia had texted that Benny's surgery had been a success and the surgeon was pleased, but that Benny was exhausted and had been sleeping all afternoon. So, no visitors today, please.

'Sure, go see Frankie,' he said. 'Do you think you'll be there long?'

'I doubt it. I just want to stop by and see how she's doing. Persia made a casserole and some cornbread after I told her about Paul, so I'm going to drop those things off and also tell her we're taking care of a luncheon after the funeral. I'll call you when I'm leaving. What about you? Do you think you'll be here late?'

'Not as late as if we were going to begin processing tonight. There's probably another ton left to pick tomorrow,' he said. 'So we can manage with our crew. We should be done by noon.'

His way of saying we didn't need Chiara again.

'She did all right,' I said, prickling, because, for someone with no experience, she'd held her own and actually had done more than all right. 'Orlando told me she was a quick learner and that she hardly needed any help once she got started.'

'That would be because *Orlando*,' he said, emphasizing his name, 'fell head over heels in love with her. He couldn't take his eyes off that chick. Which, of course, slowed *him* down. Good thing she's got a boyfriend.'

'Since when do you know something like that?'

Usually that kind of information went in one ear and out the other with him. He could tell you the batting average and pertinent statistics of every player on the San Diego Padres, his beloved California hometown baseball team, although lately I was glad to see he also seemed to have memorized the same information for the Washington Nationals. But he never remembered the name of someone's husband, wife, girlfriend, child, or significant other, and I'd get a nudge or *the look* that meant he had no idea who he was talking to and could I please help him out.

'I know something like that because Valeria made it her business to tell me everything on their lunch break when Orlando was acting like a hormonal teenager every time Chiara so much as crooked her little finger at him. She's seeing Hunter Blake. Apparently it's serious.'

'*Hunter*? Are you sure about that?'

Nash Blake and Violet Rossi – Hunter's father and Chiara's mother – had heartily disliked each other, partly because they were on opposite sides of the don't-pave-Loudoun issue, but also for reasons that were twined through a tangled relationship between generations of the Rossi and Blake families. Where you wondered whether the feud had become more important than remembering how it started or what it was about.

Hunter and Chiara.

Like Romeo and Juliet. Tony and Maria. Star-crossed.

'You mean because of that thing between their families?' Quinn asked.

'Yes. That *thing*.'

'Valeria says Hunter's different from the rest of the Blakes. He didn't want to go into the family business, so he went to vet school instead. Nash was pissed since Hunter is his only kid, but Hunter didn't care. He loves taking care of animals, not building shopping malls and subdivisions. Came home a few months ago and started working at the animal hospital with Doc Harmon, so he helps out at Serenità.'

'How did I not know that?'

'Obviously you don't keep up with all the latest gossip like I do.' He flashed a smug smile.

I hooted. 'Even if that were remotely true – which it is *not* – you'll have forgotten all of it by tomorrow.'

He grinned. 'Probably. But I have you to remind me, don't I?'

'If you're lucky.'

He turned serious. 'The truth is they're keeping it quiet because Chiara doesn't want to upset Marco, and Hunter doesn't want to piss off Nash any more than he already is.'

'So how did Valeria find out?'

'By accident. She was helping out a friend who is a house-cleaner. Chiara and Hunter had rented an Airbnb out in Paris and she happened to see them leaving the place together first thing in the morning when she came by to clean, so she put two and two together. Chiara asked her not to say anything.'

Paris, Virginia was a sweet little village – a hamlet, really – that was even smaller than Atoka. There were accounts that it got its name to honor the Marquis de Lafayette's home town of Paris, France when he returned to the US after the War of 1812, though some people said that was a romanticized version of the real story.

'How come Valeria decided to share all of this information with you?' I asked.

'Because she knew I wasn't happy that her brother – Orlando – was falling all over Chiara while he was supposed to be working. So she told me not to worry because Chiara already had a boyfriend. Plus she said she'd handle Orlando.'

'I hope it works out for the two of them. Chiara is still really grieving Violet's death.'

He slipped an arm around my waist, pulling me to him. I lifted my face for his kiss.

'Love you,' he murmured.

'Love you more. I'd better go. See you at home.'

Usually Quinn and I told each other everything, like he had

done just now. For some reason, though, I wasn't yet ready to tell him about the tiny seed Chiara had planted in my brain: that Violet Rossi's car crash might not have been an accident, and Paul Merchant's death by drowning might not have been, either. Based on pure speculation and perhaps fueled by the need to explain something she wouldn't believe and didn't want to accept.

Despite the irrefutable fact that the Sheriff's Office investigation had reached the exact opposite conclusion in Violet's case: it was an accident.

Frankie looked pale but composed when she opened her front door half an hour later. I got a whiff of alcohol on her breath the moment we hugged and, since it's my business to know, I also knew she'd been drinking Cabernet Sauvignon, the grape we picked today. And that she had started drinking early.

'You OK?' I asked and then wished I could take back such a dumb question. Of course she wasn't.

'I'm . . . coping.'

'Yale and Lily?'

'They're devastated. As I knew they would be. Lily will be home in an hour. Yale's plane gets in at eleven. Lily will pick him up at Dulles.'

'Persia made dinner for you. Her homemade chicken pot pie and corn bread. An apple pie for dessert with apples from our trees. There's enough for three.'

Frankie took the heavy carrier bag out of my hands and peered inside. 'Looks like there's enough for thirty. Please thank her for me. Come on in. Would you like a drink?'

'Um . . . sure.'

We walked into her spacious, well-laid out kitchen decorated in shades of blue and cream. A large Viking stove dominated the room next to a refrigerator with a touchscreen door. There were two wall ovens, a wine refrigerator, and a counter with a large stand mixer, a food processor, a magnetic strip lined with a dozen sharp knives, and jugs filled with wooden spoons, spatulas, and other utensils. It was the kitchen of a serious cook.

She set the carrier bag on a large central island made of labradorite, which she'd chosen because she loved the colors that blazed from deep within the dark gray stone – cobalt blue, iridescent green, turquoise, and a rich yellow-gold. She'd also chosen it because of the native American myth that labradorite had fallen to earth from the frozen fire of the Aurora Borealis and that it possessed mystical healing properties for anyone seeking knowledge and guidance.

A nearly empty bottle of Cabernet Sauvignon sat on the island next to an empty wine glass. Frankie picked up the bottle. 'Let's finish this and then I'll get another.'

'Frankie—'

She got out a second wine glass from a cabinet above the butcher-block kitchen counter. 'Please don't judge, OK? I know. Alcohol and grief don't mix well. But today . . .'

'I'm not judging,' I said. 'It's got to be brutal.'

She filled the two glasses and handed one to me. 'Lucie,' she said, 'someone else was here yesterday with Paul. I'm sure of it. It's been bothering me ever since I figured it out.'

She pulled out a bar chair upholstered in a vivid cobalt blue crushed velvet fabric from under the island and sat down. I did the same, taking the seat across from her.

'Because of that missing drink glass?' I asked.

Which, to be honest, seemed like a pretty flimsy reason to me. Except it was Frankie. A perfectionist. If she said a glass was missing, then something had happened to it.

'Walk me through it,' I said. 'Why couldn't the glass have just broken – it fell or got dropped on the tile floor and shattered – so Paul dumped it in the trash?'

'Because I went through the trash. And I didn't find any shards of broken glass.'

Of course she did. 'Could it have gone missing before yesterday and you just didn't notice?'

She looked at me over the top of her wine glass as if I had just asked her the most ridiculous question ever.

'OK,' I said. 'OK. You're *sure* it disappeared yesterday?'

'Of course I'm sure. That's why I can't figure out what happened. And it's also why I'm sure someone else was here.'

'So, do you think that person . . . took . . . their glass when they left? And if they did, then why?'

'I don't know. And I know it sounds weird.'

It did. Really weird and downright implausible: the idea that someone was here yesterday having a drink with Paul and then maybe watched him have a heart attack and perhaps tumble into the swimming pool. Then that person did nothing to save him and fled, taking their drink glass with them.

No. No way.

Besides, the glass we'd found yesterday at the bar in the Great Room when she, Quinn, and I had a cognac after the ambulance left hadn't been used. How did she explain that? The guest was drinking alone and Paul wasn't? Why would just one glass be sitting next to the bottle of gin, along with a bottle of tonic and a cut-up lime if two people had been here yesterday? That seemed even more bizarre.

What Chiara had said to me earlier in the vineyard – that her mother's death wasn't an accident and that Paul's death wouldn't turn out to be an accident either – wormed its way back into my brain like a very unwelcome guest. But I couldn't tell Frankie about that now, not with absolutely nothing concrete to go on.

I couldn't.

She got up and walked into the butler's pantry just off the kitchen, returning with another bottle of Cabernet Sauvignon. She opened it with the practiced ease of an expert.

'Can I refill your glass?' she asked.

'I'm good, thanks.'

She poured wine into her own glass. 'Father Joe was here today. We planned the funeral. It's going to be Friday at eleven. The wake will be Thursday from four to seven at BJ's.'

When anyone in Atoka or Middleburg died, the wake and the funeral were always taken care of by BJ Hunt and Sons Funeral Home. It's just the way it was.

BJ was getting on in years – he was one of the Romeos – but when someone he'd known for a long time passed away, he personally took care of the body – the embalming and then dressing the deceased person in clothes the family had chosen, the clothes he or she would be buried in. Somehow, I figured BJ would take care of Paul Merchant himself.

'How did it go with Father Joe?' I asked Frankie.

She took a long drink of her wine. 'St Mike's is really

organized about all of that stuff. About a year ago the church
staff put together a booklet called "What Do I Do Now?" to
help family members dealing with a death since it can be so
paralyzing, especially when it's sudden and unexpected. Half
the time no one has a clue what the deceased person wanted
because they never talked about it – a full-blown funeral or a
party on a beach at sunset where you send the ashes out to sea.
Plus, in the middle of all the grief and heartbreak, everyone's
panicking because no one knows the password to the computer
with all the financial information on it or whether you can use
his credit card without committing fraud. So the staff at St
Mike's put together a list of readings and hymns to make
planning the funeral as easy as possible. Joe brought over a
binder with everything in it and I chose what I wanted. Tomorrow
I'll go by the church to meet with the liturgy director so we
can finalize the program and she can get it printed.'

'So it's all taken care of?'

'Almost. I need to talk to the florist and bring Paul's dark
suit over to BJ.'

'Frankie,' I said. 'Nikki and I figured you would want to
have something to eat and drink for everyone who comes
to the funeral after the Mass is over, so we're organizing a
luncheon in the tasting room, OK? Goose Creek Catering will
take care of the food as usual. Dominique is personally supervising the menu.'

Her eyes filled with tears. 'That's so kind ... I'll
reimburse ...'

'No. Absolutely not. It's all arranged. All of us are glad we
can do something to help when you've got so much on your
plate ... especially because it's been such a shock, so
unexpected.'

'Thank you. Really. I can't thank you enough.'

She looked as if she might break down, so I changed the
subject. 'Has Win finished the autopsy?'

Because no funeral could take place until the cause of death
had been determined, the death certificate had been signed, and
Paul's body had been released to the care of Hunt & Sons
Funeral Home. Not to mention that we needed to know when
that happened so we could make plans for the luncheon.

Frankie's phone, which had been lying next to her wine glass, rang and she picked it up. 'I guess I'm about to find out. This is Win now.'

I got up. 'I'll step outside, give you some privacy.'

She nodded as she clicked on her phone, her blonde head bent to concentrate on what Win was about to tell her. 'Hi, Win . . . yes, please. Tell me everything.'

The terrace lanterns and the necklace of tiny white lights Paul had wound through the wrought-iron security fence lit up the deck around the swimming pool. In the dusky twilight, the water shimmered as though someone had just skipped a stone over the surface and the sound of the pump from inside the equipment shed was a low constant hum. I sat down on a lounge chair as a click sounded and everything went quiet. That would be the timer, shutting off the equipment for the night.

The water settled down as smooth as glass. I looked around Frankie's yard in the quiet semi-darkness, and wondered what Win was telling her. Which was when I saw something glinting underneath an azalea bush next to the edge of the deck. I stood up and went over to see what it was – though somehow I already knew what I'd find.

A shard of broken glass. I pulled it out from under the bush with the tip of my cane. Even in the darkness the gold rim gleamed, and I could see a fragment of the etched floral design that matched the glasses in the bar inside the house.

A piece of the drink glass Frankie swore was missing.

She'd been right after all.

SIX

I got up and dunked my wine glass in the pool to rinse it out so there was no trace of Cabernet Sauvignon and used my cane to slide the broken shard into the bowl of the clean glass. When I walked into the kitchen, Frankie's eyes were red-rimmed and her phone was sitting on the island again.

'It must have been a tough conversation,' I said. 'What did Win say?'

She got up and pulled a tissue from a box sitting on the counter next to an electric kettle, dabbing her eyes. 'He said . . . there was alcohol in his blood, but also an abnormally high concentration of Ativan.'

'Ativan?'

'The generic name is lorazepam. It's an anti-anxiety medication.'

'I thought you weren't supposed to mix those drugs with alcohol.'

'You're not. He knew better. He went to see our doctor and got a prescription after he took over the Don't Pave Paradise Coalition because things had gotten so stressful.'

I nodded, numb. She hadn't shared any of this with me about how stressed Paul had been and the toll it had been taking on him.

'Win reckons the combination of alcohol and the amount of lorazepam in his system – way more than he should have taken – made him woozy. Out of it. He must have slipped when he was out by the pool and fallen in. Then he drowned.'

Our eyes met. Hers were filled with sorrow and heartache. Mine, I think, were filled with shock.

I didn't know what else to say. 'I'm so, so sorry.'

She cleared her throat. Stoic. Not breaking down. 'Because of what the blood test results showed, Win said they need to wait for the toxicology report to come back so they're going to keep him for a few more days until they get those results.

He's already spoken to BJ and told him the news, so we'll have to wait before we can have the funeral. As of now, though, it appears the cause of death was . . .' She put on a pair of reading glasses that were lying on the counter and picked up a piece of paper. '"Death from asphyxiation due to drowning and high concentration of benzodiazepine and alcohol in the blood." So they're talking about lorazepam.' Her voice wavered but then her gaze fell on my wine glass. 'What have you got there?'

I set the glass on the island so she could see what was inside. 'You were right. I found this under one of the azalea bushes. It matches the tumblers on the shelves in the other room.'

'I *told* you.' Her voice was sharp with irritation and frustration. 'No one believed me, but I *told* you. Someone else was here yesterday with Paul.'

She wasn't going to let it go.

'Unless Paul broke the glass, Frankie. Look at it logically. Paul dropped the glass which he had taken outside to the pool. It broke, so he cleaned it up, but he missed a piece.'

'In the state he must have been in?' She banged her wine glass down and the dark liquid sloshed like Rorschach inkblots on the labradorite. 'If that's what happened then why didn't I find the rest of it?'

'I don't know.' I tried not to sound exasperated. 'You really think someone took the missing pieces with them?'

She put her hands on her hips and gave me her most belligerent look, her comeback to the skepticism and disbelief in my voice. 'I *do*. Absolutely. Someone didn't want it known they were here – either when Paul died or before he died. They were scared, so they left. Or maybe whoever it was had something to do with his death.'

There it was. Exactly what Chiara had said. *Not an accident.* Though Frankie still hadn't linked Paul and Violet together yet.

I pushed back. 'Win just told you Paul had a lethal amount of lorazepam in his blood stream, along with alcohol. He must have slipped, fallen into the pool and drowned. So it *was* an accident.'

'If someone was here, they could have called 911. Could have pulled him out of the pool, performed CPR . . . done *something.*' Her eyes blazed, a mixture of anger and too much wine.

'What do you want to do?' I asked.

'Isn't it obvious? Call the Sheriff's Office. Tell them what you found so they can investigate.'

I shook my head slowly. 'Frankie . . .'

'*Lucie.*'

A dog with a bone. Not giving up.

'OK.' I held up my hand. Truce. 'Is there *anything* else . . . any other reason . . . that makes you believe someone was here with Paul yesterday? Something someone left behind? Or something that was out of place or missing? What about that meeting Paul had with Nash Blake? Was there something you didn't tell me – forgot or left out – about that?'

Something tangible. Though I didn't want to say it. She was already spun up enough.

'Nooooo . . .' Now Frankie was the one shaking her head, drawing out the word, but it was as if she were trying to clear cobwebs out of her brain, not giving me an absolutely-for-sure negative reply. 'Wait a minute.'

'What?'

'That briefcase I gave you to pass on to Eli. With all Paul's notes about the unpaved roads he was mapping, their history.'

'Yes?'

'It was in the coat closet in the foyer.'

'I remember. What's so odd about that?'

'Whenever Paul comes home, he leaves it on that chair by the front door. That way he can either grab it if he's heading out to do more research or pick it up and take it to the gardener's cottage where he's been working on this project. He's got huge maps of Loudoun County taped to the walls and he can putter to his heart's content out there and leave the maps as they are. No one sees them except him. And me, of course.'

'So why would he put the briefcase in the coat closet?'

She gave me the dumb-question look. 'Because he didn't want someone to see it, obviously.'

'The person who took the broken glass.'

'Of course.'

And here we were, back at square one. For about the third time.

The briefcase in the coat closet seemed almost as flimsy a reason as someone walking off with pieces of a broken tumbler.

'All right, what if I call Bobby Noland?' I said. 'It looks as if there's a film of some sort on the inside of the glass, so maybe that's something. Ivy's christening is at St Mike's on Sunday. Kit wants to talk to Quinn and me about what we're supposed to do since we're her godparents. I can ask Bobby about that, call him as a friend and not as a Loudoun County Sheriff's Office detective. I'll bring up the broken glass and see what he says, off the record. It might have more traction doing it this way than if you try to do it officially.'

Because otherwise you'll get a rookie Sheriff's Office deputy who will show up, take the broken shard, offer condolences, and then do nothing.

She nodded and said, in a crisp, tight voice. 'All right. Call him.'

Bobby was getting ready to leave work when I reached him. I walked out of the kitchen so I could have a blunt and extremely candid conversation with him out of Frankie's earshot.

'She's totally overwrought,' I told him. 'She's convinced someone was at the house yesterday and took most of the pieces of a broken drinks tumbler with him – or her – to avoid having anyone realize Paul had a guest with him before he died.'

'I've heard weirder, more far-fetched stories,' he said. 'People do the damnedest things when they're stressed or in a panic. Removing pieces of a broken glass is nothing compared to some of the wacko stuff that goes on sometimes. Except what you're telling me doesn't sound like Frankie. She's always so logical and pragmatic.'

'Agreed.'

'She's still obviously in shock,' he said. 'I heard about what happened when our guys got there yesterday. It must've been really rough. I've been meaning to call her, offer condolences. Paul was a good man. I liked him a lot. I wonder why she's so adamant about this broken glass, though.'

'Paul had a fairly unpleasant meeting with Nash Blake in Washington yesterday. The two of them apparently went at it about the Don't Pave Paradise plan to stop the Pro-Loudoun Progressives' push to pave the roads out here. Frankie said Paul said Nash threatened him. Told him to back down and stop trying to get the gravel and dirt roads listed on the Historic Register. Or else.'

'It's a very, very long way between making a threat in the heat of an argument and actually doing something about it, Lucie. We've talked about this before. And Nash Blake? What'd he do, dash out to Middleburg from his office in D.C., go over to Paul's for a chummy drink right after their meeting in Washington and – then what? Break a glass tumbler and leave with it after Paul went into the pool?'

'I know, I know. It sounds crazy. Look, Bobby, could you please talk to her? I think it will help. She won't listen to me. Also, there's something on the inside of the glass, like something dried in it.'

'Sure,' he said, stifling a yawn. 'Of course I will. My heart breaks for her. If it'll help, I can come by now. I was on my way home anyway.'

'Thank you,' I said. 'I owe you. I'll tell her. And I'll be here, too.'

I'd known Bobby since I was five years old and he was seven and Eli's best friend. They were inseparable; he practically lived at our house, in part because his own wasn't such a happy place. I'd trailed after him with the slavish devotion of prepubescent puppy love, which had been totally unrequited and mostly ignored. Not to mention he and Eli kept making me their Union prisoner when they played Civil War, a favorite game. Of theirs, not mine. They were always Confederates and, in their version, won every battle. As their prisoner they were constantly locking me in the burned-out shell of an old tenant house we called 'The Ruins.' Eventually I'd learned how to escape after getting locked in one too many times. I'd also gotten over Bobby and moved on to someone whose name I've now forgotten when I was in fifth grade. But it was my best friend Kit Eastman, the Loudoun bureau chief for *The Washington Tribune*, who Bobby had fallen head over heels in love with and married.

He looked tired when Frankie opened her front door half an

hour later with me standing right behind her. Khakis, a light blue polo shirt with the Sheriff's Office logo stitched on it where a pocket would have been, navy blazer. And chewing gum, a habit he'd acquired to help him quit smoking. Now he couldn't quit the gum.

He and Kit knew Frankie from our tasting room, of course, but they were also friends and the two of them had been to the Merchants' holiday parties as well as many of the other parties they'd hosted. So I wasn't surprised when he immediately enveloped Frankie in a big bear hug, murmuring quietly in her ear.

I heard her say, 'Thank you . . . I know . . . he was. You're very kind.'

She invited him inside and offered him a drink once the three of us were back in the kitchen. 'I wouldn't say no to a beer,' he said, sitting on one of the blue crushed velvet chairs. 'I'm officially off duty and it's been a hell of a day.'

'What'll you have? You know Paul and beer. We have everything.'

'Sam Adams?'

I'd switched to water. Frankie was still drinking, but she'd slowed the pace of the wine.

'So,' he said after Frankie handed him his beer. 'Tell me what's going on. Lucie explained some of it, but I'd like to hear what you have to say.'

When she was done, Bobby said, 'I'll take the piece of glass with me and call in a favor to get it analyzed. We can lift fingerprints, if there are any, and determine whatever was in it, particularly whatever seems to have coated the inside of the glass. I can let you know what they find.'

'Thank you. I appreciate that.'

'It will take a while. I'm afraid there's always a backlog. So don't hold out your hopes for an instant answer, OK? This isn't CSI, Loudoun.' He tried to temper his admonishment with a half-smile that wouldn't have convinced a toddler.

She nodded, looking grateful for the lifeline he'd thrown her. 'I won't.'

'And . . .' He reached over and placed his hand on her arm. 'There might not be anything unusual or out of the ordinary.

Paul's fingerprints on a glass that had some kind of alcoholic drink in it. It might just be what it is. A piece of broken glass that didn't get cleaned up when it shattered on the pool deck. Paul's gone, so unfortunately we'll never know.'

'I know.' She accepted the explanation with grace and some resignation. 'Thank you for doing this, at least.'

Bobby and I exchanged looks. 'Frankie, I would do anything for you and Paul, you know that,' he said. 'And now I probably ought to go home to my wife and daughter. I texted Kit that I was stopping by your place, but I think she's at the end of her rope with a colicky baby. She sends her condolences, by the way. She's devastated.'

'I should go, too,' I said. 'See if Quinn has finished with the Cab Sauv for the day. When are Lily and Yale due back?'

'Any minute, I'm sure. They've been gone over three hours. They were just going to go for a walk, have some brother–sister time together so they could talk about what happened,' she said. 'Speaking of what happened, did all the grapes get picked? You didn't have Benny, Nelia, or me.'

'Chiara Rossi helped out, and no, we didn't get everything picked. We'll finish tomorrow.'

'Chiara,' she said in a thoughtful voice. 'She's been coming by quite often since Violet died, to see how Paul was getting on with mapping the unpaved roads. She called me this morning in tears, just heartbroken about the news.'

I nodded and waited to see if Frankie would make any connection between Violet and Paul, but she didn't. Maybe Chiara hadn't broached the subject with her. Yet. I had no doubt it was only a matter of time before she did.

When we were outside and Frankie had shut her front door, I told Bobby about my conversation with Chiara this morning.

'She doesn't buy the official report that her mother's death was an accident. Now she seems to think there's some kind of conspiracy and that Paul's death is part of it,' I said. 'Only six weeks apart.'

'Does she have any proof? If she does, she should have brought it to us.'

'No proof. Just that a lot of people didn't want Violet to map the unpaved roads, research their historical significance, and then apply for Historic Preservation status.'

'People who were upset enough to kill her in order to stop her? There are other, more civilized ways to do this, you know. Like using a court of law.'

'I know. Of course I know.'

He had sealed the piece of glass in a plastic ziplock bag that he now held between his thumb and forefinger as if it contained something radioactive. 'The detective who handled the investigation said Violet Rossi's accident was a case of speeding and that she lost control of her car when she took that blind corner after First Bridge too fast and the car ended up in Goose Creek. There's not much room for error even if you know that turn – it's on a hill to boot. Unfortunately she must have passed out, since the cause of death was drowning. It's pretty open-and-shut. Driver error. One hundred per cent.'

I gave him the look I used to give him when we were in high school and I was tutoring him in algebra for honor society hours. *That's the wrong answer. Try again.* 'It's also two deaths by drowning within a pretty short space of time.'

'Lucie, come on—'

'Bobby, couldn't you just take another look at the accident report? See if there's anything someone might have missed? Please?'

'If I go back and start poking into someone else's case, I'm going to get some pushback. As if I don't believe he did his job correctly, that his work was sloppy. So I'll need to talk to him first.'

'But you'll still talk to him, won't you?'

He huffed out a sigh. 'Yeah, OK. But, look, just so you know the job's hard enough without everyone second guessing everyone else. We're short-staffed. Instead of three shifts in a day, everyone's now working a twelve-hour shift, so it's only two shifts a day. If you catch a case an hour before you're supposed to go off, you could work a sixteen-hour day.' He rubbed the hand that wasn't holding the plastic bag over his face and I saw the weariness and fatigue.

He went on. 'The board of supervisors wants results from the sheriff. *Expects* them. Especially in an election year like right now when he's in an ugly pissing match with his opponent. Solved cases mean we've got crime under control. Unsolved cases are a pile of dog poop my boss doesn't want to step in and which the other guy is trying to stir up. So there's pressure from everyone to up the solve rate. I'm sure you get it.'

'I do. But thanks for being willing to take another look at Violet's case. Also, I know it's possible Frankie is out on a limb with this, but you are going to have the glass analyzed, right?'

'Yeah, that too. Like I told her, though, this isn't CSI on television where after the commercial we wrap it all up. I don't know when we'll get results. I'm doing this based on no evidence and the wish of the wife of the deceased. Hopefully I can dance it past my boss – and it just so happens a guy in the lab owes me a favor.'

'You're a good man, Bobby.'

'I'm going to remind you that you said that someday. And now I'd better get home. You should, too. If you don't mind my saying so, you're looking pretty beat. I know harvest can be a bear, especially at the end. Go home and get some sleep. You need to be bright-eyed and bushy-tailed on Sunday to handle your goddaughter who, let me tell you, is keeping us on our toes.'

'She's adorable. I can't wait.'

After he drove off, I thought about what Frankie had said about Paul hiding the briefcase that contained all his notes. Last night when I got home, I'd put it in the library at Highland House. Frankie wanted me to turn it over to Eli so he could start drawing the maps, but maybe I'd take a look and see what was in it before I gave it to my brother.

Maybe I could figure out what might be so important Paul felt it necessary to tuck it out of sight where no one could get a look at whatever was inside.

SEVEN

'So now Bobby believes Frankie's broken glass theory, too? He thinks someone else was at the house yesterday with Paul?' Quinn asked me.

'Not exactly,' I said.

We were sitting at the oak trestle table in the kitchen finishing a dinner of leftovers from the meals Persia had fixed for us over the last few days. Even Persia's leftovers were a banquet feast. The room smelled fragrantly of sugar and peaches from the pie she had baked this afternoon for our dessert – the very last peaches of the season, she'd informed us.

'What does "not exactly" mean?' Quinn asked, reaching for an earthenware bowl that contained a few spoonfuls of watermelon, mint, and feta salad. 'Want to split this with me? There's only a little bit left.'

'No, thanks, it's all yours. It means Bobby doesn't really buy Frankie's story. There's nothing concrete to back it up, no evidence.'

'Then why is he having that glass analyzed?'

'He's doing it for her. Someone in their CSI unit in the latent examiners' department will lift any fingerprints and run them through their database to see if they get a match. He also has a friend, a scientist who works at a private lab and owns a gas spectrometer, so he can analyze the contents of the glass. Bobby warned Frankie it might take a couple of days, maybe longer, before he has any information since everyone's got official business that takes priority. He told her not to get her hopes up.'

'Which of course means her hopes *are* up.'

'Well, yes,' I said. 'He threw her a lifeline.'

The flickering candles on the dinner table and the glow of the under-cabinet lights cast Quinn's face partly in shadow. In the soft, dreamy light, Frankie's certainty that someone had been with Paul just before his tragic death seemed like a hard, jarring disconnect.

'I still don't understand what she thinks happened,' he said. 'And what I do understand doesn't make any sense.'

'I know,' I said. 'Except . . .'

When I didn't finish, he tilted his head and squinted at me, an expectant but concerned look on his face. 'Except what?'

'If it were anyone else, I'd agree with you, but it's Frankie. You know how logical and meticulous she is. You know she can be a little OCD sometimes.'

'A little? Sometimes? The woman who insists every charcuterie plate we serve has to be arranged in the exact same way? Not to mention there are some of us who apparently *load the dishwasher at the Villa backwards*.' He was smiling but his eyes were grave.

'OK, she's more than "a little" OCD. Which is why if she swears the rest of that glass disappeared yesterday and isn't in some trash bin somewhere . . .'

'Whoa, wait. Are *you* starting to believe her?'

When I didn't answer immediately, he threw me a scrutinizing look. 'You know something.'

'If I tell you, you're going to tell me it sounds – I don't know – sort of woo-woo.'

I got a blank stare. 'Woo-woo.'

He wasn't going to make this easy. 'OK. You know, out there. Far-fetched.'

He folded his hands together and leaned toward me. 'Try me.'

'It's something Chiara told me.'

He blew out a breath like a tire that had suddenly deflated. 'Oh. Chiara.'

'See? You already sound cynical. By the way, she didn't do a bad job of picking grapes today, in case you didn't notice.'

'I knew you were going to bring that up. Again.'

'Yeah, well, I'm right, aren't I?'

He gave me a grudging look. 'She did OK. So what did she tell you?'

'When I was driving her out to the vineyard this morning, she told me she's convinced her mother's death wasn't an accident. And she believes Paul's death won't turn out to be one, either.'

'Huh.'

'Huh, what?'

'It does sound . . . woo-woo.'

'I knew you were going to bring *that* up. OK, forget I said anything.'

'No . . . wait. I'm sorry.' He reached over and squeezed my hand. 'Please. Go on.'

I *wanted* him to know. Wanted him to think there was a sliver of possibility she could be right. 'I told Bobby what she said. Chiara, I mean.'

'What did he say?'

'He listened. He's going to pull Violet's accident report.'

'Seriously?'

'Yup.'

'I thought her accident was ruled as driver error,' he said. 'No question about it. She was speeding when she took that turn on Crenshaw Road. You come over the crest of that hill after First Bridge and miss that blind elbow turn – boom, the creek's right there. There's no way to correct your mistake or pull out of it. The water was pretty high since we'd just had a couple of freak rainstorms, so the creek was even closer to the edge of the road than it normally would have been at that time of year.'

'I know all that. But I'm telling you, Chiara's not convinced it was her mother's fault.'

'Come on, the road's barely wide enough for one car. If two cars meet head on, someone has to either back up or else try to move onto the shoulder – if they can.'

'I know that, too.'

'Plus, there wasn't any evidence of a collision with another vehicle. Even a motorcycle would have left a scape or a transfer of paint somewhere.'

'I'm aware.'

He folded his arms across his chest and sat back, eyeing me. 'Then what exactly does Chiara think happened? And why do you sound like you believe her?'

'I don't know. It's just weird that the two people who were trying to get the unpaved roads around here listed on the National Register of Historic Places both end up dead within six weeks of each other,' I said. 'Chiara's right about that. Once is a tragic accident. But two people? You know Bobby always says there's no such thing as coincidences.'

'Yes, but there's zero evidence to back up either one of those deaths being anything *but* accidents. Speeding on a dirt road and missing a blind turn. A drug overdose and then Paul tumbled into a swimming pool and drowned. I just don't get how those two deaths could possibly be related. Or who would have orchestrated something – masterminded, is probably more like it – a plot to have two people knocked off just to keep a bunch of roads from being paved.'

'It's not the why or the how that links them together,' I said. 'It's the *who*. Both of them were working on the same project. Paul stepped in and immediately took over the Don't Pave Paradise Coalition after Violet died.'

At least he didn't shoot me down this time. 'Did you tell Frankie any of this?'

'God, no. She's already spun up enough.'

'Well, you seem to have some traction with Bobby if he's going to take another look at that accident report.'

'Maybe. We'll see. He's worried about pissing off the detective whose case it was – as if the guy didn't do his job.' I stood up and took our dinner plates over to the sink. 'Do you want a piece of peach pie?'

He patted his firm, lean stomach. 'You bet. I saved room.'

I got Persia's pie while he got dessert plates, forks, and the pie server. I cut two pieces – an extra-large one for him.

He ate a mouthful of pie, chewed, and said, 'Do you want to come out tonight with me and watch?'

A major shift in the trajectory of our conversation, but I knew what he meant.

He'd been talking about it for days: a total lunar eclipse that would occur tonight when Earth would come between the sun and the moon and all three would align perfectly. When that happened, Earth would completely block the light of the sun, which normally illuminates the moon and turns it into the silvery disc we see at night. Although it would seem logical that the unlit moon would disappear into the blackness of the night sky, a phenomenon called Rayleigh scattering meant that a small amount of light – red light, the longest wavelengths which came from the violet end of the spectrum – would filter through Earth's atmosphere and indirectly reach the moon. When that happened the moon would either turn an eerie shade of coppery orange or else a deep, dark red. Normally the October full moon was known as the Harvest Moon because it was said that farmers could gather in their crops at night, thanks to the bright shining light that flooded their fields. This moon, however – the moon of the lunar eclipse – would be known as a Blood Moon because of its color.

For the last week Quinn had been constantly checking the weather on his phone as well as reading the astronomy blogs he followed to see if the sky would be cloud-free, or at least not completely overcast. As tired as he was after a long day of harvest, and even though we had to be up at the crack of dawn tomorrow, I knew he wasn't going to miss this. Fortunately, moonrise wasn't going to be too late: nine-oh-three, to be precise. And the eclipse would be over by midnight.

One of the most surprising and unexpected discoveries I'd made about my husband when we first met was his fascination with the stars, the planets, our galaxy, and generally anything that happened in the night sky. My wedding present to him last spring had been a Celestron telescope after a violent tornado-like storm known as a derecho had wiped out the back garden where we'd planned to have our ceremony, as well as flattening the small wooden summerhouse where he'd kept his old telescope.

It also happened that the best view of the night sky was a bluff behind Highland House with a wide-open view of a valley of horse and cattle farms that stretched clear to the low-slung Blue Ridge Mountains. When the two of us had been starting to get to know each other, he'd invite me to see some nighttime phenomenon like the Perseids meteor shower or an unusual opportunity to view the rings of Saturn, explaining it all and teaching me what to look for through his telescope lens. I think that's when I fell in love with him, on those peaceful nights as we sat side by side in my mother's old Adirondack chairs, often finishing the last of the dinner wine or an after-dinner drink, talking quietly as we slowly learned about each other. Sometimes he'd smoke a cigar, since I had a firm absolutely-no-smoking-in-the-house-or-else rule, its tip glowing like a mini orange moon, the mingled aromatic scent of wood, leather, and dark, strong coffee filling the night air.

He'd taught me how to identify the planets, their moons, constellations, exoplanets, and, on incredibly clear nights, how to look for the Milky Way. He'd also explained how outer space wasn't a nice, gentle place with twinkling stars, constellations romantically named for gods, goddesses, and creatures of mythology, and meteors that flashed through the sky in graceful arcs like shooting stars. On the contrary, scientists had known for a long time that our Milky Way had a voracious, cannibalistic appetite for brutally devouring other galaxies, and showed no signs of being sated. The cosmos was a mostly empty, cold, and desolate place of everlasting night – and what happened out there was something over which we had no control.

'I'll join you for the eclipse,' I said to him now. 'But first I want to take a look in the briefcase Frankie gave us yesterday before I turn it over to Eli.'

'What are you looking for? Don't tell me you think you'll find the rest of that broken glass?'

'No, but that's a thought, even though it would be completely crazy if I did.'

'Then what are you expecting to find?'

'I don't know. Maybe I'll know it when I see it. *If* I find anything.'

We finished the dishes and then Quinn went outside to set up his telescope and smoke his cigar. Though the moon would hang low and fat in the sky so it would be clearly visible as it rose – actually it would be huge – viewing it through his telescope meant it would be possible to see its craters, mountains, and valleys, which he, of course, wanted to do. I promised to join him when the eclipse was far enough along that it looked as if something had taken a large bite out of the moon, like a bite out of a cookie. He said he'd either text or call me when that happened, so I left him and walked down the hall to the library.

It was the room that had always been the sanctuary of my

father, Leland, when he was alive – the built-in floor-to-ceiling bookcases filled with his books, many of them rare first editions, on the history of colonial Virginia, the Civil War, and an extensive collection of books about and by Thomas Jefferson, whom he had revered nearly to sainthood. There was also his gun cabinet, a substantial piece of furniture that had been custom carved of mahogany and veneer woods by a talented Amish carpenter, which he then brought to Atoka and assembled on site. The two glass-fronted doors were etched with a majestic-looking buck and the seal of the Commonwealth of Virginia – the Roman goddess Virtus standing over a vanquished foe with the words 'Sic Semper Tyrannis' – Thus Always to Tyrants – written underneath.

A fire not long after I moved home from France five years ago had destroyed much of the room, although the gun cabinet had been untouched, so I'd hired a carpenter who specialized in restoration work to rebuild the bookcases and repair the charred carved woodwork. When he was finished, you'd never have guessed that there had been any damage except for the loss of Leland's irreplaceable collection of first editions. Quinn and I had begun slowly filling the shelves with our own books, a few pieces of sculpture we'd acquired, and several small, framed paintings which were mounted inside the shelves. I'd also framed and hung several oil paintings I'd found in the back of a closet that my mother, who had been a talented artist, had painted of the farm, the house, and the vineyard. Slowly, the room began to feel more like mine. A new sofa and two comfortable club chairs pulled around a vintage coffee table I'd found at the old Luckett Store. An antique quilt rack, another find over which I draped quilts my grandmother had made so there was something warm to snuggle under in winter along with a book and a cup of tea as a fire burned in the fireplace.

A few months ago, I'd finally decided that the gun cabinet had to go. Though generations of my family had been hunters, I am not martial by nature – although I have continued the Montgomery family tradition of allowing the Goose Creek Hunt to ride through our land during fox-hunting season and consider it part of their territory. I also know how to shoot a rifle and a pistol thanks to Leland, but that was a skill that was almost considered a necessity out here in the country where we had bears, coyotes, and rattlesnakes. Actually, I am a pretty good shot.

Eli told me he would take the gun cabinet off my hands and move it to his studio in the carriage house because he could repurpose the long shallow drawers where guns and ammunition had been stored as a place to keep his architectural drawings. As for the guns, I kept two – the rifle and pistol I had learned to shoot with – and bought a plain vanilla metal gun safe to store them. The rest – especially the antique guns – I had no trouble selling to the Romeos.

Paul Merchant's leather briefcase was leaning against the large partner's desk where I'd left it last night. I set the glass of wine I'd brought with me on the coffee table in front of the rolled-arm sofa at the other end of the room and brought the briefcase over so I could open it and look through what was inside. If Paul had indeed taken care to hide it so someone – perhaps even his wife – wouldn't go through the contents, then maybe it contained a secret, something he wanted to keep hidden.

I sat down on the couch and rested my cane against one of the seat cushions. The briefcase was old, well worn, beautiful buttery soft leather. Italian, no doubt. His initials – PJM – must have once been embossed in gold, but it had long since rubbed off and now there was just the faint indentation of the letters. I pulled out the papers, which were neatly arranged in a series of folders by region or town. I opened a folder with 'Upperville' written on the tab and, sure enough, there was a rough drawing of Crenshaw Road and a two-page narrative about its history: where it had gotten its name, how it had been laid out, the history of the two early-twentieth-century one-lane stone bridges that were built where Goose Creek cut across Crenshaw Road, and the history of Phipps Polo Field, which dated back to the early 1900s. It was the road Violet Rossi had been on when her Jeep veered off after she came over a small precipitous hill, lost control around a blind corner, and plunged into Goose Creek. Some of the text had been typed and printed out, but a lot was handwritten. Two different handwritings – the sharp angular writing I figured would be Paul's; the more fine, delicate penmanship had to belong to Violet.

The last folder I came to had nothing written on the outside. When I opened it, I found a black and white photograph of a beautiful young woman dressed in the clothes of another era – a pretty, feminine dress that showed off a slender hourglass figure, fitted and cinched at the waist with a flared skirt, exaggerated shoulder pads, and big butterfly sleeves. She was lovely, leaning against something that looked like a stage because I could see part of a heavy velvet curtain above her in the background. I turned the photo over. Someone had written *Eleanor, circa 1940* in faded old-fashioned script on the back. The other item in the folder was a newspaper account of a fire at the Hollywood Theatre in Middleburg in 1941.

This must be Eleanor Blake, the woman who had died in that fire: Nash Blake's grandmother and Hunter's great-grand-mother. The theater had been located on Washington Street – Middleburg's main street, which was named for George – next door to the Red Fox Inn. Outside Middleburg, Washington Street became Route 50; for years it had been known around here as Mosby's Highway but now, with the old Civil War names disappearing, it had reverted to its former name: Little River Turnpike. Route 50 was also the longest transcontinental highway in the US, stretching from Ocean City, Maryland to Sacramento, California – and, though it was of historic interest, it was paved. So what was this story doing in a folder of information about unpaved roads? And why was the photo of Eleanor Blake here as well?

Paul had just had an ugly fight with Nash Blake before going home and ending up at the bottom of his swimming pool. Which made me wonder if the two of them had argued not only about the unpaved roads in Loudoun County, but also about something more personal that Paul had discovered concerning Nash's grandmother and the deadly fire that had killed her.

If that's what had happened, I wondered what they had talked about. And if whatever it was had upset Nash so much that somehow, in some way, he was directly or indirectly responsible for Paul's death.

To shut him up.

EIGHT

Quinn texted me as I finished re-reading the newspaper article about the fire at the Hollywood Theatre that had killed Eleanor Blake.

The game's afoot. Come *now.*

I smiled and wrote back. Be right there, Sherlock.

The moon had started to rise behind the Blue Ridge Mountains, big and fat and so close that I felt I could reach out and grab a piece of it. As we watched it began to slowly give off a reddish glow that looked like the embers of a dying fire. It took another half hour before Quinn pronounced that the moon had moved into the umbra, the deepest part of the Earth's shadow.

'This is totality,' he said. 'We get to see the whole thing. It will stay red like this for another forty-five minutes.'

And so, for the next three-quarters of an hour, I got a refresher lesson on the moon's geography since everything was blown up to gigantic size. Mountain ranges like the lunar alps, the Caucasus, the Apenninus and the so-called seas, or 'mare,' which I knew weren't really seas at all, but rather lava covering up old craters that had settled and cooled into basalt rock so smooth that the indentation looked like the floor of an ocean.

'You can see the Man in the Moon perfectly tonight,' Quinn said. 'Take a look.'

'He probably looks like he has apoplexy since he's all red,' I said and leaned down to take a look through the viewfinder.

I had been surprised the first time Quinn told me about the Man in the Moon – I'd always thought he was someone who only existed in children's nursery rhymes. But in fact there were a lot of cultures that believed you could see a human face on the moon's surface; almost all of them believing the face belonged to someone who had been punished for some egregious deed they'd done or else they'd been banished from earth altogether. It was a phenomenon known as pareidolia.

'Do you see him?' Quinn asked.

'I think so. He's huge.'

'Yeah, but he still looks like a tilted Halloween pumpkin. His eyes are the Mare Imbrium and Mare Serenitatis. His nose, which looks like a hook or a backwards C, is still off center. The Sinus Aestuum.'

'I see them.'

'Look further down and left. His mouth is open so it's two seas that are melded together, the Mare Nubium and Mare Cognitum.'

'I still say he looks different because he's so big. And so red.'

'Yes, but since we always see the exact same side of the moon, you know where to look to find him.'

'I don't understand why that happens.'

'Simple. The moon rotates on its axis exactly like Earth does, but it also happens to be perfectly in sync with us. So both the moon and Earth make a complete rotation at exactly the same time and end up in exactly the same place.'

'It's weird how they're so in sync.'

'A lot of things in outer space are weird. There's plenty we can't explain.'

And that was what he loved, what fascinated him. Why he was out here so many nights with his telescope looking at stars and planets and pricks of light that just *were* even though we couldn't explain them. Which was why I decided not to bring up the subject of Eleanor Blake and the Hollywood Theatre fire until after the moon was ending its trajectory through Earth's shadow and regaining its customary silver hue. By the time the eclipse had ended, it was nearly midnight, we were both yawning, and I could hardly keep my eyes open.

'Are you ready to go inside?' I asked, suppressing another yawn.

'Yup. It's over.' He started to disassemble his telescope.

'This was a long one.'

'I know. We were lucky we got to see totality for as long as we did. It doesn't happen often. The next one like this won't be for another fifteen years.'

'I thought a blood moon was supposed to mean that the

second coming is near. Or the end of the world. Or we'll all
be swept up in the Rapture and float into heaven to join Jesus.
Take your pick.'

'What have you been reading? Or who have you been talking
to? You aren't serious.' He eyed me. 'Are you?'

'No, of course not. But isn't there something in the Bible
about the world coming to an end when the moon turns red?'

He sighed. 'Yeah, there is. "The sun will be turned into
darkness and the moon into blood before the day of the Lord
comes, that great and terrible Day." It's from the Acts of the
Apostles. The people who believe that are the same ones who
believe in alien abductions, that kind of wacko stuff.' He
twirled his finger next to his temple. 'I wouldn't worry about
the world coming to an end tomorrow if I were you. Or Jesus
returning to straighten things out – though it wouldn't be a
bad idea if he did.'

I smiled. 'All right, but people *do* act differently when there's
a full moon, you know.'

'Oh, come on.'

'I'm serious.'

'Not. True.'

'What about doctors and nurses who claim that emergency
rooms always get busier when there's a full moon? There are
plenty of sane, normal people who are convinced a full moon
changes human behavior. You know, moon madness. It's a thing.'
I folded the log cabin quilt my grandmother had made, which
I'd brought outside to bundle up in when it got cooler. '*I* believe
it. I can always tell when there's going to be a full moon because
people drive like maniacs that day. *And* at night. It never fails.
I'm never wrong.'

'*Science*,' he said, emphasizing the word, 'does not back up
your Spidey sense.'

'Ha! I don't care. People *are* more reckless when there's a
full moon. The Latin name for moon – *luna* – means "crazy."
Where do you think that came from if there's not some truth
in all this?'

'I think it came from people with overactive imaginations
who convince themselves that a series of coincidences validates
their unsubstantiated-by-fact theory. That's what I think.' He

snapped the case of his telescope shut. 'Are you ready to go inside?'

'I am.' We threaded our way past the rose garden and cut across the lawn. The moonlight was still bright enough to light our path as if it were daytime.

'We ought to think about rebuilding the summerhouse so we can store some of this stuff there like we used to do.' Quinn abruptly changed the subject, ending any further discussion about aliens, the Rapture, and moon madness.

'I'll talk to Eli and ask him if he could come up with a design, maybe something larger than what we had before and that we can electrify so it's more than a glorified shed,' I said. 'I need to give him Paul Merchant's briefcase so he can start drawing the maps for the National Register of Historic Places. I'll ask him then. Speaking of that briefcase, I did find something inside it.'

'Oh, yeah? What was it?'

I told him about the photo of the woman named Eleanor, who I was certain had to be Eleanor Blake, and the newspaper article about the Hollywood Theatre fire in 1941 in which she'd died.

'How did she die?' he asked.

'She was in the theater by herself in the projection room and there was a short in the electrical wiring. The whole place was made of wood, so it went up in flames immediately. By the time the Middleburg Fire Department got there, they managed to get the fire under control but it was too late to save most of the building. They found her body inside afterwards. It seems she died from smoke inhalation but they also found the door to the projection room locked – apparently the lock had jammed. They had to break the door down to get to her.'

We climbed the steps to the veranda. Quinn opened the kitchen door and held it for me.

'She didn't escape because she couldn't? Jesus, what an awful way to die,' he said, following me inside.

I shuddered. 'I know. Her husband – Redmond Blake – was the one who found her. She said she was going to stop by the theater and, when he heard about the fire, he raced over there, but it was too late.'

'God, that's awful.'

'I know.' I set our wine glasses on the counter next to the sink to wash in the morning and put the bottle in the recycling bin. What *had* happened to Eleanor Blake? She must have suffered as the oxygen left the projection room, greedily consumed by the fire. Had she been overcome by smoke before the fire reached the projection room where she was locked inside? She probably had been terrified, pounding on the door, screaming for help . . .

'Are you ready to go upstairs?' Quinn cut into my thoughts. 'Are you OK?'

'Yes, sorry. Just thinking.'

When we were in our bedroom he said, 'What do you think that photo and the article were doing in a briefcase full of maps and notes about the unpaved roads?'

'I don't know. I wonder if Paul – or Violet – found out something while they were doing their research and told Nash about it since Eleanor was his grandmother.'

'You told me Frankie said Paul said Nash had threatened him at that meeting in his office in D.C.'

'Frankie was under the impression the threat had to do with the Don't Pave Paradise Coalition's plan to get the unpaved roads designated as historic landmarks,' I said. 'Maybe Paul didn't tell Frankie the whole story. Maybe the threat had to do with whatever he and Violet found out – *might* have found out – about that fire and Eleanor's death.'

'That doesn't sound good,' Quinn said.

'No,' I said. 'It doesn't.'

On Wednesday morning, in spite of everyone's grogginess, we figured it was only going to take a couple more hours to finish bringing in the last of the Cabernet Sauvignon grapes. Quinn and I weren't the only ones who had stayed up to watch the blood moon. Dante, Orlando, and Jesús had gone over to the farm manager's cottage where Antonio and Valeria lived, not far from the winery, and watched from their front porch. This morning there seemed to be more than the usual amount of teasing banter in Spanish as they were getting ready to go out to the field to pick grapes, all of it directed at Orlando, who, I'm pretty sure, was telling them where they could stick their comments.

Finally I said to Antonio, 'Why is everyone giving Orlando such a hard time? And what are "calzones rojos"? All I know is that it means red something.'

'Underwear. Red underwear.'

'What?'

'Orlando wore red underwear during the eclipse last night. To keep evil spirits away.'

'Seriously?'

'It's a Mexican superstition,' Antonio said. 'He doesn't exactly believe in evil spirits, but you don't want to take any chances, do you?'

'I guess not. Does he also believe in the Rapture or that a blood moon means the end of the world is near?'

'Isn't the Rapture that craziness about people floating up to heaven? Nah, that's too weird.'

'Unlike wearing red underwear to keep away evil spirits, which is not too weird.'

Antonio grinned. 'To each his own, Lucita.'

We finished picking the grapes just before noon on another scorching October day. Nikki brought sandwiches, chips, water, and sodas down from the tasting room and everyone sat in the shade of the crush pad, tried to cool off, and wolfed down lunch.

Even though deciding *when* to pick can be a crapshoot involving a lot of guesstimating, once the grapes are in, we need to work fast to get them processed. And we absolutely had to keep them cold because if they weren't refrigerated or packed under a layer of dry ice, they would warm up and begin fermenting on their own. If that happened, we'd end up with vinegar.

For all the loosey-goosey, should-we-or-shouldn't-we decision making that happened in the vineyard – since we never knew what the weather might bring in a few weeks or even a few days – once the grapes were in the wine cellar or on the crush pad, everything revolved around careful calculations and math. A *lot* of math – along with about nine hundred decisions, give or take, that had to be made. Plus every year we started from scratch since the one thing we could always count on in Virginia was that we couldn't count on the weather. Our growing season was never the same from one year to the next, unlike California, land of endless sunshine and consistent glorious weather. Our first winemaker, Jacques Gilbert, who came from France, used to scoff that you could stick just about anything in the soil in California and it would grow, no questions asked. In Virginia, he'd said with characteristic Gallic ego, we had to *work* to get our grapevines to grow and produce. And with the acceleration of climate change we had to work harder, become even more flexible.

This year, for example, it had been so wet that Quinn and I had already had the somewhat heartbreaking discussion about the need to bleed off some of the juice before the grapes began fermenting – a process known as saignée. Though we would make less red wine – the pale pink juice would be used to make rosé instead – the tradeoff was that we were increasing the amount of skins relative to juice in the tank, so we'd end up with richer wine with more color and tannins. In other words, better wine.

Or at least that was the plan.

The process of sorting the grapes and removing the MOG – material other than grapes – so the fruit was clean was going to take hours. It always did. Once it was finished, we would move the grapes into tanks and, when we ran out of tanks, into one-ton bins that were then covered with a layer of dry ice.

Making red wine is a labor-intensive process that is nothing like making white wine. For white wine you press the grapes as soon as you pick them and, voilà, with the juice you've extracted you make wine.

It's more complicated with red grapes. First, they need to be inoculated with yeast to start fermentation and then they need to sit on the skins in the tanks and bins for days or maybe even a couple of weeks, a process called maceration. They also need to be mixed and stirred so you don't end up with a giant pulsing tumor of vinegar somewhere in the middle of a tank. Because you begin with a mass of grapes, seeds, and skins – called the 'must' – which is as dense as a block of concrete, you need to punch down the cap on a regular basis, which means you have to push down the grapes floating on the top so they stay wet and fermentation can continue. When Jacques was here, he used Eli's old baseball bat. Now we have the right piece of equipment – a pole with a wide, flat paddle, which goes by the clever name of 'wine punch down tool.'

As soon as the grapes have softened and are no longer a hard block, we begin pumping over which means twice a day everything on the bottom of the tank gets moved to the top via a pump and a couple of hoses. Eventually the must stops bubbling like something out of the witches' brew in Macbeth and fermentation is done. Finished. Complete. Only then can you press the grapes and extract the juice.

There was a point at which I knew Quinn and Antonio and the rest of the crew had everything under control – the easy-going banter flying back and forth in Spanish mixed in with the driving beat of a boombox that set the rhythm and pace of the work that needed to be done so somehow it all looked seamless – effortless, even. Though it was most definitely not. It was hard work, but we had a good crew, people who worked with heart, who cared about the work, about the quality of the wine they were making, who didn't see this as a job. Last year, Quinn and I had started asking all of them to participate in wine tastings and blending sessions, giving them more responsibility in the decision-making process, teaching them what they needed to know. It had paid off because no one left at the end of the season. Everyone stayed. Now they felt like family.

'I want to check on Frankie and Benny,' I said to Quinn. 'Do you need me right now?'

He slid a kiss across my lips. 'I need you all the time. Go ahead. Call them. We're good here.'

I kissed him back and went outside. It was quieter in the courtyard, so I sat on the stone wall, my feet dangling over the edge, the view – always one of my favorites – of rows of vines lined up like soldiers bracketed by the Blue Ridge Mountains. In summer the canopy in the vineyard was leafy and green but today it was more sparse and what leaves remained on the vines were rust, bronze and copper-colored, like the colors of the moon at the beginning of the eclipse last night.

In another month the vines would be bare and go dormant for the winter.

The first person I talked to was Nelia, who said that tomorrow afternoon Benny would be moving to a rehab hospital in Aldie where he'd spend the next ten days, learning how to get around without putting any weight on his shattered knee.

'Can we come visit him?' I asked. 'You've been asking us to hold off, but – please?'

'Why don't you come tomorrow morning before he's trans-ferred to the rehab hospital?' She sounded exhausted and I knew she'd been sleeping in a recliner in Benny's hospital room ever since the accident because she didn't want to leave him. 'His doctor has been weaning him off the Percocet and gabapentin the surgeon prescribed for pain, thank God. I can't wait. For the last two days he's been hallucinating and talking nonsense. He has conversations with people who aren't in the room and he's so confused about where he is and what's going on. It's scary. I didn't want you to see him . . . like that. He wouldn't want it, either. By tomorrow morning he should be better when the drugs are out of his system.'

Benny, who was so proud, talking to invisible people, talking nonsense. Nelia doing her best to protect him so we wouldn't see him in such a vulnerable state.

'I'll call you before we come,' I told her. 'You can let us know then if he's up for visitors. We'll wait until you tell us it's time.'

Her voice was soft with gratitude. 'Thank you for under-standing.'

'Of course. Look, if you need anything . . .'

'I know,' she said. 'Thank you. And don't worry, Lucie. He's going to be fine.'

I disconnected, took a deep breath, and called Frankie. She answered, her voice muted.

'I'm at the funeral home,' she said. 'I brought Paul's charcoal suit so they can dress him when the time comes. He always looked so good in it. I've got a minute before BJ returns.'

'How are you holding up? Is there anything I can do? Do you need anything?'

'I'm OK – though I'm probably still in shock. As for what I need? Answers from Bobby about that wine glass.'

'Have you heard from him?'

'Not yet . . . BJ's back. I'd better go.'

She hung up. There hadn't been a chance to ask her if she knew what a photo of Eleanor Blake and an article about the Hollywood Theatre fire was doing in Paul's briefcase.

The fire had happened a long time ago, so long that hardly anyone who was alive would remember. There was, however, one person who might know *something*. In fact, she would probably know more than anyone in Middleburg and Atoka about what had happened that day because she was the self-appointed keeper of all news.

I went back to the crush pad, got the keys to the Jeep, and told Quinn I needed to pick up a few things at the General Store.

Among them, hopefully, was information about Eleanor Blake.

NINE

The General Store sits in a curve on Atoka Road within spitting distance of the turn-off from Route 50. The road splits as you come around the corner from 50, so a left turn puts you on Rector Lane, and if you stay right, you're on Atoka Road. There are three signs at that junction: one says the speed limit is twenty-five; the second that these roads are part of Virginia's historic Civil War Trails. A cardinal sitting on a branch of dogwood blossoms – our state bird and flower – are painted on the bright blue background of the third sign, which is my favorite: Atoka Road – the peaceful, pretty country road I live on – is designated as a Virginia scenic by-way.

A modest white clapboard building with a dark-green hipped roof and large picture window with a neon Open sign, or 'Ope' since the 'N' burned out years ago, the General Store sits at this intersection, which is appropriate because it is also the pulsing nexus of news in our little corner of the Old Dominion. For as long as I can remember, Thelma Johnson, owner and purveyor of all information – though some would call it gossip – has gently but firmly wrapped her velvet-gloved fist around the wrist of anyone who walked through her door, drawing them in to talk to her and, in the nicest possible way, grilling them as if it were the Spanish Inquisition. Part of her quirky charm is her disarming and uncanny ability to get you to tell her things you never intended to say. Sometimes they were things you never realized you knew, often because she swore by the otherworldly powers of her Ouija board which, she claimed, allowed her to speak with your loved ones from the Great Beyond.

I've always thought of myself as a relatively sane, normal, rational person, but let me tell you, on more than one occasion, Thelma has managed to convince me that she has had honest-to-God conversations *with my mother*. Less frequently with my father, who was a curmudgeon, a rascal, a gambler, and a womanizer. Leland, she said, didn't often show up for a chat

– from wherever he was on the Other Side. She never elaborated. I never asked.

When the Middleburg Safeway opened years ago, Thelma didn't worry one bit about the potential competition and what it might do to her little business. After all, Safeway didn't carry ammunition, live bait, or horse hoof polish – items that were necessary and essential for her clients. She also prided herself on never running out of the other essentials – milk, toilet paper, and bread – or what she liked to call 'the white stuff you need when the other white stuff starts falling from the sky.' Plus there were her three coffee pots – Plain, Fancy, and Decaf – along with a selection of freshly baked muffins, croissants and donuts that arrived each morning from a bakery in Leesburg, making the General Store undeniably attractive as *the* meeting place for everyone who wanted to know what was going on in Atoka, Middleburg, and even as far away as Winchester and Culpeper.

You could say Thelma was a woman of an *un*certain age, or as she liked to tell you in her coy, coquettish way, 'I'm not as young as I look.' She dressed with the va-va-voom sass, flair, and daring of a teenager who would immediately get sent back upstairs to change into something less short, tight, and revealing, young lady, if a parent caught her trying to sneak out of the house. Her makeup was applied with a gardening trowel, her hair was a color not seen anywhere in nature, and her tortoise-shell trifocal glasses gave her a vaguely bug-eyed look. But all in all, Thelma Johnson was a force of nature and someone not to be trifled with.

I parked the Jeep out front in the postage-stamp area she called the parking lot and was pleased to see mine was the only vehicle, so I could ask my questions about Eleanor Blake without anyone else around. The sleigh bells hanging on the front door jingled as they always did when I walked in and, as usual, there was a buzz of voices in the back room that sounded as if the participants were in the midst of discussing an important, weighty matter. More than likely, the voices belonged to the actors and actresses on *Tomorrow Ever After*, Thelma's favorite soap opera, and the discussion probably revolved around whether the hot-looking polo player would remember anything when he finally emerged from a coma that had lasted two seasons, or if the dark-eyed beauty who might also be a jewel thief would finally go to bed with the foxy, silver-haired business mogul who might also be a spy.

The voices stopped abruptly, followed by Thelma calling, 'Hold your horses out there. I'm coming.' A moment later she emerged with the theatrical drama of a diva making her entrance on a Broadway stage, dressed from head to toe in Barbie pink. A slinky knit minidress clung to her like a second skin; her pink kitten heel sandals had feathered propeller-shaped bows on them. Pink eye shadow. Bubblegum pink lipstick. Two bright spots of pink blush. A lot of pink.

'Lucille,' she said, stepping behind the check-out counter, her face lighting up like a child who has just seen the gifts under the tree on Christmas morning, 'Why, I *knew* you'd come by. I started thinking about you earlier today and, I have to tell you, my psychotic powers kicked in right away – there are some things I just *know* are going to happen.' She tapped a pink lacquered nail against her pumpkin-colored hair. 'So I've been expecting you. In fact, I saved a raspberry jelly donut for you, and today's Fancy is a real peppy one: Dejá Brew. You're looking a bit tuckered out, child. Come sit a spell and we can have a nice chat.'

Damn. I had come by to ask her about Eleanor Blake. She'd probably heard that I'd been with Frankie after Sonny dragged Paul Merchant's body out of the swimming pool and the Sheriff's Office deputies and EMTs had shown up. She was going to grill *me* for information about what had happened.

If I wanted her to answer my questions, the quid pro quo would be that I had to share what I knew about Paul. Since she was probably the only person still living who would remember anything about the Hollywood Theatre fire that had killed Eleanor, it was pretty clear how this was going to go.

She got my donut while I fixed my coffee.

In the back corner of the store next to a pot-belly stove that warmed the place in winter was a small circle of rocking chairs where Thelma liked to hold court – usually with a couple of the Romeos. Her rocking chair was an elegant antique Lincoln rocker that was closest to the stove. The one I always thought of as mine was a beautiful old Bentwood rocker. We took our seats, me balancing the powdered sugar-coated jelly donut precariously on a napkin I'd draped over my knees while I drank my coffee and wondered how I was going to eat the donut without ending up looking like I'd been dunked in powdered sugar myself.

Thelma wasn't one to beat around the bush. 'I heard – and this is between closed walls, you understand – that you were over to the Merchants' house after the pool boy pulled poor Paul out of his swimming pool. It must of been turrible, child, just turrible.'

I wondered who her 'closed walls' source was. A picture flashed through my mind of Paul's lifeless body lying on the pool deck as Frankie knelt next to him looking utterly bereft and in tears.

'It was.'

She waited and gave me a moment to compose myself. Then she said, 'I don't understand. Paul was such a strong swimmer. You wouldn't think he'd get in a swimming pool if he wasn't completely *tempus fugit* and, well . . . drown.'

'You mean "compos mentis"?'

'Well, yes, that too. So what really happened, Lucille? Had he been drinking? Was he taking medication that affected his mind? Except he didn't seem like the type to, you know, take his own life – to commit suicide. I just don't see it, not Paul Merchant.'

Small towns.

'Of course he didn't commit suicide. They don't really know what happened. Yet.' I shouldn't have snapped at her, protested so vehemently, because she picked up on it right away, finding the chink in my armor: the little white lie I'd just told.

Of course they knew what happened and it involved an overdose of drugs – with all the taint of scandal that would bring. But until the Commonwealth Medical Examiner finished his exam, it wasn't written in stone as the absolute cause of death.

She arched an eyebrow that disappeared under a heavily lacquered row of bright orange bangs. 'Oh?' she said. 'And how do you know that?'

It hadn't even taken her a minute to try to worm what I knew out of me. If I told Thelma what Win had already found out, everyone in town would know faster than a speeding bullet. And the speculating and gossip would begin in earnest. The word *suicide* would rear its ugly head.

'I know because the medical examination on Paul's body isn't finished yet,' I said and hoped we could leave it at that.

Thelma took off her glasses and wiped a finger under her heavily mascaraed eye, smearing it just enough to give her a vaguely goth look. 'I'm so sorry. If it's taking some time, Win obviously found something and now he wants to be sure. You know whatever he says will be God's truth, Lucille. All doctors swear by that Apothecary's Oath. But it must be heartbreaking for Francesca and those two beautiful children. And for you. I know you're very close.'

I nodded. If I spoke, my voice would crack. Thelma wasn't often weepy. We both were on the verge of tears.

'At my age,' she said in a soft, sad voice, 'it's not such a surprise when someone dies, especially if they're, you know, *older*. You think, well, that person certainly had a good long life and so when it's time to go, you just need to leave him lay where Jesus flang him. No tears, no regrets, no remorse, because the good Lord knows when everyone's time is up. But when it's a young person – and Paul wasn't that old – that, Lucille, *that* is hard to bear. Of course I'm thinking about your sainted mother as well, child. You know how much I loved Charlotte.'

One of Thelma's more unconventional eccentricities is her habit of calling someone by a name that was almost but not quite their actual name. My mother's name was Chantal, not Charlotte. I had become Lucille. My father, Leland, was Lee.

'I know you loved my mother,' I said. 'She loved you, too, Thelma.'

A blob of raspberry jelly landed on the napkin on my lap along with a tiny blizzard of powdered sugar. I tried to scoop it up with my finger and lick it off. Instead I smeared powdered sugar everywhere. Thelma had given me a sliver of an opening when she'd brought up friends and relatives who had passed away over the years. Perhaps now I could ask her about Eleanor Blake without making her suspicious or curious at my sudden interest in the death of someone I hadn't known, an event that had taken place more than eighty years ago.

'You must have a lot of memories of the family and friends you've loved and lost,' I said.

She nodded. 'Every one of them recorded in my book of remembrance. That way I won't forget anyone.' She tapped her finger against the side of her forehead. 'Though I do have to say I've got a photostatic memory for . . .'

'Wait – what? You keep a *book*?' I sat up, suddenly alert. 'Of everyone you know who passed away?' Thelma knew *everybody*. I wondered when she'd begun keeping those records, how many years ago it had been.

'I do, indeed.'

'Would it be possible for me to see this book? Please?'

She looked so surprised and even a little shocked that for a moment I thought she was going to turn me down outright. Absolutely *not*. You may *not* see it. It's *private*.

I should have finessed my request more gracefully. Except Thelma herself had brought up the book. I had not. I waited and held my breath.

She gave me a sharp, knowing look. 'You want to read about your parents,' she said with flat finality. 'Lucille, I told you I loved your mother. I did *not* love your father. He was a difficult man and your mother had a hard life with him, putting up with his shenanigans. That man never could remain in a monotonous relationship. What I wrote was not kind.'

'I know what he was like, Thelma. I'm sure nothing you wrote would surprise me.'

She tapped her fingers on the arms of her rocking chair. Thinking. Considering what I'd just asked. Finally, she stood and smoothed out the wrinkles in her pink minidress. 'Give me a moment.'

I waited, crumpled my napkin, brushed the powdered sugar off my jeans as best as I could, and finished my coffee. Thelma was gone a lot longer than a moment, but when she finally emerged from her back room, she was carrying a book that was as thick as a dictionary. It looked as if the reason it had swelled in size was the addition of newspaper clippings and papers that bristled out of the edges of many pages – what I guessed were probably death notices and perhaps funeral programs.

She handed it to me as carefully as if it were one of Shakespeare's most valuable First Folios. 'No one else has ever seen this before, Lucille. Until now.'

I took the book from her with equal reverence and set it on my lap. The faded richly tooled maroon leather cover had the words 'Births and Deaths' inscribed on it, though like Paul Merchant's briefcase, most of the gold embossing had rubbed away. 'I'm honored you trusted me enough to let me look at it.'

The binding barely held the book together because it had been stuffed so full with other papers. Many of the newspaper clippings – death notices as I'd suspected – were yellowed and brittle with age. There were also photographs with some of the entries: the early ones were black and white, the later pictures were in color, including a few faded Polaroids.

'How did you get the idea to do something like this?' Even though the book's title said 'Births and Deaths,' the only thing recorded in it were deaths.

She walked back over to her rocking chair and sat down. 'Well, to tell the truth, it wasn't my idea,' she said, blushing, as if she were confessing a guilty secret. 'My mother started the book during the Great Depression when it seemed as if everyone she knew was losing everything they owned or cared about – money, homes, jobs. Hope. She said it felt as if she had an Alcatraz around her neck with so much sadness.' She shrugged. 'Some members of our family and many of her friends and acquaintances were passing away, either from polio since the vaccine hadn't been invented yet or else from severe depression and broken hearts. The Depression years were so awful, Lucille. Mother decided she didn't want to forget anyone, so she started writing down names. Then she began adding memories and cutting out the death notices in the newspaper. After she died, I found the book and decided to keep it going.'

If Thelma's mother had begun the book during the Great Depression, what were the odds that there would be an entry for Eleanor Blake, who had died in 1941, the year the Japanese bombed Pearl Harbor, dragging America into what had previously been a European war? I turned the pages until I came to the entry for April 4, 1941, the day of the Hollywood Theatre fire that had killed Eleanor. And discovered an abundance of riches.

Not only was there a newspaper article about the fire, there was also a long tribute in *The Washington Tribune* about Eleanor's life – what a tragedy that such a beautiful woman had died so young – and her generous philanthropy. Thelma's mother must have been a huge fan because there were numerous black and white newspaper photographs of Eleanor along with a few color pictures that had obviously come from magazines. Eleanor sailing effortlessly over a jump at the Upperville Horse and Colt Show, completely at ease on her horse, a beautiful gray Thoroughbred. Another photo of her on horseback again, but this time dressed in the formal hunting attire of the Goose Creek Hunt, lifting a stirrup cup along with a group of fellow hunters and surrounded by their hounds, a toast for luck before setting off for a morning of fox hunting. A color photo from a magazine that showed her standing at a podium with a backdrop of the Hollywood Theatre logo emblazoned on a red velvet curtain, looking earnest and impossibly beautiful, as she spoke to a packed house. In the final photo she wore a dazzling off-the-shoulder décolleté cobalt-blue evening gown. Redmond Blake, her husband, stood next to her, dressed in white tie and tails.

Eleanor was a knockout, all right, absolutely stunning. I looked at the list of people who surrounded her in the Goose Creek Hunt photo and recognized some of the surnames, though the faces were unfamiliar since they were of an earlier generation – people my parents probably would have known. One name stood out: Lorenzo Rossi, who would be Chiara's great-uncle, someone I couldn't stop staring at because of his darkly handsome looks and a profile that could have been the relief of an ancient Roman coin. The camera had caught him and Eleanor, perhaps in an unguarded moment, looking at each other with so much longing and smoldering chemistry you couldn't help but focus on them as if they were the only two people in that photo and everyone else was just in the background.

So maybe the Rossi family and the Blake family hadn't always been mortal enemies. Eleanor and Lorenzo. And now Hunter and Chiara. I wondered what had started their family feud. Or if anyone who was alive today even remembered why they were still at loggerheads.

I looked again at the picture of Eleanor and Redmond. She looked young enough to be his daughter; Redmond, distinguished-looking and gray-haired, had a proprietary arm around his pretty wife's shoulder, pulling her firmly to his side as if to say 'She's mine.' Except their body language reminded me of the forlorn-looking photos of Charles and Diana that popped up on every anniversary or when there was some 'shocking new development' in the lurid story of Diana's death. The pictures in which they were visibly bored and unhappy to be in each other's company, forced to be together at some public event at which the frenzied paparazzi couldn't get enough reporting on the tattered condition of their marriage.

But the reporter who'd written the story about the fire that killed Eleanor had stated that Redmond had been absolutely beside himself with grief when his wife's body had been discovered inside the projection room of the movie theater. 'In complete shock and utterly devastated' was how he'd described Redmond. Maybe the weary, put-upon expressions on their faces in that photo of them in evening dress had been due to something that had nothing to do with how they felt about each other.

There was one final article – a few terse lines – about Eleanor's funeral. There had been no wake, nothing at Hunt and Sons Funeral Home. She had been cremated. A private service had been held for immediate family at Connemara, the family estate. Her ashes had been scattered over the grounds of the home she'd loved so much, rather than buried in the family plot at Union Cemetery in Leesburg, which seemed odd. According to a family statement released to the press, that had been her request. She'd been all of twenty-six when she died, when her whole life should have been ahead of her. Not an age where you'd imagine she'd be thinking about her burial wishes so specifically.

I turned the page. That was end of the entry about Eleanor

but there was one more photo of her, again looking incredibly radiant and happy. Actually it was half a photo, as someone's arm – a man's – was around her shoulder. Whoever he was would remain a mystery: the picture had been literally cut in half with a pair of scissors.

'What's this?' I looked up from the book. 'What happened to the other half of the picture?'

Thelma took the photo. 'I don't know. It belongs with the others. I don't know who took it or how it got in there.'

'I wonder who he is. Or was.'

'I guess we'll never know.'

'I heard the Blakes have been talking about restoring the Hollywood Theatre,' I said. 'In honor of Eleanor.'

'That would be Nash. Wyatt's not . . . up to handling that any more,' she said and twirled a finger next to her temple to indicate the current state of mind of Nash's father, Wyatt Blake. 'But Nash wants to do it as a tribute to his grandma. She did a lot for Middleburg and Atoka, even though she died so young. He wants her to be honored in the same way we honor Jackie.'

She meant Jacqueline Kennedy, who had spent time in Middleburg with her husband and children, even building a home, in the 1960s during John F. Kennedy's presidency. Later, after Aristotle Onassis's death, she came back by herself to ride and fox hunt with the Orange County Hunt. A pretty little park on Madison Street near the Middleburg Museum had been named for her.

'Do you remember anything about the Hollywood Theatre fire?' I asked her.

She stared at me as if I'd just stabbed her through the heart. 'Me? Lordy, child, I was just a little girl back then.'

I rushed to backtrack. 'Of course. I know that. I meant do you remember your mother saying anything about it when you were growing up?'

'Oh.' She looked mollified. 'Well, yes, I remember plenty. Mother was one of the ushers at that theater. And she adored Eleanor.'

'What did she say?'

'She thought Redmond had influenced the fire marshal's investigation, getting it wrapped up so quickly.'

'Influenced how?'

'He didn't want it to drag on. He said it was painful enough losing his beloved wife and now he was a single father raising a little boy – Wyatt was just a toddler, you see – all by himself. Redmond wanted it to be over.'

'Was there any reason to suspect it was anything but an accident?'

She eyed me. If I kept pushing, asking so many questions, Thelma being Thelma, she was going to wonder why. But she answered in a matter-of-fact way. 'Mother heard a story afterwards from one of the maids at Connemara who said she'd overheard Redmond and Eleanor shouting at each other that day. She said it was a dreadful fight.'

'What were they fighting about?'

'A medical test – Mother thought it had to do with him, not her. Whoever it was, apparently the result didn't come back so good.'

'Redmond lived for a good long time – years and years – after Eleanor died. The test result must not have been life-threatening, if it was a test he'd taken.'

'I know, but then he died so suddenly and tragically. Just like that.' Thelma snapped her fingers. 'Took a bad fall while he was skiing in Colorado and died not long after the paramedics got him to the hospital. I think his family was in shock for weeks. Especially Wyatt. The two of them were so close.'

'That must have been heartbreaking, losing both of his parents in accidents.'

'The older you get, the more you remember that death is a natural part of the cycle of life, Lucille. You're young, just married and in love with that handsome husband of yours, so of course you don't want to think about it now. What you hope when the time comes, though, is that you don't have any regrets, that you've lived a good full life. You know what they say, don't you? "The bitterest tears shed over graves are for words left unsaid and deeds left undone."'

There was a faraway look in her eyes that made me wonder if she was speaking from experience.

'I think it's especially hard when someone's death is *not* at the end of a long life. Like Paul's was,' I said.

'I know. Grief is hard, Lucille; sometimes it's unbearable. Because the people who are left behind, the ones who have to carry on, have to find a way to fill the hole in their lives after someone they loved so much is gone.'

Like Frankie would have to do. Like Redmond might have done.

'I don't think I've gotten over my mother's death yet – and that was years ago.'

'Course you haven't. She was wonderful, a beautiful woman inside and out. Everyone loved her.'

Talking about her could still bring me to the edge of tears. I cleared my throat and said, 'Redmond never remarried after Eleanor's death.'

'Because he lost the great love of his life, that's why. And though you'd see him out and about at hunt balls and parties and such with someone, it was never anything serious.'

I closed the book, which felt much heavier than when she'd given it to me – weighted with all the sorrow and sadness it contained – and handed it back to her. 'Thank you for letting me look at this. It's nearly full.'

'Oh, there are still a few more pages,' she said, tapping the leather cover with a fingernail. 'Room for Paul and a few others. His entry will go right after Violet Rossi.' She clicked her tongue against her teeth and shook her head. 'Now that was another tragedy and only six weeks ago.'

'Chiara's still taking it really hard.'

'I know she is. She was in here the other day. We talked.'

I wanted to ask Thelma what they talked about, but there was no way I was going to touch that third rail and ask if they'd discussed Chiara's theory that Paul's and Violet's deaths were somehow connected and related to their advocacy work with Don't Pave Paradise. And that Chiara thought neither one of them had been an accident.

'I showed you this book for a reason, child.'

'What would that be?' I could feel the hair on the back of my neck pricking because I had a feeling where this conversation was going.

'The last page is going to be my entry, Lucille. I would like you to take care of adding it.'

The final entry in a book that contained so much loss and sadness. 'Thelma, I don't know . . . maybe you should ask someone else—'

'I want it to be you. *Promise me.*'

I had written my father's obituary. And I had helped him write the obituary for my mother. Thelma wasn't going to take no for an answer, I knew that.

'All right,' I said. 'I promise.'

'Good,' she said with a small, satisfied smile. 'Now, do you want to tell me why you didn't look up either of your parents' entries?'

That it had been a ruse to get her to show me the book of deaths so I could look up the entry for Eleanor Blake? 'No. Not really.'

I thought she would push back, but instead she said, 'You know what they say about death, don't you?'

Another aphorism about dying? I didn't think I wanted to know, but I asked anyway. 'What?'

'Never two without three. Violet and Paul – that's two. There's going to be a third death. Someone else is going to die before long.' That was either the absolute certainty of an all-knowing sage or else she was Cassandra whose warnings were ignored and disbelieved by everyone.

'Thelma—'

She cut me off. 'It could be me. Or it could be someone else. I don't know *who* it's going to be. But mark my words. It will happen soon.'

TEN

On my way home from the General Store I called Kit Noland and asked if she could search the archives of *The Washington Tribune* for any stories or information about the 1941 fire that killed Eleanor Blake, as well as the skiing accident that had taken Redmond Blake's life. Specifically anything written *after* both accidents. Also articles about the two of them together, which I suspected would be in the society or lifestyle section of the newspaper – especially since the Blakes had hosted so many parties for Eleanor's famous friends who came to Middleburg when their movies were playing at the Hollywood Theatre. The expressions on Eleanor's and Redmond's faces in that hunt ball photo in Thelma's remembrance book suggested their relationship might not have been especially happy. Then there was her mother's story about the maid overhearing an ugly argument between the two of them the day Eleanor died, which had something to do with the results of a medical test.

What I really wondered, though, was what the article about the Hollywood Theatre fire and the glamorous photo of Eleanor were doing among Violet's and Paul's notes and maps of Loudoun's unpaved roads. Who put them there – Paul or Violet? For some reason, my money was on Violet. She had done it – for a reason I still couldn't figure out.

Thelma's mother said Redmond had used his considerable influence to bring the investigation into the fire to a swift conclusion, citing personal anguish over his wife's tragic death as one of the reasons not to drag it out. And then there was his unusual decision not to have a funeral for Eleanor, cremating her remains and scattering them at Connemara rather than placing her urn in the family vault at Union Cemetery where family and friends could go to mourn her.

At the top of a hill at Highland Farm, from which there is a breathtaking view of the Blue Ridge Mountains, is a small cemetery surrounded by a low brick wall where every member of the Montgomery family is buried, beginning with my ancestor Hamish, who had chosen that site in the late 1700s precisely for that view. My parents are there. Someday I will lie there and so will Quinn. The idea of cremating anyone in our family and scattering their ashes to the four winds – even if it was somewhere on the farm – was something I couldn't imagine.

I wondered why Redmond had chosen to do that with his wife's remains. I also wondered whether Paul and Violet had learned something that the Blake family wanted covered up – something to do with the fire. Maybe Paul had confronted Nash about what they had learned the other day at their meeting in his office in Washington. Maybe that was why Nash had threatened him – Paul had tried to blackmail Nash, and it had backfired.

But even if that's what had happened, did that mean Nash had resorted to murder to keep Paul from talking? And Violet? *Two* murders? Because of a fire that happened eighty years ago? I'd already been over this with Bobby and he didn't see anything there. Still, there had to be a reason for that photo and article to be mixed in with the other papers – it wasn't just random.

Unfortunately, I had no idea what that reason was.

Kit Eastman Noland and I go way back. We met when we were five and we have remained umbilically tied together ever since, closer even than sisters. We know each other so well we can finish one another's sentences, breathe for each other. I'd been her maid of honor and she'd been my matron of honor when we each got married at the vineyard. On Sunday, Quinn and I would become godparents to Kit and Bobby's daughter, Ivy, and we had already promised that if anything ever happened to them, we would raise Ivy as our own.

Kit was the Loudoun County Bureau Chief for *The Washington Tribune* and technically still on maternity leave for another month, but I knew her well enough to know that she was checking in on things at the office, a small brick cottage with a wraparound front porch on Harrison Street in Leesburg. Especially because the *Trib*, like every news organization in the country, had been making savage cuts among their staff of journalists, leaving their newsrooms critically understaffed. Kit had done her best to shield her staff from the draconian cuts that would be coming at Christmas, though no one knew about them, and she'd had a lot of push back from the bosses in Washington. She'd confessed all of this to me in the strictest secrecy one afternoon when we were together at the old Goose Creek Bridge, a Civil War battle site that was now a historic landmark. It was a place we'd always gone, ever since we were teenagers, because there was never anyone else there and we could share confidences and confess things no one else could know, usually lubricated by a bottle of Montgomery Estate Vineyard wine.

'You have to tell some of your staff they're getting fired – and you have to do it at *Christmas*?' I'd been incredulous. 'Why do you have to let people go then, for God's sake? Who are your bosses? A bunch of Scrooges? That's cruel.'

She'd turned misery-filled eyes on me. 'So we can start with a clean slate in the New Year and those salaries won't be on our books. And you can't tell *anyone*, Luce. I shouldn't even be telling you.'

'The people you have to let go don't know what's coming?'

She shook her head. 'They don't. Some of them have been with the *Trib* their whole career. At least those folks will get decent severance pay, a whole year. The younger ones will get the usual two months. God knows where they'll find jobs. No one's hiring any more.'

We hadn't spoken about the upcoming carnage since that day, but I knew it grieved her heart and she was dreading what she would have to do in just over two months. The fact that she had to keep it a secret while still working with people she thought of as family only made it more heartrending, more of a burden she carried around.

Kit being Kit, she immediately asked why I wanted to know about Eleanor, the fire, and Redmond's accident. 'I'll check our archives, of course, but you know you're going to have to tell me what's really going on. Bobby already told me Frankie is convinced someone was at her house with Paul before he drowned, and that you told him Chiara believes her mother's accident *wasn't* an accident. Are you thinking all those things are related?'

I told her about finding the article about the fire along with Eleanor's picture in Paul's briefcase.

'Wait a minute,' she said. 'You lost me. What does all this have to do with the unpaved roads?'

'I don't know. I wonder if Violet or Paul thought Eleanor's death and the fire were related. Or maybe they knew something.'

'Lucie, that fire happened eighty years ago.'

'I know, I know.'

'Do you have any idea what you're looking for?'

'No, but I'm hoping if I find it, I will.'

I heard her sigh through the phone. 'You know, Bobby thinks you're way out on a limb bringing up the possibility of foul play in both Violet's and Paul's deaths.'

'I know he does.'

'If you're right, you're talking about murder. Maybe two murders. And then dragging in the ancient history with the fire and Eleanor. Sweetie, it's pretty hard to connect the dots, you know?'

I knew she was trying to let me down easily, but I also knew she was skeptical about everything I'd told her. Not like the friend I'd grown up with who would always, *always* give me the benefit of the doubt. Now she was the wife of a Loudoun County Sheriff's Office detective, and her allegiance had shifted. Now she believed Bobby's solid logic over my unsubstantiated hunches.

I suppose I couldn't blame her.

I made one more stab at trying to persuade her there was something to this bubbling stew of conjecture and it wasn't just a collection of unrelated events. I told her what Thelma had said about the maid's story that Redmond and Eleanor Blake had argued ferociously the day she died. And about the hunt ball photo in which she and Redmond looked thoroughly miserable standing next to each other.

No dice.

'Hey, Bobby and I argue. We have our moments. So do you and Quinn. So what? As for Violet's and Paul's deaths, the Sheriff's Office said they were both accidents. Case closed.

The movie theater fire was also an accident – faulty wiring. Also case closed.'

I gave up. 'You will check your archives, won't you, even though you think I'm nuts?'

'I will,' she said. 'Although I'm not sure whether I hope it will turn up something or not. Sleeping dogs, Luce. Sleeping dogs.'

My half-brother David Phelps' black SUV was in the driveway when I got home, parked outside the carriage house where Eli had his architecture studio. Before I went over to see Thelma, I'd left Paul's briefcase next to Eli's drafting table and sent him a text telling him it was there, minus the photo and the newspaper article, which I hadn't mentioned.

I hadn't known I had a half-brother until a few years ago when I decided to spit into a vial and send off my DNA to one of those ancestry websites, somewhat for a lark but also out of curiosity since our family history in Virginia dates back to the French and Indian War and, before that, the Montgomery clan's story is deeply woven through the warp and weft of Scottish history.

It was Leland, my father, who had had the affair thirty-four years ago with David's mother, a stunning young woman, a head-turner. Now she was the first African American Speaker of the House of Representatives and she'd already been on the cover of *Vogue* twice.

Apparently, Leland never knew about David – at least that's what we all believed, though we'll never be able to prove it. When Eli, Mia, and I found out we had another brother we were stunned. Doing the math, we worked out David was born when my mother was pregnant with me.

That had hurt. Deeply. I wondered if Mom had known or maybe *sensed* that Leland was already cheating on her so early in their marriage, and if she had been aware, how devastating that must have been.

To be honest, I was glad I didn't know the answer to that question, nor would I ever know since both my parents were dead. What I really didn't understand was how my mother stayed with my father through so many rocky, difficult years, though it probably boiled down to one simple fact.

Or three.

Eli, Mia, and me.

She was French but she was raising children who were born in America, lived in America, had deep roots in America. *Were* American. France was an annual summer holiday to visit my mother's family – our aunts, uncles, cousins, and grandparents – but home was Virginia. If she left Leland, she'd probably end up going back to her close-knit family in Bordeaux and she wasn't going to uproot us and take us away from everything and everyone we knew. So she stayed.

As much as I had been prepared not to like David – frankly, I expected to resent him even though he had nothing to do with my father's and his mother's liaison – it was just the opposite when we met: an instant click. It was so obvious we were related because we were so much alike – our mannerisms, how we moved, talked, thought, our sense of humor – which is when I realized that when it came down to nature versus nurture, or genetics versus how we'd been raised, genetics won every time.

He was an award-winning professional photographer living in Washington, D.C., though he often came out to Atoka when he wasn't traveling on assignment for *National Geographic* or *Smithsonian* or one of his many A-list clients, and we had grown closer. A few months ago he had photographed our wedding and the photos were, as expected, amazing. On one of his pre-wedding trips here to scout locations he learned about the Don't Pave Paradise Coalition and the plan to present a list of Loudoun's unpaved roads that were of historic interest to the National Trust for Historic Preservation. He'd immediately gone to Violet and offered to take photos pro bono for the project. She'd been over the moon. Now Violet was dead and so was Paul. David was probably out here regrouping, talking to Eli about his photographs and Eli's maps. Discussing who was going to pick up the pieces and get this project going again without its two main champions.

I saw David, Eli, and my five-year-old niece Hope, Eli's daughter, through the floor-to-ceiling windows that had replaced the original double doors of the carriage house. The three of them were huddled around Eli's drafting table, engrossed in studying something that was laid out in front of them. David was holding Hope who rested on his hip, clinging to him like a little monkey as he pointed to something on the table.

For the last two years my niece had been allowed to choose what she wore each day, whether it was mismatched socks, the cat tail from a Halloween costume, or the sparkly blue Elsa dress and crown from *Frozen*. Today she looked relatively subdued, almost monochromatic: Kelly-green tutu, lime-colored leggings and the green sneakers that lit up when she walked, all wrapped in a neon green satin cape so bright it vibrated. I couldn't decide whether she looked like a little gypsy or one of the leprechauns on the Lucky Charms cereal box.

The front door to the studio creaked when I walked in and the three of them looked up at the same time. Hope wriggled down from David's side. I knelt and held out my arms as she threw herself at me in a stranglehold hug that nearly knocked us both over. So much love from this adorable little girl.

She lifted her face for a kiss and began fiddling with a lock of my shoulder-length brown hair, avoiding my eyes. 'Aunt Lucie, my Barbie needs new clothes. So she can go ice skating.'

Ah. Sugarplum innocence wrapped around sweet manipulative guile. She glanced up through long dark eyelashes, checking to see if I'd bitten into that apple.

'Hope,' Eli said in his no-nonsense, knock-it-off dad voice. 'Do *not* ask Aunt Lucie for another outfit for Barbie. Barbie has enough clothes to open her own department store.'

'She doesn't have an ice-skating outfit.' She was starting to sound petulant.

'Hope. *No.*' She got the don't-push-it-or-else look this time.

Her lower lip thrust out and I tousled her long dark hair. 'Christmas is coming, pumpkin. It's too warm for Barbie to go skating now anyway. I think she should get an ice-skating outfit for Christmas instead. Come on. Let's go see what Daddy and Uncle David are looking at.'

She didn't budge. 'Do you want to see my eye roll?'

'What?'

'My eye roll. I just learned how to do it.'

Eli did his own version of an eye roll. 'She's good. Uses it *all* the time. Very effectively, too.'

'Show me,' I said, and she did. 'Where'd you learn that?'

'From my friends,' she said and rolled her eyes again. 'Daddy, I want to go home.'

'Momma will be here in a minute. I just texted her. You can go home with her.'

'Come on, sweetie.' I leaned on my cane and pulled myself up. 'I want to see what you and Uncle David and Daddy were looking at.'

'We're looking at Uncle David's pictures,' she said. 'Of trees.'

Ten photos of Loudoun County's unpaved roads were spread out on Eli's drafting table. Though our region has become a major IT hub and data center for the US, Loudoun is – thank God – still also a farming community, as it has been since colonial days and even earlier than that. With our rolling hills, charming villages that date back to the seventeen- and eighteen-hundreds, Civil War era stacked stone walls lining winding country roads, and fields where Thoroughbreds and Angus cattle graze, this is where people decamp from the relentless intensity of D.C. on weekends to pick berries and fruit at our farms, drink our wine, and wander our pretty main streets to shop and dine. They come in droves for Christmas in Middleburg Weekend, the farm tour, the stable tour, the garden tour, hayrides and pumpkin patches in the fall, outdoor summer concerts, and sidewalk art shows to satisfy their nostalgic longing for small-town America. To be reassured there are still places where moseying, lingering, or tarrying are acceptable – even required – and life is simpler and sweeter. David's photos captured so perfectly the unspoiled beauty and lifestyle we were fighting to preserve that I wondered how anyone in their right mind could be in favor of paving these roads and forfeiting what made us unique and so appealing.

'Your photos are gorgeous,' I said.

'Thanks.' He threw an arm around my shoulder and gave it a squeeze. 'How are you doing? I heard about you and Frankie finding Paul the other day. That must have been rough.'

'It was.'

'So what's going to happen now?' he said, glancing from me to Eli. 'Who's taking over the Don't Pave Paradise Coalition now that Paul's gone? And Violet?'

'I don't know,' I said. 'It's still too early to think of a successor.'

'I disagree,' David said. 'The two of them fought hard for this project. Someone needs to pick up the torch and keep going. You know that's what they'd want.' His eyes locked on mine. 'What about you?'

'*Me?* No . . .'

'Yes, you.' Eli had perked up. 'Miss I-Majored-in-Environmental-Studies-and-Conservation-in-College. You worked for that lobbyist firm that specialized in climate change and conservation issues for a couple of years after you graduated. You were good. Really good, Luce. You'd be perfect for this.'

His grin was too fast and too easy, a dead giveaway he was trying to sweet-talk me.

'Now I know where Hope learned how to wheedle and get her way, Eli. Thanks, but come on, you two. I don't know—'

'We'll help you.' David cut me off.

We. So they had talked this over.

'Look, Paul and Violet did all the heavy lifting to pull together the history of these roads,' Eli added. 'David's taken the photos and when I finish the maps we're almost done. You can write the proposal to the Historic Preservation people in your sleep. Piece of cake, Luce.'

'You make it sound like there's nothing to it.'

'Oh, come on,' he said. 'You know this stuff. It'll be easy.'

I looked at my brothers who were so obviously waiting for me to say yes. The last two people who had been in charge of this project were dead. Neither Eli nor David knew about the possible link between the Don't Pave Paradise Coalition and the fire that had killed Eleanor Blake – if there was one. I was already involved, having just asked Kit to search the *Trib*'s database for more information on that fire.

'All right.' I held up my hands, surrendering. 'I'll do it. I'll write the proposal.'

I caught the fleeting look of triumph that passed between them.

I'd been set up twice in the last fifteen minutes. First Hope. Now Eli and David. They'd planned this outcome before I even walked through the door.

'Daddy. When is Momma going to be here? I want to go

home.' Hope folded her arms across her little chest, the impending meltdown of a five-year-old's boredom, angst, and general state of being overwrought that was beginning to escalate from simmer to slow boil.

'Right . . . now. She just got here,' Eli said, with obvious relief as we all looked out the large picture window to see my sister-in-law Sasha Vaughn pull up in a dark gray Volvo and park next to David's car.

But when she walked through the front door a moment later, Sasha looked every bit as upset as her daughter, throwing her keys down on a file cabinet next to Eli's drafting table. They made a clanking sound of metal on metal and bounced, falling to the floor. She bent and picked them up.

'Grayson.' Her dark eyes flashed with anger and she looked as if she was about to erupt. 'I could . . . *throttle* . . . him.'

My big-eyed niece said, 'What's throttle, Momma?'

Eli threw his wife a warning look and said, 'Ixnay this conversation in front of the ild-chay, sweetheart. Let's talk about it when I get home.'

'Daddy's talking that funny pig language again, Momma. He does that when I'm not supposed to know something.'

David looked as if he was working hard at keeping a straight face while Hope fixed her gaze on her mother, waiting for her answer. I knew Sasha would tell Hope the truth. You don't lie to kids. Especially smart ones who've figured out you're trying to do an end run around them.

'It's, well, I shouldn't have said it, sweetie. It means I'm cross with Uncle Grayson,' Sasha said.

'Why?'

Another poignant pause and more looks exchanged between Eli and Sasha. Grayson Vaughn was Sasha's older brother. Eli had been dropping hints recently about trouble between his wife and brother-in-law. What Sasha had just said sounded as if it had ratcheted up to the next level.

She took a deep breath as if she were trying to dial down her anger. 'Because he wants to sell his farm to some people, and I don't want him to.'

Hope processed that information, eyes still like saucers. 'Will he move away? Won't we see him any more?'

'We'll see him. He just wants to sell part of the farm and keep the land with his house on it for himself. So he's not going to move, or at least I don't think he is. Come on, sugarplum, let's get you home. It's way past time for you to take a little rest.'

After they left, I turned to my brother. 'What was all that about?'

Though I had a pretty good idea.

A few years ago, Jamison Vaughn, former presidential candidate, successful businessman, and Sasha and Grayson's father, had been killed in a tragic car accident in Atoka. To everyone's surprise, Jamie had left Sasha and Grayson the three-hundred-acre farm in Upperville that had been in the Vaughn family almost as long as my family had owned Highland Farm, bypassing their mother – his second wife – as well as twin sons by a previous marriage. The will had been contested, of course, but once the dust settled, the farm still belonged to Grayson and Sasha.

Grayson, who wanted to move there with his new wife and raise Thoroughbreds, had bought out his sister. Unlike the settlement of the will, the sale had been amicable. Sasha and Eli had decided to build their own home on our land and Sasha's settlement money had made a significant dent in reducing the cost of their construction loan. So, it had worked out well for both of them.

But last year, while Grayson was out of town looking at a couple of horses he wanted to buy, his wife had gone into premature labor two months before their baby was due. The ambulance that had been dispatched after she called 911 had hit a deep pothole lurking in the shadows of Williams Gap Road, an unpaved road a mile and a half from the Vaughn home, and had broken an axle. By the time the backup ambulance arrived, she was hemorrhaging badly and the paramedics from the first ambulance who had walked to her house hadn't been able to stop the bleeding. She and the baby died on the way to the hospital.

Grayson's grief had been so crippling that Sasha had been worried about his mental health, even his sanity. Over the next few months it had morphed into anger and outrage, which he directed at the county, blaming them for neglect and for failing to take care of the roads. If they'd been kept up – or better yet, if they'd been *paved* – his wife and child would be alive today.

Eli got up and went over to a coffee pot that sat on top of a mini fridge across the room. 'Anyone want a cup?'

'I'm fine, thanks,' I said. 'Is this a delaying tactic while you figure out what you're going to tell us about what's going on?'

'This is the need for caffeination.'

'I'll take some,' David said. 'Thanks.'

Eli filled two mugs and gave David the one that said 'World's OKest Architect.' His mug said 'I Draw Things and I Know Stuff.' Both Christmas gifts from me.

He came back to the drafting table after dousing his coffee with enough vanilla coffee creamer from a carton in the refrigerator to turn it into creamer-with-some-coffee instead of the other way around. David did the exact same thing. Then Eli dragged stools for David and me over to the drafting table.

He sat down on his own stool and said, 'To answer your question, Luce, what that was all about is that Grayson is planning to subdivide the farm and sell parcels of land before the new zoning laws come into effect.'

'You're joking,' I said, but of course I knew he wasn't.

'Oh, that's not the worst of it. He's planning to sell everything to Nash Blake. Do you know what that means?'

Nash Blake. *Again.* His name was certainly popping up a lot these last few days.

'That he'll be able to build a lot of houses on pristine land,' I said, feeling numb.

'Three hundred and fifteen houses to be precise,' Eli said. 'That's the maximum. He doesn't have to build that many, but he can if he wants to, according to the way the land was zoned way back when.'

'That many homes could be a small town,' David said. 'It's going to be an eyesore sitting in the middle of all this gorgeous farmland.'

'Tell me something I don't know.' Eli sounded morose.

'Nash absolutely will build that land out,' I said, my voice flat with disbelief and shock, 'just like he has everywhere else he's bought land and put up his cookie-cutter subdivisions.'

'I don't know whether Sasha is angrier with Gray for selling the land or herself for letting him buy her share of the farm. Because if she hadn't sold, she could stop him from selling. The two of them have been having arguments that are epic. She's so upset she's not sleeping.'

'Why is Grayson doing this? Why is he selling to Nash, of all people? Is he that hard up for money?' I asked.

'No,' Eli said, 'but if Nash does put up all those homes, the county will come in and pave the roads.'

'It won't change what happened to his wife and baby,' I said and then wished I hadn't because it sounded cruel. 'Sorry. I shouldn't have said that. It was unkind.'

'It's OK. I know. He knows. But he says that maybe it will save someone else's life, perhaps someone else's child.'

David leaned against the back of his barstool and folded his arms across his chest, assessing Eli. 'So, what's the other thing you aren't telling us?'

'What do you mean?'

'Come on, bro.'

Eli looked like he did when Leland caught him hanging out his bedroom window trying to smoke a cigarette and not get caught. Not realizing he was stinking up the place and my parents could smell tobacco as it sifted through the floorboards of our two-hundred-year-old house.

'OK, but this is . . . sort of speculation. On my part and Sasha's.'

'Spill it,' I said. 'You can't stop now.'

He let out a breath like air leaving a tire. 'Before she died, Violet Rossi had talked Gray into putting all his land into a conservation easement. It hadn't happened yet, but things were moving in that direction. The other thing is that I think there might have been something going on between the two of them – you know?' He waggled his eyebrows suggestively. 'Sasha thought so, too, but Gray was pretty close-mouthed, so we didn't know for sure.'

'You're talking about a romantic relationship,' I said, and he nodded.

'So what happened?' David asked.

'Well, if Gray had put the land into easement, he would have forfeited the right to allow those three hundred and fifteen homes to be built on his farmland. Ever. Plus, he would have made a lot of money in tax benefits. The quid pro quo was that he'd only be allowed to build twenty houses on his property – *if* he wanted to. Violet managed to persuade him that he was doing the right thing for the future of Loudoun. That saving the land for future generations was for the greater good, even if it meant he'd walk away from how much he could make selling his land so those houses could be built on it – which would have meant more money than he would have gotten from the easement.'

'What made him change his mind?' David asked.

Eli shrugged. 'Simple. Violet died. Another accident involving a car on an unpaved road. Grayson lost someone he cared for – again. Nash stepped into that vacuum and persuaded Grayson that it was more important than ever to pave the roads out here. Plus, Nash managed to convince him that selling his land – only a portion of it, as he reminded Gray – was *progress*. That new homes could coexist quite well with the old farms and that it could be good for everyone. Not to overstate the point – as I said – that he'll make a ton more money doing this than if he'd put the land into easement. This whole situation has made life at my house not exactly a bowl of cherries, either. My wife is upset with me, too.'

'Why?' I asked.

Eli threw out his arms encompassing his entire studio. 'Hello? What do I do for a living? I'm an architect. I build buildings. And I have to tell you, I'm not 100 per cent against new construction out here. Look at Highland Farm. It was zoned so we can still build another ten homes on our land – if we want to. It's something to think about. But do I want to see Nash come in and clear-cut Grayson's land so he can plunk down three hundred and fifteen cookie-cutter McMansions on half-acre lots? Hell, no. In the meantime, Sasha and I keep trying to refine our definition of what "progress" is, but with this whole Grayson situation, it's become an instant third-rail conversation. She can't talk about it without getting upset – and that includes being pissed off at me.'

'That must be rough,' I said.

He gave me a you-don't-know-the-half-of-it look.

The possibility that we could build ten houses on our land had come up when Eli and Sasha built their home last year. Ever since I'd taken over the vineyard, I'd had visions – hopes – of my cousin Dominique moving to the farm, building a place, and living nearby one day. Mia building a home where she could have a proper art studio with floor-to-ceiling windows and perfect daylight for painting. More recently, maybe David leaving D.C. and coming out here, setting up his studio as well. *Family.* All of us together. But absolutely *not* selling the land to strangers.

'So now what?' I asked.

'Well, there's nothing Sasha can do to stop Gray from selling if he wants to. Or anybody else, for that matter. I think he's going to make a deal with Nash, if he hasn't already.'

My phone vibrated in my jeans back pocket and I pulled it out, expecting it to be Quinn wondering where I was.

'It's Bobby,' I said as his name flashed on my display. 'Probably something about the baptism on Sunday.'

'Go ahead, take it,' Eli said.

I answered the phone and punched the dial for speaker. 'Hey, Bobby,' I said. 'I'm in Eli's studio and David's here, too. You're on speaker. Is everything still OK for Sunday?'

'For . . . what? Oh, Sunday. Yeah, everything's fine. That's not why I'm calling,' he said and the ominous tone in his voice made me sit up straighter.

'What's wrong?' I asked because something obviously was.

'That glass shard you found by the pool at Frankie's house yesterday? There's good news and bad news, depending on your idea of good and bad. We lifted prints off the outside of the glass. Unfortunately, they belong to someone who's not in the CODIS database.'

'You mean, not a known criminal?'

'Well, just no one whose prints ended up in the database.'

'Is that the good news or the bad?'

'The good. I told you it depended on your idea of good or bad.'

'What's the bad news?'

'We found traces of lorazepam and gin on the inside of the glass.'

'What's lorazepam?' David asked.

'Lorazepam is in a class of drugs known as benzodiazepines. They're anti-anxiety meds. Valium, Librium, Klonopin – they're benzos, too. Lorazepam is also a very fast-acting sedative,' he said.

'The lab found traces of this drug on the *inside* of Paul's glass?' I asked. They'd already found it in his bloodstream, but the inside of the glass? Didn't that change the dynamics of everything?

'Right. It was ground up and added to the gin and tonic.'

'Well, obviously Paul didn't do that, right?' Because it would have meant he intentionally took an overdose of his medication mixed with alcohol.

'Look, I can't say what he did or didn't do,' he said. 'I'm not going to get into speculating.'

'Oh, come on, Bobby,' Eli said. 'Any normal person is going to pop a pill in his mouth and wash it down with a glass of water. Not grind it up and put it in a G and T.'

'I know, Eli.' Bobby sounded irritable. 'I know. But we've got to do this step by step.'

'Did the drugs belong to Paul?' David asked. 'Was it his prescription?'

'It was. We found a bottle of pills with his name on it on a lazy Susan in the kitchen. Apparently, he kept his meds there along with his vitamins and supplements instead of in the bathroom medicine cabinet, where you'd think it might be. Frankie confirmed it.'

'Don't all these things also confirm someone else was with Paul before he died? Another set of fingerprints? Whoever it was must have put the ground-up pills in his drink. Especially since they were so accessible.' I couldn't stop pushing it, that Paul had *not* tried to end his own life.

'I know it might seem obvious.' Bobby was still irked. 'Believe me, I *know*. The bottle of lorazepam had no prints on it. Not even Paul's. So it was wiped clean. Which is why our guys are over there now going over every inch of that house with a microscope and tweezers. Unfortunately, Frankie had her cleaners come in to get the house ready for Paul's funeral.'

I groaned. 'Of course she did. She's Frankie.'

'Oh, jeez,' Eli said. 'So now what?'

'We'll see what we can find, but the Commonwealth ME also wants to re-examine Paul's body, so Win is handing his autopsy off to them. Now it definitely means postponing Paul's funeral a few days.'

He let that sink in. I looked at my brothers whose faces were as stunned as I'm sure mine was. 'How did Frankie take that news?' I asked.

'Not well,' he said. 'On the one hand, she's feels like she's vindicated because she's still convinced someone else was at the house with Paul – and sooner or later we're going to find out who it was. On the other hand, she's pretty upset.'

'Because she probably removed any trace of whoever was there?'

'Well, there's that. Plus the obvious,' he said. 'If someone else was with Paul that evening, it's very probable his death wasn't an accident, that he didn't slip and fall after taking an overdose of lorazepam mixed with a gin and tonic.'

'Meaning he *was* murdered,' I said.

'Well, if someone else was there, then it's something we've got to consider. Yes, it's possible Paul Merchant was murdered.'

ELEVEN

All I could feel was anger. And disbelief.

'So maybe a guest in Paul's home – someone he *invited in* – drugged him with his own medication, making him so confused and disoriented he fell into his swimming pool and drowned. Unless, of course, he was pushed, which is even more awful,' I said. 'And then that person left with almost all the pieces of Paul's broken drink glass. Letting Frankie believe Paul deliberately took an overdose combined with alcohol because he wanted to end his life. What kind of person does that?'

'Someone who, when we find them – and we will if that's what happened – will do jail time for a very long time,' Bobby said with such grim certainty I knew he'd personally plan to be there when they slammed the door to the prison cell, if not slam it shut himself.

'Do you have any idea who you're looking for? Who might have done it?' Eli asked.

'I've already told you more than I should have, but Lucie was the one who found the broken glass and pushed me to examine it, so I felt I owed her an explanation about what we'd discovered. People who commit suicide usually leave notes and there was none, so there's that. As for suspects, I can't really get into that since this is an ongoing investigation. Unless you have any information to add that would help us out?' Bobby said.

'Only that Paul had a target painted on his back when he took over the Don't Pave Paradise Coalition after Violet died,' Eli said. He started ticking a list off on his fingers. 'Business owners. Builders. Developers. Hell, people who move out here for the country lifestyle and then go nuts because their cars get so dirty they have to go to the carwash every week. All of them want VDOT to come out here and pave the roads.'

'I know, but is one of them mad enough to commit murder

because of a couple of truckloads of asphalt?' Bobby said. 'Anyway, with Violet and now Paul gone, that coalition doesn't have anyone running the show any more.'

'Not exactly,' Eli said. 'I'm drawing the maps for the National Trust for Historic Preservation application from the notes and drawings Paul and Violet made. David took photos. And Lucie volunteered to draft the application. So we're going ahead with it.'

I ignored 'volunteered,' but Bobby immediately picked up on what Eli said about the notes. 'I'm going to need those notes. And anything else that was with them.'

Anything else.

That would include the photo of Eleanor and the article about the fire.

'There was something else.' My voice came out as a squeak.

Bobby's groan was audible. 'You want to tell me about it, Lucie?'

I did, as Eli and David both shot me puzzled looks.

'What the . . .?' Eli mouthed at me, a frown creasing his forehead.

I shook my head and mouthed back, 'Later.'

'Well, that explains why Kit is trawling through the *Trib* archives for information about that fire this afternoon,' Bobby said. 'Lucie, leave the investigating to us, OK?'

'Bobby, I told you Chiara thinks her mother's death wasn't an accident, either. Just like Paul's,' I said. 'You and I talked about this. We also talked about the Hollywood Theatre fire.'

'That was then. This is now. I told you I'd pull the file on Violet's accident. As for that fire, it happened a very long time ago – in the 1940s. Anyone who remembers it well is pretty old – I'm talking about people in their nineties. And they would have been very young when it happened. My first priority is finding out how Paul died – whether he took an overdose or he was deliberately drugged. Because if it's the latter, someone is walking around right now believing they got away with murder.'

After Bobby hung up, I got what-the-hell looks from both of my brothers, Eli's expression dyed darker than David's because he knew me better and knew I wasn't above being sneaky. David looked more curious than upset. I knew Eli – as an architect – would be focused on the Hollywood Theatre fire. He'd grown up here like I had and he was intimately familiar with the history of every building in Middleburg and Atoka. As for David, a photographer who had not grown up here and didn't know any of this, he was already googling pictures of Eleanor Blake on his phone.

When her photo popped up, he let out a long, low whistle. 'She was stunning. What a knockout.'

'I know,' I said. 'She was.'

'So how does what happened to her relate to Paul's death? If she died in that fire, it happened a long time ago like Bobby said,' he said.

'Exactly,' Eli said. 'What *does* the Hollywood Theatre fire have to do with all this, Luce?'

'I don't know the answers to either of those questions,' I said. 'It could be nothing at all.'

'You found the photo and the newspaper article in Paul's briefcase?' Eli asked.

I nodded. 'I don't know whether Violet put them with those maps or Paul did.'

'Does it matter?' David asked.

'I think it does,' I said. 'You heard me tell Bobby that Chiara is convinced her mother's death wasn't an accident. Plus, she speculated that Paul's death wasn't an accident, either. If Violet put the article and the photo there, she probably had a reason. But what was her reason and did Paul also know what it was? That's what I'd like to know.'

Eli picked up a pencil and started spinning it around between two fingers like a confused compass that couldn't find true north. 'OK, let's say Paul did know about it,' he said. 'If that's true, what it probably means is there's a connection between the picture, the article, and the Don't Pave Paradise Coalition. In other words, something to do with not paving the roads.'

David got up and walked over to set his empty coffee cup on the mini fridge. When he turned around to face us, he said, 'Maybe it's not a connection to the roads.'

'What do you mean?' Eli asked.

He came back and took his seat on the barstool. 'Eleanor Blake was Nash Blake's grandmother, right?'

'Right,' I said.

'And Nash Blake is one of the leaders of the Pro-Loudoun Progressives who want the roads paved out here?'

'Also correct.'

'And Nash,' Eli put in, 'managed to talk my brother-in-law into selling him a parcel of his farm on which he will be able to build over three hundred houses.'

'Which Paul was vehemently against,' I said. 'Violet would have been as well – though from what you said, Eli, Grayson didn't change his mind about selling to Nash until after Violet died. Violet had persuaded him to put the land into a conservation easement.'

Eli's turn to nod.

'The connection – if there is one,' David said, sounding thoughtful, 'has to be something to do with Eleanor . . . and most likely Nash.'

'Eleanor *and* the fire that killed her,' I said. 'Violet or Paul found out something that must have upset Nash.'

'Maybe it wasn't an accident she died in that fire.' David's statement fell into the silence as if he'd lit a match to a snake trail of kerosene and a pile of old rags.

I felt the breath go out of me. Now we were getting somewhere.

'If that's true, maybe she was murdered and the fire was a way to cover it up,' I said.

What had Thelma told me? Redmond pushed to have the investigation brought to a swift conclusion – the fire was caused by faulty electrical wiring – to put an end to his grief and suffering.

Or maybe not.

'And now all these years later, someone possibly murders Paul. And also Violet. To keep them from talking,' I added.

'Wait. Hang on.' Eli held up his hand. 'If we keep going down this road, no pun intended, you're almost implying Nash Blake might have killed Paul Merchant in cold blood because of something Paul knew about his grandmother's death. And maybe he killed Violet Rossi as well. Bobby's still not convinced Paul was murdered, never mind bringing Violet into this scenario.'

'I didn't say it was Nash . . .'

'The man's a billionaire, an incredibly generous philanthropist. If Paul and Violet found out something that was unflattering about his family, Nash could get it quashed like that.' Eli snapped his fingers. 'I can't see him going over to Paul's house, drugging his drink enough to make him tumble into the swimming pool and drown, and then taking off with the remnants of a broken glass. Plus, the fire happened eighty years ago.'

'I know. But maybe Kit will find something in the *Trib* archives, something that might shed more light on all this,' I said.

'Maybe, but you heard Bobby.' Eli gave me a warning look. 'Leave the investigating to him and the Sheriff's Office, Luce. They'll figure it out.'

'Eli's right,' David said. 'Paul and Violet are dead. If Violet's death wasn't an accident and Paul's turns out not to be, that's two murders. Don't paint a target on your back, Lucie. Someone's not playing games. You don't want to be victim number three.'

I shivered. Thelma had just warned me about that: never two deaths without three. *There will be a third death*, she had said. *Mark my words.*

'I know,' I said. 'But there's something else.'

'What?' Eli asked.

'If Paul did invite someone into his home and that person ended up killing him, there's a good chance it's someone in this community. Meaning we all know him or her, too. In other words, the killer is one of us.'

The Goose Creek Inn is hidden like a secret – a jewel tucked around a bend on Sam Fred Road just outside Middleburg. It is surrounded by mature cherry, dogwood, and magnolia trees so that in spring, when everything is flowering, the old half-timbered building seems to be floating in a cloud of pink and white blossoms. It is aptly named because Goose Creek runs along one side of the inn as it makes its meandering way to the Potomac River. In early spring, when the creek is swollen with rain and snowmelt, the water tumbles over rocks and down little waterfalls, but by the end of the summer it has become a thready trickle and you almost wonder if it's still there. Now in October – especially after the deluge we'd just had – the creek had perked up after its near dormancy and turned into a desultory stream as it burbled its way past the inn.

Quinn had texted me just as Bobby was leaving Eli's studio and suggested meeting there for dinner this evening, a break from the frenetic pace of the last couple of days. I know my husband. There was something else, another reason for suggesting we dine out. But when I texted back and asked if everything was OK, he sent a smiley emoji and wrote that he'd meet me at the inn around six thirty.

He'd ducked my question, which meant everything was not all right. Something was up and he wasn't going to tell me in a text. I didn't push it. I would find out soon enough.

Hassan, the inn's maître d', was waiting at his usual station behind a carved oak podium in the middle of the lobby, when I arrived a little before six thirty. We greeted each other in French as we always did and then he kissed me on both cheeks, what the French call 'faire la bise.' His old-school black reservation book, thick as a family Bible and filled with years of observations, notes, birthday reminders, and details of his guests and their family members, was open in front of him. Dominique called the book 'pure gold' because it probably contained more secrets about who was doing what and with whom in Washington, D.C. than the FBI and CIA knew put together.

When online reservation apps popped up as the new way to book a table, Hassan and Dominique said thanks-but-no-thanks, agreeing that there was no replacing the decades of information and knowledge that lived in Hassan's head: who should sit where, which politicians not to seat in the same dining room, or what to do when someone showed up with a guest who was not his or her spouse and asked for a table with 'a little privacy.'

Their guest list was a Who's Who of Washington power brokers and deal makers: senators, congressmen, ambassadors, cabinet officers, K Street lawyers, lobbyists, influencers – even two former presidents and their wives – all of whom appreciated the off-the-record discretion they found here. It was one of the reasons people returned so often. Two other reasons were the inn's coveted Michelin star and its reputation as the most romantic place to dine in the entire D.C. metropolitan region.

After Hassan's kiss and heartfelt condolences about Paul's death – plus a request to give Frankie and the children his love – he told me Quinn was already waiting in the green dining room. It was the inn's most private room and also, I thought, its most beautiful, tucked away at the end of a hall on its own. The walls were painted a rich hunter green, a working fireplace with a Provençal tile surround dominated one wall, and oil paintings of fox-hunting scenes mixed in with landscapes of the Blue Ridge Mountains and the farmland of the Piedmont hung on the other walls, one more reminder why we didn't want more roads paved over: if that happened we would lose this beautiful, bucolic countryside.

I gave Hassan a side-eyed look when he mentioned the green dining room. The staff's nickname for it was the 'Room of Secrets.' Confessions, trysts, confidences, things you couldn't or shouldn't share happened there. Everyone knew that's what went down because in that room the walls did *not* have ears.

'Do you know something?' I asked Hassan.

His kind face gave away nothing. 'I thought you might like some privacy tonight. Go join your husband. He just arrived.'

The dining room was practically empty when I entered a few minutes later. Quinn stood up and came around the table to kiss me, pulling me close. As he did, I caught a glimpse of his left hand. The dark tan lines where his wedding ring had been were sharp and distinctive.

The ring was gone.

'What . . . happened . . . to your wedding ring?'

He froze. 'Wow, you spotted that fast. It came off today when we were punching down the cap on the Cab Sauv. I caught it on the lip of the tank. It flipped off and I watched it spin in the air and arc into the juice. It sank and disappeared before I could grab it. I'm so sorry, sweetheart. I really am.'

'It's . . . OK,' I said, trying to remember if a lost or missing wedding ring signified bad luck or a premonition of something about to go wrong in a marriage. His ring, a one-of-a-kind hammered gold band that we'd bought from an artisan jeweler in Leesburg, had been perfectly plain except for the engraving I'd chosen for the inside: Je t'aime – I love you – and the date of our wedding. 'We'll replace it. Don't worry. Neither of us should probably be wearing our wedding rings on days we do labor-intensive work, especially in the wine cellar. We're asking for trouble.'

'Eventually,' he said, 'my ring had better turn up, hopefully after fermentation stops. Either when we press or when we move the juice into barrels. At least I know where it is. I don't want someone finding it in the bottom of a bottle of wine like they won a prize in a box of Cracker Jack. Or worse, swallowing it.'

'I'm sure it'll turn up,' I said as we sat down, though actually I wasn't. 'Is that what you didn't want to tell me when you texted me?'

He nodded, looking sheepish. 'Also that we managed to process most of the Cab Sauv this afternoon. We'll finish the rest tomorrow.'

Our waiter, who had been hovering in the background, materialized at our table and introduced himself before filling our water glasses and asking if we'd like a drink or a cocktail before ordering dinner. Quinn raised an eyebrow at me and I shook my head.

'We'll just have wine with dinner,' he told the waiter. 'Give us a minute to look at the menu before we order, please? And I'd like the wine list.'

'So how was *your* day? It has to be better than mine,' he added, with a rueful look after the waiter had recited the day's specials, produced the wine list, and vanished again.

My day had been a never-ending ride on the craziest merry-go-round in the amusement park. Things I hadn't thought were related suddenly connecting in the weirdest ways. Everything moving and changing so fast that figuring out where it began and ended gave me the world's biggest headache.

Were Eleanor Blake and the Hollywood Theatre fire that took place eighty years ago related to Paul's and Violet's deaths because the two of them discovered something that the Blake family didn't want known? Did whatever it was have anything to do with the photo in Thelma's book of death remembrances, the picture that seemed to imply that maybe Eleanor and Redmond Blake hadn't had the happiest of marriages? Was whatever had happened in 1941 so serious that it caused nearly forgotten memories to bubble up into a nasty stew that spilled over into the present day?

Then there was Bobby's bombshell: Finding the ground-up sedative on the broken shard of Paul's glass, along with remnants of gin from Paul's gin and tonic. Whatever Bobby said or thought, I now believed with my heart and soul that Frankie was right, and someone had been at the Merchants' home that day. Whoever it was had put a toxic amount of lorazepam in Paul's drink, enough that it had ultimately killed him.

'I don't know where to start,' I said.

'As bad as that?'

'I'm afraid so.'

'Let's order first – I'm starved – and then you can tell me. By the way, Dominique said she'd stop by later. She wants to talk about the lunch after Paul's funeral.'

'The funeral,' I said, 'has been postponed.'

'What?' He looked stunned. 'Why?'

I'd jumped in at the deep end, so I told him about Paul after our waiter took our orders. The news hit him harder than I had expected, his eyes locked on mine registering total shock – and then turned into outrage that someone had so callously and cruelly taken Paul's life and then walked away. Over dinner – rack of lamb for him, mushroom risotto for me, and a bottle of New Zealand Sauvignon Blanc – I told him the rest of it.

He was silent until I finished. His first question surprised me. 'What do you expect Kit is going to find in the newspaper archives?'

'I don't know. Maybe nothing.'

'If Paul and maybe Violet were killed because of something they found out about that fire, you don't want to get involved, sweetheart. You don't *need* to get involved. That's Bobby's job. Let him put the puzzle pieces together, figure it out. Because after what happened today – you finding that piece of broken glass after Frankie insisted someone else was at their home with Paul – now the Sheriff's Office has got to be considering murder as a possibility. You've done enough. As for that fire, it's another story.'

'I know that.'

'So let it go, OK?'

He reached across the table and tipped my chin so I was looking into his dark, serious eyes. 'I don't want anything to happen to you,' he said. 'Someone's not playing games, and it seems to be over this unpaved roads issue. It's got everyone so stirred up that people aren't behaving rationally.'

He wasn't going to let me look away until I told him what he wanted to hear. 'I know. OK. I promise. I'm done.' He nodded, releasing me. 'Except for one more thing.'

'What?' It sounded like a growl. 'You just promised . . .'

'I know. But before we let it go completely, it looks like this has something to do with the Blake family. Do you think . . .?'

'That Nash Blake is a murderer, that he killed Paul Merchant? Or Wyatt is? Or Hunter?' He shook his head. 'I do not. Although you never know about people; you never know who might be living a secret life that no one has any idea about.'

'So is that a no or a yes?'

'It is.'

I smiled. 'OK, I'm done. But I *am* curious.'

His eyes were still grave, troubled. 'Lucie.'

'Aren't you?'

'I'd just like whoever did this to be caught.'

'Whoever did what?'

We had been so engrossed in our conversation that neither of us realized my cousin had entered the room and was standing at our table. The angels in heaven who had created Dominique Gosselin had designed a woman of great beauty – slender, petite, alabaster skin, enormous green eyes, short, spiky auburn hair – along with a quick wit, a good heart, and a sense of humor. But they had forgotten to give her an off switch, like the Energizer Bunny when things went haywire.

Dominique and I exchanged kisses – the French *always* kiss, it's what we do instead of a handshake, even if it's two men – and then Quinn got a chair from another table so she could sit with us.

She didn't sit though, she perched as if she might bolt at any second because of a problem in the kitchen, a guest who needed soothing, or some crisis only she could solve. 'Have you two ordered dessert?' she asked.

We had not. I chose the chocolate mousse with Grand Marnier; Quinn had the inn's legendary Died and Gone to Heaven Chocolate Triple Layer Cake. Three espressos, Quinn's a double.

The word hadn't gotten out about a toxic amount of medication being mixed in with alcohol as the probable cause of Paul's death, nor that someone else might have been there with Paul that day. But Dominique needed to know that the funeral luncheon was going to be postponed for a couple of days while the Commonwealth Medical Examiner's Office did a more thorough examination of Paul's body in case they discovered something Win Turnbull had missed.

And of course, she wanted to know the rest of it.

'Murder.' Her expression was a mixture of horror and shock when I was done telling her. 'Paul was such a good, kind man. Who would *do* such a thing?'

Murders don't happen in Atoka, Virginia. They just don't. Out here we recoil watching the evening news, where it's a given there will be yet another story about a homicide somewhere in D.C., ratcheting up the numbers and setting another new record in a city where the murders seem random and brazen and senseless. But here in our corner of the Old Dominion, a little over fifty miles west of where that violence and killing and crime were taking place, we felt safe. Cocooned. Insulated. People left doors unlocked and no one worried about walking home alone at night. Crime was generally of the petty theft variety – someone's tools stolen out of the back of their pickup, shoplifters caught at one of Middleburg's upscale boutique stores, usually someone from out of town visiting for the day – that sort of thing.

Dominique had spoken quietly, but even so the word *murder* floated into the air and caught the attention of the other guests in the dining room. A few swiveled their heads like startled birds and stared at our table.

I leaned toward my cousin, lowering my voice. 'Bobby said he's still not convinced it's murder, but he definitely intends to find out what happened.'

'How is Frankie doing?' she asked.

'She's devastated. Grieving. Like you'd think.'

She absorbed that news and then said, 'Do you think Paul's death had something to do with the project to keep the roads unpaved?'

I couldn't keep the astonishment out of my voice. 'What made you think of that?'

Dominique couldn't have known about the stormy meeting between Nash Blake and Paul Merchant the day he was killed – could she? Then why – how – had she managed to zero in with such laser-like accuracy on the exact subject Quinn and I had just been discussing, the same reason we had speculated someone would have wanted Paul out of the way?

Quinn nudged me under the table. I knew what that was for: *Don't bring up Eleanor and the Hollywood Theatre fire. Don't throw gasoline on a blaze and turn it into an inferno.*

Our desserts arrived along with the three espressos.

'I have my ear to the grindstone,' Dominique said, dropping a cube of raw sugar into her espresso. 'Especially here. Sooner or later, I run into just about everyone who comes for lunch or dinner or goes to the bar. I hear things.'

Even though my cousin had become a citizen a few years ago and her English had improved enormously since she had first arrived in Virginia, our idioms still flummoxed her.

'What kind of things?'

'Well, for example, the Pro-Loudoun Progressives meet here. Nash Blake dines here so often that Hassan has reserved a table just for him.'

My cousin, as the owner of a small business, was on the pave-the-roads side of the aisle with the Pro-Loudoun Progressives. I didn't blame her – it made sense for her bottom line. But at least she wasn't a rabid do-anything-to-win supporter. She didn't have campaign signs stuck in front of the inn where people could see them as they drove by, especially the more militant, combative signs.

Don't Pave Paradise: Eco-Fascists and Tree-huggers Against Progress

Don't Pave Paradise: Taking Us Back to the Good Old Days of 1787

*Don't Pave Paradise: Supporting Car Wash & Auto Repair
Businesses Near You*

Unpaved Roads: Great for Horses, Lousy for Humans & Cars

'Do you sit in on those meetings?' I asked, trying not to make it sound like an accusation.

Even though we were on opposite sides of this issue, so far we'd treaded lightly whenever the subject came up – in fact, mostly we avoided discussing it. It had already leeched into Eli's marriage and poisoned Sasha's relationship with Grayson. That was bad enough. But as Virginians, we were also deeply dyed Southerners who couldn't help wearing our hearts, our beliefs, our convictions on our sleeves because it was baked into our DNA. Our history was a long trail of passionate differences that had life-changing consequences for family relationships. Union or Confederate. Republican or Democrat – especially lately. Pro- or anti-NRA. Pro-life or Pro-a-woman's-right-to-choose.

Pave the Roads or Don't.

I didn't want anything to happen to my relationship with my cousin and I don't think she did, either. After my mother died and Mia turned into a hell-raising teenage rebel who was too much for Leland to handle, Dominique had quit her studies at Le Cordon Bleu in Paris and moved to Atoka to help us out, a life-saving angel. It hadn't taken long for her to realize my sister needed a Mother-Superior-cum-Marine-Corps-drill-sergeant to rein her in rather than a loving, gentle hand. In addition to keeping Mia from being expelled from school or doing a stint in juvie, she also landed a job as a sous-chef at the Goose Creek Inn. When Fitzhugh Pico – my godfather and the owner of the inn – died a few years later, he left it to Dominique, who had become his de facto business partner. Within a few years she had turned it into one of the most sought-after restaurants in the region. She'd also started a wildly successful catering business.

'I do sit in on some of the Pro-Loudoun Progressive meetings,' she said, stirring her espresso until I thought her spoon might melt. 'Although it depends on the night, how busy we are. And yes, I know things have gotten pretty heated between the Progressives and the No-Pavers. Especially after Violet died and Paul took her place. That made things even more . . . intense, since Paul was also campaigning for that open seat on the board of supervisors. If he won, he'd be pushing the non-paving agenda, along with his beliefs about climate change, which were also controversial. It got a lot of people worked up, angry. Still, everyone's entitled to their Sixth Amendment rights here.'

'The right to a speedy trial?' Quinn asked.

'Uh, no. The one about freedom of speech.'

'That would be the First Amendment,' he said.

'Right. That one.'

'Did things get so . . . heated . . . intense . . . during those discussions that someone might have wanted to silence Paul?' I asked.

'I . . . hope not.' Her face was troubled. As if she were replaying a video of some of the meetings in her head, running through who had been especially upset or outraged, saying something that, at the time, had seemed like blowing off steam.

'You hope people will be . . . rational,' she went on. 'Anyway, Nash's not here only for business meetings. He proposed to his girlfriend the other night. Got down on one knee and gave her a ring in front of everyone. It was right here in this room, actually. At that table over there.' She pointed to a table for two in the corner. 'All the guests applauded and cheered. He ordered champagne for everyone – it was . . . charmant.'

It had been an abrupt, purposeful change of subject. If my cousin had any suspicions about who was angry enough to go after Paul, she wasn't going to say so based on nothing but hotheaded talk.

'Wait,' I said. 'His *girlfriend*?'

'Lucie, chérie, where have you *been*? Zoey Ainsworth. The daughter of his financial manager, Dallas Ainsworth. Dallas has been hoping this will happen for *years*. Zoey marrying Nash would secure their relationship into the future, especially since Hunter isn't interested in the family business. And Zoey . . . she's been waiting for Nash to come around, even though he's so much older, at least twenty years older than she is. He dated other women, but she was patient. She's been in love with him since she was a little girl.'

The last time I remembered seeing Zoey Ainsworth, she'd

been at the vineyard for a hen party for one of her girlfriends where she'd gotten overly boisterous after a few too many glasses of Chardonnay. Frankie had cut her off – nicely. It was one of many reasons we didn't allow tour bus or party bus groups in the tasting room, because they usually had one goal in mind. Go home buzzed – at a minimum. Especially if they showed up late in the day and we were the last stop. After the hen party episode, we had another meeting with the tasting room staff and the vineyard crew to discuss yet again the perennial problem of what to do when people didn't *drink responsibly* like the sign at the entrance to the vineyard specified.

'I guess I didn't realize she was carrying a torch for Nash all these years,' I said.

Dominique nodded. 'Dallas did a lot to encourage it. He wanted the Ainsworths and Blakes to be family. I think he really hopes Nash and Zoey will have a baby, even if Hunter is closer to Zoey's age than his father is. A grandchild for Dallas and another son or a daughter for Nash would cement their ties.'

Our waiter showed up to ask if we wanted anything else.

'Just the check, please,' Quinn said. 'When you have a chance.'

'Dessert and the coffees are on the house,' Dominique told the waiter.

'You can't . . .' Quinn protested and she waved her hand at him.

'It's my restaurant. I can.'

The waiter left and I said, 'Has Nash been in here with Grayson Vaughn?'

Dominique arched a surprised eyebrow. 'Why do you ask?'

'Grayson and Sasha have practically come to blows because Gray decided to sell some of his land to Nash.' When she nodded, I added, 'So you know about that, too?'

'I know who my guests are. *You* know that.'

'Did you ever see Grayson having dinner or lunch with Violet Rossi?'

She frowned. 'You know we don't discuss who comes and goes here. Everyone's entitled to their privacy.'

'I'm aware of that. But Paul is dead and there was something going on between Gray and Violet before she died – apparently a romantic relationship. Violet had persuaded him to put his farm into a conservation easement, even though he would make more money selling it to a developer like Nash who would turn it into cookie-cutter McMansion land. After Violet died, Nash stepped back into the picture and persuaded Gray to sell him the land after all.'

She sat back and surveyed me, not happily. 'You know quite a lot, chérie.'

'Yes, but not everything. I understand your rules about respecting your guests' privacy, but this is different.'

Next to me I could feel Quinn growing restless. But I also knew he was drawn into this story just as I was, its magnetic pull. Dominique knew things. She had *answers*.

'Why don't you tell me what you know first?' she said to me.

Fair enough.

'OK. All of us know Violet died because she lost control of her car on Crenshaw Road, on a dirt and gravel section after First Bridge where it runs along Goose Creek. According to Eli – who found out from Sasha – apparently Violet and Grayson were also involved romantically right before she died. So now Gray lost two women he cared about . . . both times because the roads were unpaved. If Nash built his homes on Grayson's land, the odds would be pretty good the county would step in and pave them for the new subdivisions.' I paused. 'How am I doing so far?'

'Fine,' she said. 'What about the rest of it?'

I gave her a blank stare. 'The rest of what?'

'The *beginning* of the story.'

'I don't know what you're talking about,' I said.

'Me, neither,' Quinn added.

'I don't want to open a box of Pandoras,' she said.

'Don't worry,' I said. 'Whatever you tell us stays between the three of us.'

Her smile was twisted. 'All right. Before Violet persuaded Grayson to put the land into easement, Nash had persuaded Gray to sell it to him.'

'Wait,' Quinn said. 'Grayson was going to sell to Nash, then he backed out and agreed to the conservation easement with

Violet, and then he went back to Nash and said, "OK, I'll sell."
Is that what happened?'

'Not exactly.'

Clear as mud.

'You want to explain?' I asked.

'Grayson wasn't the one who changed his mind and told Nash
he wasn't selling. Violet went to Nash and got him to back off.'

Quinn said, 'What?' as I said, 'You're kidding.'

'I'm not kidding.'

'What happened? How did Violet get Nash to walk away
from a deal to build over three hundred homes on beautiful,
pristine land?' I asked.

'I have no idea. All I know is that he was as mad as a wet
blanket for weeks.'

'Did the two of them ever have dinner together here?' Quinn
asked.

'Mon dieu, *no*. Ils ne pouvaient pas se voir dans un tableau.
They couldn't even stand seeing each other in a painting. After
Violet stole Grayson from Nash, it was practically open war
between them. It took all of Hassan's diplomatic skills to make
sure they never ran into each other if both of them were here
on the same evening. I always wondered what Violet said – or
knew – to make Nash walk away from that deal with Grayson.'

I couldn't look at Quinn because we *knew* what she'd said.
Or at least we thought we did. Violet had discovered something
that had to do with Eleanor Blake and the Hollywood Theatre
fire. And whatever it was, she succeeded in getting Nash to
back off from buying Grayson's land so she, in turn, could
persuade Grayson to put his land into a conservation easement.

Blackmail.

There weren't too many possibilities that I could imagine
would be of an order of magnitude to get billionaire philanthropist Nash Blake to walk away from a deal worth many
millions of dollars. Although there was one possibility that was
so glaringly obvious it was screaming *look at me*. And it didn't
take a rocket scientist to figure it out.

Murder.

Again.

TWELVE

The trip home from the inn was headache-inducing. So many questions, not nearly enough answers. Quinn and I had driven there in separate vehicles – me in the Jeep, him in the pickup. My phone rang and his name flashed on the screen on my dashboard the moment we turned out of the parking lot onto Sam Fred Road. Our conversation picked up seamlessly from where we'd left off in the restaurant.

'I think it's a good thing you didn't mention Eleanor and that fire to Dominique,' he said. 'We don't know anything for sure, so right now it's all speculation.'

At least he'd said *we*.

'I know. I wonder if Kit's going to find anything in the *Trib* archives that will give us a clue about what Violet found out. If she managed to blackmail Nash and make him back off from buying Gray's land, *she's* the one who made the discovery. Either she told Paul what it was before her accident, or he learned about it afterward. Or figured it out.'

'What do you think this "discovery" was?' he asked. It was a half-rhetorical question.

'The same thing you're thinking. The fire was a cover-up for Eleanor's murder. Redmond used his influence and maybe his money to get the Sheriff's Office to speed up the investigation and rule that the fire was an accident caused by faulty electrical wiring. And Eleanor died because she was locked in the projection room alone in the building and couldn't get out. No whiff of murder or foul play, just a tragic accident.'

'Except that what really happened was that Redmond Blake somehow arranged for his wife to die in that fire,' he said.

When he said it like that – so cold and heartless and calculating – it punched the breath out of me. '*Why?* Why would he do it?'

'I don't know. It couldn't have been money, because wasn't he rich even though he married an heiress? We already know it probably wasn't another woman. He never remarried, so you have to assume there wasn't someone else.'

'Maybe. But it still feels as if we're missing something. Except . . .'

Not just a small puzzle piece so that everything would tumble neatly into place once we realized what it was, but something big. In fact, it seemed we were so lost we couldn't see the forest for the trees.

'Except what?' Quinn asked.

'I don't know. Except everybody involved is dead. Except even if Redmond did arrange for Eleanor to die in the fire, no one is going to jail. Except what would the consequences be now, eighty years later?'

He was silent for a moment. 'I think there would be consequences for Nash. Shame. Humiliation. A revelation that his grandfather – or in Wyatt's case, his father and, in Hunter's case, his great-grandfather – who was the patriarch of a wealthy family of philanthropists wasn't such a nice guy after all, arranging for his wife's death which he then covered up by setting a fire – or arranging for that to happen, too. Who wants that legacy? He's a cold-blooded *murderer.*'

'I agree. It's awful,' I said. 'But I don't think Redmond potentially being guilty of murder – probably second-degree murder – is enough of a reason for Nash to back off from buying Grayson's land. First of all, it's ancient history. And second, after a couple of news cycles, people are going to forget all about this, as sordid a story as it is. At best it'll be a footnote or maybe an asterisk by the Blake family name in the future. You know as well as I do that anybody can be rehabilitated if they just wait it out long enough, let enough time pass. You see it in politics all the time. Everybody gets another chance at redemption.'

We were approaching the entrance to the vineyard and the turnoff for Sycamore Lane, our private road named for a two-hundred-year-old tree that stood at a junction where the road split and turned into a big loop. I put on my turn signal and behind me Quinn did the same.

'OK, I'll agree that's possible, that Nash might not care about something that happened such a long time ago,' he said. 'But it's also possible that he wanted to spare his father and his son the pain that a revelation like this might cause.'

'And he did that by committing another murder? Maybe two? To shut up two people who uncovered the biggest family skeleton in the closet,' I asked. 'Really?'

We were home.

'Do you think Nash is responsible for killing Paul?' I asked. We were back to that again. 'That he was the one who was over at the Merchants' house the other day and drugged Paul, leaving him in the swimming pool when he fell in – or worse, he pushed him in?'

'You mean like grandfather, like grandson? Redmond and Nash? Both of them committing homicides?' he said. 'Honestly, no. I don't think Nash killed Paul.'

'Unless he had someone else take care of it for him. Murder for hire.'

'You're forgetting one thing,' Quinn said. He clicked his phone off as we both got out of our vehicles and walked to the front door.

'What's that?'

'Paul knew his killer. He let him in. So Nash didn't hire some thug.'

Above the entrance to Highland House, the Montgomery clan motto had been carved into the lintel: Garde bien.

Watch well. Watch out for us. *Don't turn your back.*

It was a warning to be vigilant.

Paul Merchant had turned his back on someone. I was sure of it, just as Frankie was. Someone else had been in the Merchants' home that day.

And whoever it was had killed him.

'I have no idea where that leaves us,' I said. 'It seems the more we know, the less we know.'

Quinn was sitting up in bed with his pillow propped up behind him, the book he was currently reading lying face down on the covers. Yet another sobering treatise on climate change, which, to me, was like reading horror before bedtime and then hoping to have a peaceful night's sleep without nightmares.

I climbed into bed, a small velvet box nestled in the palm

of my hand, and knelt beside him. 'What are you thinking about?' I asked.

'Rising sea levels, places that become so hot they're uninhabitable. A shortage of drinking water. Not enough food.'

'Quinn—'

'It's here. It's only going to get worse unless we do something radical to slow it down.'

'I know,' I said. 'Look, it's been a rough day. So much awful news. Can we leave it for now? Besides, I have something for you.'

He closed his book and set it on his bedside table. I handed him the box.

'What is it?'

'Open it.'

The eighteen-carat solid-gold ring was engraved with the Montgomery family crest, although after so many years the image had grown softer, fainter. Still, you could tell there was a woman holding a sword in one hand and a severed head in the other.

He looked up. 'What is this all about?'

'Until you find your wedding ring. with the family crest on it It's something from me. It belonged to my grandfather. Since it had already been decided that Eli was going to get Leland's ring with the family crest on it when he passed away, my grandmother gave this ring to me. I think it might fit your ring finger.'

He slipped it on the third finger of his left hand. A perfect fit.

He took it off again and held it out to me. 'I already lost one ring that's precious to me in a vat of wine. I don't want to lose another. Especially this one.'

I put both my hands over his large strong hand and closed it around the ring. 'Please.'

He tilted his head, a shadow briefly flitting across his face. 'Wait a minute. You don't think I lost my ring . . . on purpose, do you? Because I didn't want to wear a wedding ring to begin with?'

He had balked when we talked about the subject of two wedding rings, but eventually acquiesced when he saw how much it meant to me.

'No, no . . . of course not. Not at all.'

'Then, what?' he asked. 'Is there some . . . superstition . . . about losing a wedding ring that I don't know about? Like maybe it signifies that the marriage might be over?'

When I didn't reply, he leaned forward and kissed me, long and tender and deep. When he pulled back from his kiss, he whispered in my ear. 'How could you even think such a thing? We're just beginning . . . we have a lifetime together ahead of us. I love you more than anything in the world, Lucie.'

'I love you, too,' I whispered back.

He slipped the ring on again and laid me back against the pillows, pulling my silky nightgown over my head and tossing it onto a chair. Then he slipped off his underwear and moved on top of me. 'I don't want you to doubt me,' he said, his mouth against mine. 'Tell me that you don't.'

When I could breathe, I said, 'I don't.'

And for a very long time after that, he proved it.

Quinn was up before me the next morning. When I woke up, I smelled coffee and found the note he left for me on his pillow that was fairly explicit about what we'd done last night in bed and just how good the sex had been. I rolled over and found my nightgown. He wasn't in the kitchen when I came downstairs, nor was the Jeep in the driveway. Another note was propped up against the coffee maker. He'd made his usual sludge but the rule was the first one up made the coffee and the other one couldn't complain. He thought I brewed dirty dishwater. He'd scrawled that he'd gone over to the barrel room to pump over the tanks of Cabernet Sauvignon with Antonio now that the task of pigéage – punching down the cap – was finished and the solid mass of grapes had started breaking down and slowly turning into juice, and eventually, wine. From now until the grapes finished fermenting, it was something that needed to be done twice a day.

We had breakfast together when he returned.

'You're very quiet,' he said as he got up to get the coffee pot. 'Everything OK? You want another cup of coffee?'

I set my fork down on my plate. 'No, thanks. I'm not looking forward to this morning. I don't know what to say to Frankie

– Bobby's news about the tox results of the contents of the drinks glass and needing to re-examine Paul's body has got to be devastating. And Benny is apparently driving Nelia nuts because now he has to go to a rehab hospital. I don't blame him. Hospitals are full of sick people.'

He smiled as he poured himself another cup of coffee. After he sat down again, he said, 'I know you hate hospitals, sweetheart. We don't have to stay long. Benny won't want us to, anyway. As for Frankie . . .' His voice trailed off. When he spoke again, he didn't look at me. 'I don't know what to say, either. I'm terrible at stuff like this.'

Emotions. Women. Emotional women. Emotional women crying. Quinn came unraveled. I knew this from experience. And when it was someone like Frankie, who we all thought of as Superwoman? It was as if gravity suddenly stopped working and nothing was as it should be.

How would we comfort her? What could we say?

'I don't think she's sleeping,' I said. 'I got a couple of texts from her this morning with time stamps all through the night. Having her housecleaners come in to get the house spick and span before the funeral and then finding out she might have accidentally removed all the evidence from a crime scene – if there was one – has really knocked her off balance. Especially because Bobby seems more and more convinced that Paul was at the house by himself – no one else was with him – and he added the drugs to his drink either by accident or on purpose. Meaning there's no crime.'

'I don't believe that he ground up those pills and put them in his drink. Not Paul,' Quinn said. 'He wouldn't be that careless. Or dumb. Besides, someone else's prints were on that piece of broken glass you found.'

He picked up our plates and loaded them into the dishwasher.

'I don't believe he would take his own life, either,' I said.

When we walked outside a few minutes later, Quinn looked up at the sky. 'Another storm's coming,' he said as he opened the passenger door to the Jeep for me. 'It's been a hell of a harvest, one for the record books. This one's going to end with a bang.'

I got in and buckled my seatbelt. 'I think a lot of things are going to end with a bang,' I said. 'Not just harvest. And there's no way to MacGyver any of what's broken back together and make it whole again, either. Not Frankie. Not Benny.'

'I know,' he said. 'I guess we've finally run out of tricks and solutions.'

I recognized Father Joe O'Malley's dusty black Honda CR-V in Frankie's driveway when Quinn and I pulled in half an hour later after stopping by the Goose Creek Inn to pick up a picnic basket filled with chicken hummus wraps, vegetarian club sandwiches, a Caprese salad, a fruit salad, and hazelnut tiramisu for dessert. Dominique had also tucked in a box of homemade macarons and a note for Frankie.

Quinn turned off the engine as a rumble of thunder sounded ominously in the distance. 'She's got company,' he said. 'Maybe this isn't a good time.'

I reached for my cane. 'It's Father Joe,' I said. 'They're probably talking about a new day and time for the funeral and the wake. Or more likely . . .'

'More likely what?' He picked up the picnic basket from the back seat.

'They're talking about the other thing. Actually, it's probably *exactly* what they are talking about.'

'The other thing. Bobby saying either Paul's death was an accident – or else it was intentional?' He paused. 'Suicide. Not murder.'

I nodded as we got out of the Jeep. 'Yes. *That* other thing. Frankie and Paul are devout, practicing Catholics. I don't know how she will find any peace or consolation if it turns out to be suicide. Although she and Father Joe go way back. If anybody can help her get through this, he can. And we can always just drop off the picnic basket and leave if they're really involved in a heavy conversation.'

The kind on conversation you never in your life want to have. Did the person you love most in the world kill himself because demons you didn't know about were too much to bear any more?

I wouldn't know where to begin.

In fact, it was Father Joe O'Malley who answered the door,

coffee mug in hand, dressed in his clerical blacks, here in his official capacity to provide comfort, support, and solace.

'Lucie, Quinn,' he said. 'Frankie said you were planning to stop by this morning. Come on in. I'm glad to see you both.'

'Is this a good time? How is she?' I asked.

'She needs to lean on her family and friends more than ever right now. So, it's a very good time. Not only losing a beloved husband of many years, but all the news and conjecture swirling around Paul's death. Come. She's waiting.'

'Father,' Quinn said before he could turn around and lead us down the hall to the kitchen. 'Can I ask you something?'

He nodded, watching Quinn, a somber look on his face. 'Of course you can.'

I usually didn't see Quinn flustered but right now he was totally nonplussed. 'Before we see Frankie, I wanted to ask you *if* – and I mean *if* – Paul took his own life – I don't believe he did, but in case he did – don't you – I mean, doesn't the Church consider it a mortal sin, meaning Paul can't have a Catholic funeral?'

He didn't add 'and if he killed himself Paul burns in hell for all eternity,' but I knew from the look on his face that he was thinking it. His Spanish mother, a single mom after his dad left when he was a baby, had been the kind of Catholic who went to daily Mass and had a small altar in their linen closet where she said novenas for herself and her son. Once Quinn admitted to me that he'd briefly been an altar boy. But after the sexual abuse scandal and the subsequent cover-ups and lies that had followed, he had left the Catholic Church and never went back.

Father Joe laid a hand on Quinn's shoulder, and I knew what he was going to say would be consoling. Not damning or judgmental.

'Maybe if Paul died in the thirteenth century, it would have been. Back then St Thomas Aquinas called suicide an act against God and said it was a sin for which one could not repent. But not today. There's no blaming anyone for taking their own life. Instead, we focus on the family – the survivors – because they need so much care after the trauma they've just been through. As for the person who killed him or herself, you have to ask yourself what made them believe death was a better option than facing whatever awful thing was tormenting them. Which is why we believe that these individuals who were so tortured and desperate deserve all of our understanding and compassion. Perhaps they were suffering from some kind of serious psychological instability or an overwhelming feeling of fear and confusion. We don't know and we'll never know. It's not for any of us to judge. Nor should those left behind blame themselves for missing a warning sign, a clue, not doing more to prevent such hopelessness and despair from spilling over into a final end to it all.'

It was a long speech and for a moment I wondered if Father Joe had only been talking about suicide and compassion or whether he was also obliquely referring to the Church and how it had learned its lesson, or so one hoped: that forgiveness was available to everyone, however heinous the crime, that no one should judge the actions of another, because you could not look into another person's soul and know what resided there. His eyes were riveted on Quinn's just as Quinn's were locked on his.

'I'm glad to hear that,' Quinn said finally. 'Because the Church means everything to Frankie.'

There was so much subtext in those words I almost winced. *Be there for her. Don't let her down.*

'I am aware of that,' Father Joe said. 'Believe me, I am. I can tell you she is leaning heavily into her faith right now with everything that's happened. But she still needs everyone she loves around her, including you two. Come – she's in the kitchen, waiting for you. And I'm afraid there's some bad news. I'll let her tell you.'

Frankie was sitting on one of the barstools at the labradorite counter, her hands wrapped around a coffee mug. She looked so despondent and bereft it hurt. I walked over to where she was sitting as Quinn set down the picnic basket on the counter. She got up and fell into my arms.

'I. Am. So. Sorry,' I said. 'What can I do? What can we do?'

Her arms tightened around me and she fought back a sob. 'Bobby just called. He says they're going to rule Paul's death as an accidental overdose – I think as a kindness to me and the kids. They're not going to say it was suicide – because they don't know for sure.'

'Oh, Frankie—'

'He didn't kill himself.'

She stepped back, her eyes roving between Quinn and me, asking us to believe her, wondering if we did.

'I know,' I said. 'I know.'

'And it wasn't an accident, either.' Her voice was fierce with anger. 'I don't know why Bobby just doesn't . . . get it.'

'What else did he tell you?' Quinn asked as Father Joe set down two more mugs of coffee and the four of us settled onto barstools.

I caught a whiff of alcohol on Frankie's breath as she sat down. Not strong, but enough. It was barely ten o'clock in the morning. Day drinking. We drank at all hours in our job – tasting wine, selling wine, making wine. It was a constant worry whether all that alcohol – even if you spit when you were only tasting – might veer from something you had under control to something that controlled you.

'He said there's no evidence – no *physical* evidence – to support anyone else being at the house that day.'

'Because you had your cleaners here?' I asked.

'My cleaners weren't out by the pool,' she said in a flat, dull voice. 'The investigators who were here didn't find *anything*. Anywhere.'

'What about the broken glass – what about not finding the rest of it except that one shard under the azalea bush?' I asked. 'And someone else's prints.'

She shrugged. 'Paul could have gotten rid of the rest of the glass somewhere none of us have found yet. His prints were on the glass as well.' She made small concentric rings with her mug on the bar, her eyes downcast, fixated on what she was doing. 'Bobby says that he's seen enough instances where someone puts a lethal dose of something – sleeping pills, anti-depressants, opioids – in an alcoholic drink and then drinks it knowing what's going to happen. It's a lot more painless than some of the other choices – guns, hanging, jumping off a bridge. Finding lorazepam residue in the gin and tonic glass doesn't necessarily mean someone else put it there.'

I met Quinn's eyes above her bowed head. Tell her our theory about Eleanor and the fire and get her hopes up, or don't tell her until we learned more? His eyes shifted briefly. *Don't say anything.* I nodded imperceptibly, acutely aware that Father Joe hadn't missed our wordless exchange.

'He didn't leave a note,' Quinn said.

Frankie shrugged again, another helpless gesture. 'I know. Apparently, there doesn't always have to be a note, though there is more often than not.' She looked up at the three of us, her eyes swollen and red-rimmed. 'Bobby says Paul wasn't thinking. He was stressed out after the meeting with Nash Blake in Washington and dumped the pills in a drink. It just *happened.*'

'Is there anything we can do?' I asked again. 'Anything at all? What do you need?'

She gestured to the picnic basket. 'I have no idea what's in there, but I know it will be delicious. Thank you for that. The funeral is definitely going to be on Tuesday morning now that the autopsy is over and done with. The wake will be Monday evening instead of tomorrow night,' she said, giving us a weary look. 'Joe and I are just making last-minute plans and adjustments.'

'We don't have funerals on Saturdays at St Mike's,' Father Joe said, almost apologetically. 'Those days are reserved for weddings and baptisms. And there's a wedding this Saturday.'

'And a baptism on Sunday,' I said. 'Ivy Noland.'

He smiled. 'Yes, that's right.'

'Sweetie,' I said to Frankie, 'we're on our way to Lansdowne to see Benny before he moves to the rehab hospital, but we wanted to check on you and bring you and the kids a meal from the inn. I'll talk to Nikki and Dominique when I get home and make sure they know the funeral is taking place on Tuesday so everything is in order for the luncheon after Mass, OK?'

She gave me a sad, grateful smile and looked as if she were close to tears again. 'That would be great. Thank you.' Her voice wavered.

'We should probably let you finish making plans.' Quinn caught my eye. He wanted to get out of Dodge before the floodgates opened.

'I'll see you out,' Father Joe said. 'Frankie, I'll be right back.'

'Is she going to be OK?' I asked him in a low voice as we walked down the hall toward the foyer. 'I smelled alcohol on her breath.'

'I know. I'm worried about her, too.' He gave us a sharp-eyed look. 'Is there something you two know about what happened that you're holding back from her?'

'I didn't realize reading minds was one of the gifts bestowed on you when you become a priest,' I said, and he smiled. 'It's kind of scary.'

'On-the-job training. You learn to pay attention,' he said. 'No magic or supernatural skills involved.'

'No one else knows about this except Bobby, and he doesn't put any stock in it,' I said. 'Obviously.'

'You can tell me anything. It stays right here.' He tapped two fingers against his heart. 'You know that.'

Quinn let me talk – he seemed more comfortable having me take the lead – so I recounted what we'd learned about Eleanor, Redmond, and the Hollywood Theatre fire. Also that we guessed that Violet, and later Paul, had learned something relating to Eleanor's death and that it was information Nash Blake didn't want to get out.

'If that's true,' Father Joe said when I was done, 'it seems as if they might have discovered something that proved the fire had been arranged to cover up Eleanor's death.'

'Which would make it a homicide,' Quinn said.

Father Joe's eyes narrowed. 'It would, wouldn't it?'

'What we don't know is what they found. Something hiding in plain sight all these years?' I said. 'Something they unearthed, turned up . . . somewhere?'

'I'm afraid my omniscience doesn't extend that far. It has limits.' His smile was rueful, but I had a feeling we had pricked something in his memory that got him thinking.

'Do you know Nash Blake?' Quinn asked him.

'Not well. In fact, hardly at all. When I came to St Michael the Archangel nine years ago, I said the funeral Mass for his grandfather, Redmond Blake. It was one of the first Masses I said at that church. I haven't really had any interaction with the Blake family since then. They're not . . . uh . . . frequent . . . rather, regular parishioners.'

'Do you remember anything . . . unusual . . . about the funeral?' I asked.

'Unusual?' His eyes had the faraway look of trying to remember. 'It was crowded, I remember that. The church was packed. Someone fainted. Also, one of Redmond's late wife's relatives – one of Eleanor Blake's relatives, I should say – showed up. A grandniece, I think it was. But it was as if she came to witness the Mass rather than grieve over Redmond's death. You know, make sure he was really dead. I remember thinking there was no love lost between her and the Blakes. You see that more often than I wish you did at funerals. They don't always bring out the best in families.'

'Do you remember the grandniece's name?' I asked.

He shook his head. 'I scarcely remember her, except that she had her arms folded tight across her chest for most of the Mass, as if they were locked in place. Between her body language and the expression on her face, you could tell there were a lot of unresolved issues and some anger.' He glanced over his shoulder toward the kitchen. 'I should probably get back to Frankie. This last call from Bobby . . .'

He didn't need to finish. She could be dumping another slug of brandy in her coffee. Trying to cope.

'If you think of anything or happen to remember the grandniece's name, would you let us know?' I asked.

'Of course. Unfortunately, I don't think you should hold out much hope – I was brand new and the funeral was almost a decade ago. I'm sorry. It's too bad you can't ask one of the Blakes who it was. They'd know for sure.'

And if we did, that question would likely stir up a hornet's nest and possibly an unpleasant awareness that Quinn and I were probing into matters that were none of our business. Not to mention that it might lead the trail back to whatever Violet and Paul knew about Eleanor's death.

Father Joe opened the front door for Quinn and me. 'Francesca needs . . . closure. She needs to be at peace with what happened, however this turns out. I pray that with God's help – and the help of everyone who loves her – she will be able to find it.'

'I don't know if that's going to happen,' Quinn said as we walked back to the Jeep. 'I don't know if Frankie's going to find peace as long as she continues to believe that whoever was in the house with Paul had something to do with his death.'

'I know.'

So, Bobby had closed the door to Paul's death being anything but an unfortunate accident. He had stopped short of calling it suicide because one, he didn't know if it had been intentional or not, and two, there was no need to put Frankie through any more grief and heartache than she was already dealing with.

Violet and Paul had uncovered a secret the Blake family was determined to keep buried. If we could find out for certain what they knew – instead of just our unsubstantiated suspicions – it might change the narrative about their deaths being accidents. But right now, I had no idea how we were going to do that.

Without also possibly putting Quinn and me in the crosshairs of a killer.

THIRTEEN

The thunder that had merely been rumbling in the background while we'd been at Frankie's grew louder as we cut across Route 15, driving from Middleburg to Leesburg on our way to Lansdowne Hospital. By now lightning had begun to fork across a lead-colored sky of clouds that hung so thick and low it felt as if we were inside a bell jar. A few minutes later, the first fat raindrops splattered across the Jeep's windshield; before long rain pelted the car like hundreds of tiny ball-peen hammers, an all-out downpour exactly as it had been the other day.

Quinn reached over and automatically grabbed my hand. 'You're hyperventilating,' he said. 'It's going to be OK. Breathe normally, sweetheart.'

'I am. I'm OK.'

He glanced over at me. 'I'll believe you when you start breathing.'

I smiled. 'All right, I promise. But I'm still thinking about Frankie and what Father Joe said.'

'I know.' He turned off 15, easing onto Route 7 and heading east. A busy highway that wound its meandering way to Washington, D.C. 'Me, too.'

My phone dinged and he said, 'Everything OK?'

I looked at the screen. 'It's Nelia. I told her I'd text her before we got to the hospital to make sure Benny is still up for seeing us.'

'And is he?'

'She said, "Bring it on."'

It had been years since I'd been at Lansdowne Hospital – for one of my own surgeries after the accident – but muscle memory kicked in and I led Quinn to the correct elevator and then down all the right corridors until we got to the surgical wing on the fourth floor. First, though, we stopped at the coffee shop in the lobby and picked up a venti mocha latte for Benny and a cappuccino for Nelia.

Benny's room was across the hall from the nurse's station and the door was ajar. We knocked and Nelia called out, 'Come in.'

A nurse with her back to us was taking Benny's blood pressure when I pushed opened the door and Quinn and I walked in. I stopped so abruptly he nearly bumped into me and sloshed the two coffees he was carrying in a to-go container.

'I'm sorry . . . I didn't realize we were interrupting. We can come back,' I said.

The nurse turned around and smiled. A pretty redhead with wide-set green eyes and a dusting of freckles across her cheeks. Our eyes met and for the briefest of seconds we both froze. Then she relaxed and said in an easy voice, 'Don't worry. I'm almost done. You're Lucie Montgomery.'

'Yes. And you're Zoey Ainsworth. I didn't know you worked here.'

'You two know each other?' Benny asked in surprise as Zoey removed the blood pressure cuff from his forearm.

'We've met,' I said.

I glanced at Quinn, but his face was blank. He didn't remember her.

'When I overindulged at a bachelorette party at your winery.' Zoey's cheeks turned bright pink, but her gaze was steady and unflinching. 'You were very kind about my . . . exuberant behavior . . . and, just so you know, it hasn't happened again. I learned my lesson.'

Kudos to her for admitting it. 'I'm glad. Really – are we intruding? We could leave until you're finished.'

'Mr Ortiz?' Zoey turned to Benny.

'No, no, they're family. They can stay.' He grinned. 'They brought me my mocha latte.'

Quinn handed Benny his coffee and I gave Nelia her cappuccino and a hug.

'All right then, I need to listen to your lungs and then I'm all finished with your vitals,' Zoey said to Benny. 'After that, I just have to give you your medication.'

She removed the stethoscope that was hanging around her

neck and bent over Benny once again. We were quiet as she listened to his chest and his back. When she was done, she said, 'Excellent. Blood pressure great. Oxygen saturation great. Chest and lungs clear. Your trauma team is putting together the paperwork to release you to the rehab hospital. Someone will be in later to give you everything you need for your new doctors and therapists.'

'Thank you,' Nelia said. 'You've been very kind.'

'She's my favorite nurse,' Benny said to us. 'I'm going to miss her.'

'They're *all* your favorite nurses. You flirt with all of them,' Nelia said, flashing a serene, unruffled look at Zoey and a teasing smile of forbearance at her husband. 'And they spoil you rotten. I should be jealous.'

'That's because we all love him.' Zoey grinned and wrapped the stethoscope around her neck again.

Benny reached for Zoey's left hand and picked it up. With an exaggerated sigh, he said, 'And then she went and got engaged.'

I had been expecting a substantial diamond on Zoey's left hand, a statement ring from a billionaire like Nash Blake. Instead, she wore a delicate gold ring adorned with a heart in the center and a crown that sat on top of the heart. A multi-faceted diamond that looked like a very old European cut stone was set in the middle of the heart.

'What an unusual ring,' I said. 'It's lovely.'

Zoey tilted her hand so the diamond caught the light. 'It's Irish, a Claddagh ring. The heart symbolizes love. The crown symbolizes loyalty. There are also two hands clasping that symbolize friendship. Nash . . . Nash Blake, my fiancé, told me this ring belonged to his grandmother. His father's mother. He said these rings were very popular in Connemara, where his family came from, which is why that's the name of their home.'

'Then it must have a lot of meaning for you. And especially for Nash,' I said.

She took the bait. 'Oh, yes. Nash told me all about his grandmother, that she knew so many famous Hollywood movie stars, how she was such a generous philanthropist, and that she could have made the Olympics team in dressage if there had been an Olympics during World War Two.' She flashed the diamond again, admiring the ring. 'It's gorgeous, isn't it? I love it.'

'It's beautiful,' Benny said, patting her hand. 'Like you.'

'Thank you, Mr Ortiz.' Her cheeks turned pink once again. 'I'll be back in a minute with your medication.'

So, Nash Blake had given Zoey Ainsworth a ring that had belonged to Eleanor, extolling her virtues to his fiancée. Did that mean he didn't have any idea that his grandfather might have been responsible for the death of his grandmother? Because if he did know about it, why would he give a ring with such an awful, tortured history to his young, beautiful fiancée?

Maybe he didn't know about Eleanor, after all. Maybe Quinn and I were barking up the wrong tree. Completely.

After Zoey left the room, Quinn said to Benny, 'How are you doing?'

Benny lifted the blankets that were covering him so he could raise his left leg and show us the brace that extended from the middle of his thigh to the middle of his calf. 'The surgeon says I gotta keep this thing on for four months, though in a couple of weeks he'll let me start bending my knee. I'm going to go nuts. Plus, I've got to go to another hospital for the next ten days.'

'Do what your doctors and the physical therapists say,' I said. 'You know that, don't you? It's the only way you're going to get better faster.'

He gave me an exasperated eye roll that reminded me of Hope.

'How about you, Nelia?' I asked. 'How are you doing?'

She jerked a thumb in Benny's direction and smiled with her eyes. 'Listening to this one moan all the time – me estoy volviendo loca. I'm going nuts. But, doing better than I was now that he's had surgery and the doctor thinks he's going to be fine. Good as new. Thank you, by the way, for the coffees. And the flowers. And the card.'

Benny held out his hand to his wife. She took it and kissed him on the forehead. He murmured something low and tender to her in Spanish and kissed her lips. Quinn slipped an arm around my waist and pulled me close as we watched the love and intimate teasing between them.

'In sickness and in health,' Benny said. 'She meant it. I'm lucky.'

'Don't you forget it, mi amor.' Nelia poked him gently in the ribs. 'Speaking of sickness and health, how was Frankie when you saw her? We're so . . . desconsolados – our hearts are broken – over Paul's death. I haven't left the hospital or I would have gone by with some food. I'm sure she's not cooking right now.'

'Frankie could feed an army with all the food everyone has been dropping off,' I said. 'She's always been there for everyone else, so now she's being repaid a hundred times over. But to be honest, she's not doing great. Father Joe was with her when we were there, and Bobby Noland called earlier today as well.'

The door opened and Zoey returned, holding a small paper cup.

'What did Bobby have to say?' Benny asked.

'The final verdict is that his death was accidental,' Quinn said.

Zoey's head swiveled in our direction but then she turned to Benny. 'Your medications, Mr Ortiz.' She picked up a large plastic cup of water with a straw poking out of it that was sitting on his bedside table and handed Benny the water and the pill cup. 'Are you talking about Paul Merchant?' she asked Quinn, her voice casual but curious.

Small towns.

'We are,' he said.

'Did you know him?' I asked.

She nodded. 'Actually, I know Lily really well. I was her riding instructor for many years at Foxfire Farm. So I also met her mom and dad. I was so sorry to hear about Paul's death. It's awful . . . the medical examiner said it was an accidental drug overdose?'

'That's right,' I said. 'And drowning.'

She frowned as if she was considering something. 'You know, it can be hard to determine whether a patient was confused about how much medication they've taken. Especially when it's

something as potent as Ativan. "Did I take that last dose or
didn't I?" Then you think – or worry – you didn't, so you take
it again. If you're not using a pill box with days of the week
and a.m. or p.m. printed on it, you can forget so easily. Or if
you didn't set an alarm on your phone.'

'How did you know about the drug overdose?' I asked. 'The
drug was called lorazepam, by the way.'

She nodded, but she looked rattled. 'Ativan's the generic
name for lorazepam. And I know about all of it because I talked
to Lily. She's taking her dad's death really hard.'

Of course she would have talked to Lily. I hadn't seen either
her or Yale since Paul's death – I'd been so focused on Frankie's
state of mind, I'd almost forgotten how devastating this would
be for their children.

'I'm going to try to go to either the wake or the funeral if I
can get off work,' she added.

'The wake is Monday night at Hunt's,' I said. 'The funeral
is Tuesday morning at eleven at St Michael the Archangel.'

'I'm working days until seven so I should be able to stop by
Monday night,' she said. 'Not sure about the funeral unless I
can get someone to switch days with me.' She turned to Benny.
'Do you need anything else? Your lunch should be here in a
few minutes, and we need to get your discharge papers in order,
so if you're OK . . .?'

'I'm fine.' He patted her hand. 'I hope the nurses at the other
hospital are as nice as you are.'

She smiled. 'Don't you worry. I know a lot of the nurses
who work there. You'll love them, too.'

After she left, I said to Benny and Nelia, 'What do you need?
What can we do?'

Nelia shook her head. 'I think we're OK now that the shock
has worn off. Though I wasn't expecting the recovery to take
so long – four months, the surgeon said. *If* this one behaves
and does all the physical therapy he's supposed to do.' She
threw a sidelong glance at Benny. 'Right, mi amor?'

Benny returned her look with a martyred expression. 'Right.'

'Once harvest is over – and it nearly is – things will quiet
down for the winter,' Quinn said. 'If you had to pick a time for
this to happen, you picked a good one.'

'We'll come visit you at the rehab hospital,' I told him. 'As soon as you're settled.'

'Bring cerveza,' he said. 'There's no alcohol in this place, no beer. Probably won't be any at the next hospital, either.'

Nelia shook her head, a mock-exasperated look on her face. 'See what I mean?' she said. 'He's impossible.'

We made our way back to the parking lot and I thought about Zoey's engagement ring. Quinn's wedding ring. What they meant and symbolized. I hadn't told Quinn much about my grandfather when I gave him the bague chevalière last night, the French name my mother used for a ring with the Montgomery heraldic crest on it. I wanted Quinn to wear the ring lightly, unencumbered by anything that had happened in the past. As for Zoey, Nash had filled his fiancée's head full of family mythology and legend about what an incredible human being Eleanor had been, binding her memory so deeply to the ring as if Zoey had a legacy to live up to.

I wondered if that made it feel heavier than it really was when Nash slipped it on her finger. As if the weight of everything that had come before was now part of the ring's provenance. If it had been mine, I think my hand would have felt as if the gravity of Jupiter was dragging it down.

Dominique said Zoey had pined for Nash for years and that Dallas had pushed their match to bind the two families together as more than just business partners. Zoey and Dallas Ainsworth had gotten what they wanted. Even though the Blake family might have some connection to the deaths of Paul Merchant and Violet Rossi – however gossamer or insubstantial it might be. So the Ainsworths would be tied in to whatever it was, especially once Zoey married Nash. Plus, there was the matter of what had happened to Eleanor in the Hollywood Theatre fire.

There had to be a connection between Eleanor, the fire, and Paul and Violet. No matter what Bobby said.

Unfortunately, I still had absolutely no clue what it was.

Kit called on the trip home. Quinn was driving, so I took the call, which came through the Jeep's speakers. I told her where we were and that Quinn was listening as well.

'I'm sorry, Lucie. I've got nothing new for you,' she said. 'Nothing to add to what you already told me. Eleanor's death was ruled a tragic accident – she died in the fire, which was caused by faulty electrical wiring. The fact that the whole building was made of wood, so it was a tinderbox, was the reason the fire spread so fast even though the fire department got there fairly quickly.'

To be honest, I hadn't expected Kit would come up with anything new in the *Tribune*'s archives, but it still didn't mean I wasn't disappointed. 'What about the Sheriff's Office investigation?'

'By the book.'

'Redmond pushed them to move it along, to bring it to a speedy conclusion,' I said, leaving the question unasked.

'Well, OK. Apparently he did some nudging – the whole town was torn up, heartbroken by what had happened. Eleanor was enormously popular – thanks to her philanthropy and the causes she supported, she was beloved – so it wasn't just the family that was grieving. Don't forget, she was only in her twenties, so her life was cut way too short. And, wow, so beautiful, she was drop-dead gorgeous. No wonder Wyatt and Nash and Hunter are so good-looking – they must take after her. But there didn't appear to be a cover-up about the cause of death, if that's what you're suggesting.'

'I just wondered.'

'The answer is no.' She was really shutting me down.

'OK, thanks. I appreciate you doing this with everything you've got on your plate at the moment.'

Quinn glanced over at me and shrugged his shoulders as if to say: 'You can't get blood from a turnip.'

'There is some other stuff, though,' she said as her voice brightened.

'You're just telling me now? What is it?'

'It's about Redmond's death.'

'The skiing accident?'

'Yeah. The skiing accident. He was on vacation in Colorado with Wyatt and Nash,' she said. 'Apparently he was an experienced skier but somehow he lost control of his skis and crashed into a pine tree head on. He had massive internal injuries along

with a serious head wound from hitting the tree. By the time
the paramedics showed up – they were skiing off-piste so it
took a while to get to him – he'd lost so much blood that he
died not long afterwards in the hospital.'

'How awful. I didn't know that,' I said. 'I don't remember
reading about it, either.'

'That's because you were living in France when it happened,'
she said.

'Oh. Is that . . . everything?'

'No, of course that's not everything.'

'*Well?*'

'Well, there were a bunch of articles, most of them in the
business section,' she said. 'The big news was that Redmond
died intestate.'

'Wow. A guy like him didn't have a will?'

'Happens more often than you think. Blake Construction had
no articles of incorporation, no documents establishing it as an
LLC that anybody could find – nothing. Nada. Redmond had
never gotten around to doing anything about setting up the
company properly, any more than he'd gotten around to having
a will drafted. Which, when you think of the size of the estate
he left, is a pretty dumb thing to overlook.'

She paused and I could hear her sucking something liquid
through a straw.

'There's more?' I asked.

'There is. Eleanor had a brother who weighed in and said
that some of her money had been used to start Blake Construction
so he – the brother, James Walsh – was entitled to a share of
what had become a very profitable business. The Blakes – Wyatt
and Nash – said "no way, buddy" because when an individual
dies without a will, everything goes to the next of kin. So that
was Wyatt,' she said. 'It got ugly, but you know how it turned
out. The Blakes won. Eleanor's family got nothing.'

She hung up and for the rest of the drive home I wondered
about Eleanor Blake and her family. Father Joe O'Malley had
said that he remembered Eleanor's grandniece who came to the
funeral and sat stone-faced and angry through the entire Mass.
Then James Walsh, Eleanor's brother, had tried to claim that
he was a partial heir to the estate of Redmond Blake because

Redmond's late wife – his sister – had provided the funds to set up Blake Construction. Then they got shut out again.

Father Joe couldn't remember the name of the grandniece, but I'd bet money it was Walsh, unless she'd married. Maybe it was worthwhile trying to track someone down – possibly the grandniece, who was very likely the daughter of James Walsh.

The Walshes had clearly dropped out of the picture after Redmond's funeral and the mess with the settlement of the estate. So they wouldn't know anything about whether there was any connection between the Blake family and the deaths of Paul Merchant and Violet Rossi.

But they most definitely might know something about Eleanor's death that hadn't made it into the newspaper, something the Blakes might have managed to keep tamped down.

Maybe the key to the present was in the past.

And someone in the Walsh family – if I could locate anyone – could tell me what it was.

FOURTEEN

Quinn wanted to go over to the barrel room as soon as we got home from the hospital.

'I'll be along in a little while,' I said. 'There's something I want to do first.'

'What's that?'

'Have a talk with my mother.'

He gave me a knowing look, wrapping an arm around my shoulder and bending down to plant a kiss in my hair. 'Give her my love.'

'I will. I wish you'd known her.'

'So do I,' he said, glancing at his phone. 'Looks like we might get more rain this afternoon according to the weather app.'

'Good thing everything's all picked. I'll take the ATV and then meet you in the barrel room when I'm done. You take the Jeep.'

'Don't stay too long,' he said. 'You don't want to get caught outside if that storm blows up all of a sudden. They're talking about tornadoes with this one.'

'I won't,' I said. 'Don't worry. I can take care of myself.'

A low red brick wall with a wrought-iron gate surrounds my family's cemetery, which is shaped like a slightly bent rectangle. It is nearly filled with graves but there are still empty places and then I suppose we'll think about expanding. A mulberry tree stands near the entrance and a grove of pines and deciduous trees shades many of the graves on the far side, across from the gate, so they don't bake in the hot summer sun. But the trees and the pines also shed leaves, pinecones, and needles, which means someone has to come by now and again to tidy up.

When my mother was alive, she was the one who used to visit regularly to sweep away the dead leaves and debris as well as leaving vases filled with flowers from her garden or American flags on the patriotic holidays. After she died, I took over that responsibility – in part because if I didn't, no one else would have done it and the place soon would have gone to seed, which would have been disrespectful. On a few occasions I could guilt-trip – er, cajole – Eli or Mia into joining me, but mostly I went alone. It also gave me time to sit quietly with my mother, who I missed every day of my life. Thelma had her Ouija board with which she swore she was able to commune with those on the Other Side, but I felt my mother's presence most acutely when I sat next to her headstone and looked out at the chiaroscuro patterns of sun and shade made by the drifting clouds on the slopes of the Blue Ridge.

I parked the ATV next to the gate, which groaned in protest when I opened it. It had been a while since I'd been here, the demands of harvest overtaking absolutely everything else for a few intense weeks. The small flags I'd placed at the headstones of my ancestors who had served in our country's wars were where I'd left them a month ago for Labor Day. I collected them all and put them on a shelf in a small shed we'd built on the other side of the stand of trees where I also kept vases, a leaf rake, and a few gardening tools.

I paid my respects to my ancestors as I always did, including a brief stop at Leland's grave, which was next to my mother's. I have Thelma-like moments, which I don't really admit to anyone, when I wonder if my relatives commune with each other when no one is around to hear them. Do they chatter, argue, laugh, tease, and gossip with the energy and passion I remember from our family meals around the dining room table every Sunday when my mother invited cousins, aunts, uncles, and grandparents to join us for a big, boisterous, and, occasionally, raucous meal?

I sat down at my mother's grave. Her epitaph was our adaptation of an Eskimo proverb: 'Perhaps they are not stars in the sky, but openings in heaven where her love shines down upon us to let us know she is happy.' She had died years ago on a beautiful Indian summer afternoon in September when she was out riding on the farm with Mia; her horse unexpectedly stumbling and throwing her while jumping over one of the many low stacked-stone walls that crisscrossed our land. Something had spooked Orion, her horse, and Mia had been practically incoherent with shock and grief, unable to explain exactly what had happened. Though Mia never said anything, I had always wondered if my wild-child rebellious sister and my mother had been arguing that day and my mother had been distracted as Orion took that jump.

Her funeral had packed the beautiful two-hundred-year-old Episcopalian church in Upperville. The Goose Creek Hunt, of which she'd been a member, had paid tribute to her skill as a superb horsewoman.

Eleanor Blake had also been a member of that hunt. I knew my mother wouldn't have known Eleanor except by reputation since Eleanor died years – decades – before my mother moved to Virginia, but she had known Redmond, as well as Wyatt and Nash.

'What I can't figure out,' I said to her headstone, 'is why Violet and Paul had that newspaper article about the Hollywood Theatre fire and the photo of Eleanor in with their drawings and papers of the unpaved roads in Loudoun County. What do Eleanor and an eighty-year-old fire have to do with what's happening now?'

Because there had to be something.

My father had been shot – murdered – by someone who had tried to cover up a decades-old hit and run accident that he'd gotten away with. If Redmond had been responsible for Eleanor's death in that fire, had it also been to cover up something else?

Something he did?

Something *she* did?

Did Eleanor know something about her husband – a crime he committed, a *murder* he'd gotten away with, something illegal that could send him to jail for years – and he wanted to silence her? Except a wife can't testify against her husband in court. And why would Eleanor have wanted to turn Redmond in – unless he'd done something that somehow directly injured or harmed her?

Think about Eleanor. She has the answer. I could almost hear my mother telling me. *It's her, not him.*

So, what could Eleanor have done to Redmond that angered – even outraged – him enough to set up her 'accidental' tragic death? Was his very beautiful, wealthy, young wife preparing to leave him and he wouldn't have it? Was there someone else – a lover – involved? Jealousy was an incredibly powerful motive.

I leaned against my mother's headstone and closed my eyes. Saw Thelma's book of remembrances and the pages of photos of Eleanor. Eleanor and Redmond, looking unhappy and bored, just like Diana and Charles had been before the divorce. Eleanor and that searing look of longing between her and Lorenzo Rossi, who must have been Chiara's great-uncle. He was also her grandfather Marco's brother and, if I remembered correctly, had left Atoka and moved back to Italy to take care of the family's estate there. Then there was the photograph of Eleanor, looking particularly glamorous with a man's arm draped possessively around her shoulder – the face of whoever it was cut out of the photo.

Had she been having an affair and Redmond found out?

A sudden furious gust of wind whipped up the few dead leaves I hadn't swept up and whirled them around the cemetery like a mini tornado. I opened my eyes and turned to look behind me at the Blue Ridge, which was almost completely obscured by a black wall of clouds. A clap of thunder that could have awakened everyone in the cemetery and a lightning bolt that forked from the sky to the ground jerked me upright and to attention.

How long had I been here? Had I fallen asleep?

The wind rattled the trees again so that the undersides of the leaves were visible. My mother always said as soon as that happened – the wind flipping around the leaves so you saw the undersides – regardless of what the weather forecasters said, meant it was going to rain. *Soon.*

More bone-rattling thunder, followed by pitchfork lightning. This time not that far apart. The storm was moving closer.

And I could not run.

Even if I could, there was no way I could get to a safe place without becoming an instant magnet for the next bolt of lightning.

I made myself as flat as I could against my mother's grave, closed my eyes and prayed as the rain pelted me like a well-deserved punishment for being such an idiot and not paying attention to the weather as Quinn had warned me to do.

I heard him holler my name above the roar of the storm and a moment later he was by my side, scooping me up in his arms and grabbing my cane.

'Come on,' he said, his mouth rough against my ear. 'Let's get out of here. They weren't kidding about tornadoes. I saw a funnel cloud in the distance when I was driving over here. You didn't answer your phone, by the way. I've been calling.'

He lifted me up as if I weighed nothing at all. We were both soaked to the skin, hair plastered to our heads, clothes pasted to our bodies as if they'd been painted on.

'My phone. I turned it on silent mode while we were in the hospital. I don't think I ever turned it back on. I didn't even feel it vibrate.'

'The Jeep is next to the gate. We're going to run for it.'

Meaning he was going to run for it. I clung to him, my arms wrapped around his neck, as he sprinted across the graveyard, sloshing through the puddles in the low spots, the rain blowing sideways and coming down almost horizontally in sheets that lashed at us. The world seemed to close down to a wet, gray blur. I couldn't even see the Jeep.

Quinn was yanking open the passenger door when I felt my hair standing on end. The storm was on top of us.

'Quinn!'

'I know. *Get in.*' He shoved me into the car as another clap of thunder rattled the ground under us. A few seconds later the bolt of lightning that followed lit up the cemetery as if it were electrified. Quinn raced around to the driver's side, yanked open the door, climbed in and put the Jeep in gear. We pulled away just as one of the tall pine trees on the far side of the cemetery split in half and toppled onto the wall, the branches obscuring the headstones of Hamish and my ancestor Thomas Montgomery who had fought in the Civil War with Mosby.

I was still breathless and, by now, my teeth were chattering. 'I . . . I think . . . that tree took out . . . a couple of headstones . . . I think it was Hamish and Thomas.'

'They can be fixed.' Quinn had turned the heater on so it was blasting out hot air. 'You, on the other hand, would have been fried like an extra-crispy onion ring if it had hit you.'

'I know. I know. Thank you.'

He glanced sideways at me. He looked and smelled like a wet dog. I couldn't have been much better, smears of mud on my hands, arms, and clothes – probably my face, too – after lying on my mother's grave as the rain turned the red clay Virginia soil between the rows of headstones into streams of ochre sludge.

'What were you *doing* out there, for the love of God? That storm blew up out of nowhere . . . you were completely out in the open.'

'I think I fell asleep.'

'*Lucie*. Jesus.' He pulled up next to the crush pad. The barrel room was probably the safest place to be in the vineyard, though already the storm seemed to be moving away from us. The thunder was more distant and the rain was no longer coming down like a waterfall from the sky.

'You don't need to tell me.'

When we walked into the barrel room a moment later, the entire vineyard crew and tasting room staff were there, hunkered down and waiting out the storm. Before anybody could say anything – their shocked, horrified expressions told me I was in for more what-the-hell and were-you-out-of-your-mind comments – I held up my hand as the lights flickered briefly.

'One, I got caught in the storm. Two, I don't want to talk about it except to thank my sweet husband for coming to my rescue. Three, I think we should open a couple of bottles of wine and have a drink until this storm passes.'

'Four, the four-seater ATV,' Quinn said in a dry voice, 'is probably up to its running board in water over by the cemetery. And five, a lightning strike hit one of the pine trees by the shed and split it in half. It came down on a couple of headstones, though we didn't stick around to check out the damage.'

Nikki and Antonio were already getting out bottles of wine and corkscrews. Valeria and Orlando got glasses.

When everyone had a glass of wine, Quinn raised his and said, 'Thank God everyone is safe. And we got lucky this time.

No tornadoes tearing up the vineyard or destroying any of the buildings. To good luck.'

The lights flickered again and suddenly the room went quiet as all the machinery stopped working and the lights went out. I held my breath and waited, praying the generator would kick in as it was supposed to do.

It did. Lights back on. Machinery whirring again. I could see Quinn and everyone else visibly relax, just as I did. There probably wouldn't be any power at the house or in the tasting room, but at least the electricity that kept the wine in the stainless-steel tanks chilling and the climate-controlled equipment that kept the barrel room a brisk, constant sixty degrees was on again and we weren't going to lose anything.

Quinn met my eyes across the room. One bullet dodged.

But out there in the cemetery I had started to feel as if maybe a few pieces of the puzzle were coming together. What had happened to Eleanor Blake eighty years ago – her death in that fire – *did* have something to do with events of the past few weeks: the deaths of Paul Merchant and Violet Rossi.

Now I just needed to figure out how to connect the dots. And, while I was at it, make sure I didn't become death number three that Thelma had warned about.

Because if I *was* right, someone out there would do whatever it took to shut me up. They wouldn't think twice about killing me.

FIFTEEN

The power didn't come back on at the house until two thirty in the morning, and when it did – with a great whoosh – lights flashed on, the alarm system beeped, the air conditioning kicked in, and we both woke up.

'There are lights on downstairs,' I said, sitting up. 'I should turn them off.'

Quinn pulled me back down with him. 'We'll get 'em in the morning. Come back to sleep. It's been a long day.'

I moved into his arms. 'I know it has. You rescued me. You saved my life.'

'I'll always save you.' His words were mumbled and drowsy with sleep. 'You know that.'

'I do. I love you so much.'

'I love you, too.'

I laid my head on his chest and felt his heartbeat, strong and steady. 'When I was out there at the cemetery, I was thinking about Redmond Blake. Wondering what would make him angry enough to want Eleanor dead – if that's what happened.'

'Sweetheart. It's the middle of the night. Let's go back to sleep. We can talk about this tomorrow . . . or later today, since it *is* today.'

'Wait – hear me out, please? I've really been thinking about this. What if Eleanor had an affair? What if Redmond found out?'

'What made you think of that?' He sounded wide awake and alert now.

'My father. Who is buried next to my mother.'

He gently lifted me off his chest and laid me back on my pillow. Then he propped himself up on an elbow and looked down at me. 'He did have an affair. You have a half-brother because of it. Your mother didn't kill your father.'

'I *know* that. I don't know if she knew about the affair – none of us know. And even if she did, my mother stayed with Leland.

But not everyone would. Affairs can destroy marriages. You didn't know Redmond Blake, my love. He was a proud man with a big ego. He may have been a philanthropist who did a lot of good, but he was also arrogant. Haughty.'

'Huh. Sounds like Nash.'

'I know. Although the ego and arrogance must have skipped a generation. Wyatt is a nice man. So is Hunter.'

'Okay. Look, you're not going to solve the mystery of what happened to Eleanor Blake tonight.' He laid down again. 'Let's try to go back to sleep, OK?'

I moved on top of him and kissed him. 'All right, we'll talk in the morning,' I said in his ear. 'Right now, I have something else in mind. I'm still wide awake.'

He lifted his head and watched as I slid down his long torso. 'And what is that?'

After a moment I said, 'You're just going to have to find out.'

He groaned and said, 'Do that again.'

So I did.

We overslept after the night's lovemaking session. I woke first. Quinn found me in the shower and stepped in behind me.

'That was nice,' he said, kissing the back of my neck.

I turned around and slipped into his arms. 'It was.'

'You were pretty wound up before we got distracted,' he said. 'Something about Redmond Blake being upset because maybe Eleanor had an affair. Where'd you get that idea?'

'When I was at the cemetery, I kept trying to figure out a motive for Redmond wanting to kill his wife . . . or else arranging to have her killed without anything boomeranging back on him. If that's what happened, he succeeded. The fire was caused by faulty wiring and Eleanor was trapped inside an empty building and a locked room so she died in the fire.'

'You really think she had an affair and Redmond got so angry he decided to kill her? Why didn't he go after her lover? How did he *know* she had an affair?'

'I don't know the answer to either of those questions.' We finished our shower and he turned off the water. I stepped out and handed him a towel.

He started to dry himself off. 'So how are you going to find out after all this time? Everyone involved is dead.'

'True. But Eleanor's son isn't. And her grandson isn't.'

'Wyatt and Nash. You think they know something? And if they did, would they tell you? You're talking about murder. No one is going to admit to that – especially a murder involving two family members.'

'I know,' I said. 'But I'm thinking another visit to the General Store might be helpful.'

I got lucky again. When I got there two hours later, the parking lot was empty. Inside the store was deserted. I had waited until after the morning rush hour when the coffee klatch group – otherwise known as the Romeos – would have left to move on to their first watering hole of the day, and I appeared to have timed it just right. My bigger concern was not arousing Thelma's suspicion if I asked to see her book of remembrances one more time so I could look at the photographs of Eleanor Blake. It would take Thelma all of one nanosecond, if that long, to start putting the puzzle pieces together before she'd ask me – quite justifiably since, after all, it was her book – what I was looking for. If I told her, I might as well take out an ad in *The Washington Tribune*. The whole world would know by the end of the morning, if not sooner. And Paul's killer – if, in fact, he *had* been murdered – would figure out pretty fast that I'd seen the photo of Eleanor and the newspaper article about the Hollywood Theatre fire that, more than likely, Violet Rossi had given to Paul. So, once word went around that I was asking about Eleanor Blake, it wouldn't take long to put two and two together.

When Thelma emerged from the back room and our eyes met, it was clear I had fretted about what she might discern for nothing. She already knew why I was here. The other day I had conned her into thinking I wanted to see her book of remembrances to read what had been written about my parents. She wasn't falling for that story a second time.

Today she was a beam of sunshine in buttercup yellow. 'Lucille. How nice to see you again. What can I do for you, child?' Her smile was as sunny as her outfit, but her attitude was no-nonsense.

'I was wondering if I could see your book of remembrances again.'

She eyed me up and down through heavily mascaraed eyelashes. 'You want to look at the photos of Eleanor Blake.'

A statement, not a question. Yep, game over.

I gave her a meek smile. 'Yes, ma'am. Please.'

She disappeared into the back room, her stiletto heels clacking on the old wooden floor, the sound drilling into my head like fingernails on a blackboard. Maybe this was a mistake. Maybe I shouldn't have come. When she returned, she set the heavy book on the counter next to the cash register. I wondered how many deaths were recorded in it. Thelma probably knew the precise number. She had counted them all.

'What are you looking for?' she asked. 'I mean, besides the photos of Eleanor. What do you think you'll find? Because I've been over them more times than you can shake a stick at, and I haven't found a blessed thing. Nothing.'

So *she* was looking for something, too? What did she know? With my straightest poker face I said, 'What do you mean?'

'Lucille.' Hands on her hips, eyes fixed on mine. 'Do you really think I'm so presumable that you can pull the rug out from under the carpet with me?'

'I . . . no. Absolutely not. You're not . . . presumable.'

'Then what are you looking for?' Each word like a sharp, staccato drumbeat.

'I was wondering whether you believe the fire was an accident . . . or not?'

Thelma opened the book and, like a well-worn entry visited many times, it practically fell open to Eleanor's obituary and the pages of photos and articles. She tapped a long, manicured nail covered in blood-red nail polish on the photo of Eleanor and Redmond looking deeply unhappy. 'My mother never believed it was an accident.' She looked up and her eyes met mine. 'So I didn't, either. Why are you interested in this all of a sudden? That fire took place eighty years ago. What happened? What do you know?'

If I told her . . .

'I don't really *know* anything.'

'But you suspect plenty.' Arms folded across her thin chest

and a grim, steely-eyed expression that could have pinned me to the wall.

Thelma was the only person alive – except maybe Wyatt and Nash – who had any knowledge of what might have happened the day of the fire. Her knowledge was second-hand, from her mother, but still, that was a pretty good source. Her mother had been friends with Eleanor. She had *known* Eleanor.

'Have you been talking to Chiara?' Thelma asked.

The question came out of nowhere. 'Yes.'

'Then you probably know she's convinced her mother's death was no accident.'

'Yes.'

'And she thinks it has something to do with Violet's campaign not to pave the roads in Loudoun County.'

This time I nodded.

Thelma placed her elbows on the counter, folded her hands, and rested her chin on them. Regarded me with that now-familiar sharp-eyed look. 'How is Eleanor's death related to Violet Rossi's death, Lucille? What is the connection?'

'I really don't know, Thelma. Honest. That's why I came here, to see if the photographs of Eleanor would spark something I was missing. Overlooking. If there is a connection. What do *you* think?'

Her eyes became distant, as if she were watching re-runs of an old movie that had played over and over in her head. Something she had kept inside for a long time, perhaps afraid that if she let it out, it would strike like a dangerous, lethal snake.

'I think,' she said slowly, 'whatever is going on has something to do with the feud between the Blake and Rossi families.'

I pounced on her answer. 'Do you know how that feud started? *When* it started?' Did she know about Chiara and Hunter, their Romeo and Juliet love story? If she did, she was being uncharacteristically close-mouthed.

'According to my mother, there was some dispute over land, something between Lorenzo Rossi and Redmond Blake,' she said. 'Also, Redmond didn't like the fact that Eleanor and Lorenzo seemed to hit it off real well. So, it kind of went from there, a little spat that just snowballed. After a while I don't think anyone remembered how it started, but the grievances between those two families just grew and grew.'

'Lorenzo Rossi? Marco's uncle? The one who left for Italy?'

'That's right.'

'Do you know why he left?'

'He didn't leave. He was *told* to go. His older brother Gianni sent him back to manage the family farm after their father died – they owned a lot of land, so it was a big estate. Though my mother thought the real reason was to keep Lorenzo away from Eleanor. Gianni didn't have much time for her, thought she was nothing but trouble.'

'So there *was* something between Eleanor and Lorenzo?'

Thelma flapped a hand as if she were shooing away a pesky fly. 'According to my mother, there was something between Eleanor and half the men in Loudoun County. She was a real beauty, Lucille. Rich, young, glamorous. And with a mind of her own. Plus, she had all those friends in Hollywood, folks who came out to Middleburg when their movies were playing at her theater.'

'Why did she marry Redmond?'

'Back in the day, Redmond was a handsome devil, all charm and good looks and considered a right good catch. Sex on a stick, was what my mother called him back then. Eleanor fell for him, hook, line, and sinker. He swept her off her feet, brought her to Middleburg and brought her to Connemara, let her fix it up however she wanted since it was a dusty old relic. She was over the moon about him, the house, her new life on the east coast where she could ride and hunt as she pleased, met so many new people – at least she was happy for a while. Course, she came from money herself, a California girl. That's where she met all her movie star friends. Apparently, she did some acting herself, but she wasn't going to be another Grace Kelly or Lauren Bacall, so she gave it up to marry Redmond. Kind of like Grace Kelly marrying that prince from Morocco, come to think of it. What was his name – Rudolph?'

'Monaco. Rainier.'

'Well, whatever. Then when Redmond started his business building houses and buying land, the marriage started to go downhill. He was working flat out to get things off the ground

– all go, that one. Eleanor found out he didn't have as much money as he'd pretended he had – she learned Connemara was mortgaged to the hilt, so she paid off the loan and then she was supporting Redmond, propping up his business. Not long after that they began going their separate ways. It happened soon after Wyatt was born.'

I looked down at the unhappy photo of Eleanor and Redmond, neither one bothering to put on a good face for the camera.

'I wonder when this photo was taken,' I said.

'Looks like a hunt ball to me,' Thelma said. 'As for when, I don't know.'

I flipped the page and found the provocative half-photo of Eleanor with someone's arm – a man – protectively around her shoulders. She looked happy. Radiant. *In love.*

'Do you have any idea who the man in this photo might be?' I asked.

She peered through her thick glasses. 'No, but he's married, whoever he is. Got a wedding ring on his finger.'

I looked closer. Thelma was mistaken – the ring was actually on the third finger of his right hand, not his left hand. The picture was backward, flipped around. It had to be, because Eleanor's wedding ring and her engagement ring wouldn't be on her right hand as they were in the photo.

And the ring he was wearing wasn't a wedding ring. In fact, it looked a lot like the one I'd seen on Zoey Ainsworth's finger yesterday. It looked like a Claddagh ring.

Zoey said her ring had belonged to Eleanor.

So, who was this guy with his arm draped around Eleanor, and was it a coincidence that he was wearing a Claddagh ring, too?

'Is there an entry in your book for Lorenzo Rossi?' I asked. 'Even though he didn't live here any more?'

'Of course there is. There was something in the Middleburg paper, since he'd lived here for so long.' She began turning pages. 'Here it is.'

A short obituary with a black and white photograph, now with a leonine mane of silver-white hair, tanned and rugged and handsome. He'd put on weight since the fox hunting photo I'd seen of him and Eleanor, but it suited him. He'd married an Italian woman. Had kids. Grandkids. His arms were folded across his chest and he stared into the camera, a confident, cocky glint in his eye. And on the pinky finger of his right hand was a Claddagh ring that looked an awful lot like the one I'd seen in the picture of Eleanor with her mystery man.

Who I now suspected was almost certainly Lorenzo Rossi.

SIXTEEN

Thelma tilted her head, a frown creasing her forehead. 'What is it? You do know something, Lucille, don't you?'

I didn't want to tell her about the two Claddagh rings, since I wasn't certain I was right. Eleanor owned one. Lorenzo owned one. Maybe it was a coincidence. Except Bobby always said he didn't believe in coincidences, not in his line of work. So maybe it wasn't.

I flipped back to the pages with Eleanor's photos and her obituary and answered Thelma's question with my own. 'Do you think the man who had his arm around Eleanor in this photo could have been Lorenzo Rossi?'

Thelma adjusted her trifocals and squinted at the photo. 'Maybe. But, as my mother said, Eleanor flirted with everyone. It's hard to tell who belongs to an arm.'

She clearly hadn't noticed the ring on the man's hand, but then her vision wasn't the greatest. She'd been putting off cataract surgery, claiming she could see 'fine, just fine, thank you,' and no doctor was going to use a scalpel anywhere near her eyes, no matter if the result was guaranteed to improve her vision.

And even if she had noticed the ring, she probably didn't know Eleanor owned an identical one that Zoey Ainsworth now wore, the engagement ring Nash Blake had given her. So it wouldn't have registered that it could be significant.

'Why do you think Violet's death might have something to do with the feud between the Blakes and the Rossi family?' I asked.

'Same reason as the way it started. Land and money,' she said with dead-bang certainty that she was right. 'The person who knows about that is your sister-in-law's brother. Grayson Vaughn. If you want answers, Lucille, go ask him. Grayson Vaughn is the key to finding out what really happened to Violet, and, if you want my opinion, he's hiding something. He's gotten real chummy with Nash Blake all of a sudden. It's not rocket surgery to figure out why.'

Dominique said Grayson got pally with Nash because if he sold his land to Nash, some of Loudoun's dirt roads would finally get paved. That it was *personal* for Grayson, who had lost the two women he loved because their deaths were directly related to the roads being unpaved. Thelma was implying something else. Not altruism motived by grief, but land and money motivated by greed.

'The Sheriff's Office investigators checked over Violet's car thoroughly for any signs of tampering. They didn't find anything,' I said.

'Maybe they didn't look hard enough.'

She'd thrown down that statement like a gauntlet. 'Is that what you think?' I asked.

'I think there's something fishy about Violet's death, that's what I think.'

'If you're right, then who was responsible? One of the Blakes? Do you honestly think it was one of them?'

Chiara had been adamant that no one in the Blake family had been involved. But that was before I found out she was in love with Hunter Blake, which would definitely color her judgment.

Thelma shrugged and closed the thick book. 'Who stood to gain by Violet's death, Lucille?'

I didn't even have to think. 'Nash Blake.'

'There's your answer.'

Even though it seemed plausible, it didn't make sense. Like I'd said, the investigators didn't find evidence that anyone had tampered with Violet's car. So how could Nash have done it? Plus, as arrogant and haughty as he could be, Nash Blake just didn't seem like he was capable of murder. With his wealth and influence he could *buy* his way out of any situation.

'The Sheriff's Office ruled her death was an accident. Driver error,' I repeated, though I didn't add that I'd asked Bobby to take another look at the final report written by one of his colleagues. 'They consider it case closed.'

'You wouldn't be here if you thought it was case closed.' She gave me a knowing look. 'Would you?'

'I . . . no. I guess I wouldn't.'

'Course you wouldn't. Look, I've tried to talk to Violet – you know how I can talk to those who've gone over to the Other Side on my Ouija board, don't you?' she asked as I nodded. 'And do you know what?'

I didn't want to know what. When Thelma started talking about how she could commune with the dead on her Ouija board, the hair on the back of my neck always stood up.

'What?' I asked.

'I *can't* talk to her.'

Of course I was going to ask. 'Why not?'

'Because she's not *there* yet, that's why. She hasn't crossed over. She's still *here*.' She sounded indignant. Outraged. 'Violet is not at peace, Lucille. She won't rest until justice is done – her spirit can't rest. Her death wasn't an accident. Someone is responsible.' She shook an arthritic finger in my face. 'And I'll bet you any amount of money that Grayson Vaughn probably knows more than he let on about what really happened to her.'

On the drive home, I kept replaying Thelma's Cassandra-like pronouncements in my head until my brain hurt. Things I didn't want to believe were true, even though I knew they probably were.

My mother always believed Eleanor's death wasn't an accident.

You know who stood to gain by Violet's death: Nash Blake.

And, last but not least, a parting shot I hadn't seen coming. *Grayson Vaughn knows more than he let on about what really happened to Violet. Go talk to him.*

Grayson Vaughn. Eli's brother-in-law. Sasha's brother, with whom she was no longer on speaking terms. Now all of a sudden the ever-growing messy spiral of what really happened to Paul and Violet had caught someone from my extended family in its huge, wide swath.

I pulled into the parking lot next to the Villa, the ivy-covered brick building my mother had designed to resemble a French mas, a long, low structure of red brick and stone quarried from our land. The Villa looked as if it could have twirled down from la France profonde – the heart of France – where my mother had grown up, landing here in Virginia. For a while I sat in the Jeep and wondered what to do, whom to talk to. Grayson? Frankie? Bobby?

In the end I knew there was only one person besides Thelma who would have answers to what I wanted to know. The bigger question was whether he would talk to me.

And, if I succeeded in getting past his gatekeepers, would he tell me the truth?

Chiara had chosen two bottles of our Viognier as a thank-you gift for helping out with the harvest, in addition to what we had paid her the other day, because it was the favorite wine of her grandfather, Marco Rossi. When I walked into the Villa a few minutes later, Nikki greeted me from behind the bar, a long undulating serpentine counter and another of my mother's unusual designs. Its most striking feature was the mosaic façade of twining grapevines made from multi-colored clear glass stones. On days when the afternoon sunlight streamed in through the French doors at just the right angle, the stones glowed as though they were lit from within.

'Lucie. What can I do for you?' Nikki asked with an easy smile. 'Is everything OK?'

'Yes . . . fine. Could you pack three bottles of Viognier for me, please? And make sure one is already chilled?'

'Sure.' She disappeared into the back room, returning with a cardboard carrier box with Montgomery Estate Vineyard and our logo stamped on it.

She gave me a sideways look as she put the bottles in the box. 'Just the wine? Do you need anything else?'

'No, thanks, I'm good.'

I didn't owe her an explanation. I was her boss. I didn't have to tell her why or for whom. Except that *look*. Along with everything that had been happening around here lately, especially the gossip that was surely going around about Paul Merchant's death probably being an accidental drug overdose. Stopping short of using the word *suicide*.

'They're a gift for an elderly friend who doesn't get out much any more.' It sounded lame, or like an apology.

Nikki knows me well enough to know when I'm lying because

I'm terrible at it. She had been the one to give Chiara the bottles of Viognier for Marco the other day. 'You're sure you don't need anything else to take to your friend? Would he like a charcuterie plate? An assortment of local cheeses?'

'I think the wine will do.'

She gave me a cheeky grin. 'I know I'm being nosy, but can I ask where you're going?'

I picked up the carrier case and reached for my cane. She knew where I was going, she just wanted confirmation. 'Sure,' I said. 'I'll be at Serenità.'

'Oh?' She waited for the rest of it.

So now she knew where. She just didn't know why.

'Going fishing,' I said.

The rolling hills and lush pastures where Angus cattle grazed peacefully came into view long before I turned into the entrance to Serenità Farm off the Snickersville Turnpike. I wondered if the realization that she had suddenly become the heiress to the largest cattle breeding farm on the east coast after her mother's death six weeks ago seemed daunting, even overwhelming, to Chiara Rossi. Earlier in the year, at the spring cattle auction, Marco had announced that at ninety years old he intended to step down as president and CEO and let Violet take over running the family business. She was ready. She knew cattle breeding inside out; she had majored in agricultural management in college. She was well-prepared and she had plans to grow what the men in her family had started into a multinational business, a woman at the helm in a male-dominated world.

Then she was gone and suddenly Chiara – who was not ready and had not been groomed to run a cattle farm – had to take her mother's place. At least she would have Carlo di Stefano, Marco's consigliere and long-time family friend, who had agreed to stay on and run the day-to-day operations. Plus, Marco wanted him to have a share in the business.

I had called before I drove over to Serenità and spoke to Carlo, explaining to him – and this was true – that Quinn and I had been considering the possibility of raising cattle at Highland Farm, an addition to the vineyard that might bring in more money. Before we did anything, I wondered if it would be possible to talk to Marco about what would be involved, get his seasoned advice because, truth be told, Quinn and I knew less than nothing about cows. To my relief Carlo said I could stop by any time. He also hinted that Marco was still grieving deeply over Violet's death and anything that would distract him from his sorrow, however briefly, would be most welcome. I told him I'd be over in half an hour.

Carlo had told me to go directly to the house; Marco hadn't been showing up at the offices near the main barn these last few weeks. He would let the housekeeper know to expect me.

An elderly woman dressed in black and hunched over as if she suffered from scoliosis or osteoporosis opened the door to the old stone farmhouse with its terracotta tile roof and whimsical conical turrets that reminded me of rockets about to launch into space. She murmured a greeting in Italian and English and invited me in, eyeing the box containing the wine.

The walls of the cheerful light-filled foyer were whitewashed, hung with oil paintings and watercolors of scenes that were clearly somewhere in Italy and others that had to be of Serenità. A multi-tiered wrought-iron chandelier descended from the two-story ceiling and an enormous vase of red roses sat on a table of inlaid semi-precious stones – lapis, tiger's eye, malachite, carnelian, onyx – that reminded me of ornate palaces I'd seen in Venice, Florence, and Rome. The faintest odor of lemon-scented wood polish and the stronger mingled odors of fragrant cooking – onion, garlic, herbs, and tomatoes – scented the air.

'I'm here to see Signore Marco,' I said. 'Carlo said he is expecting me.'

The housekeeper pointed to the sweeping spiral staircase. Polished marble stairs, the treads partially covered with a worn Persian carpet in pale blues and shades of ochre and rust. A carved wooden railing, also worn with age, led up to the second floor.

'Lui è li. He is upstairs. Le aspetto. He's waiting for you in his study. Second door on the left.'

'Thank you. Grazie.'

'Prego, signora.'

The door to Marco's study was ajar. I knocked and heard his muffled voice. 'Enter, Giulia.'

I cracked the door open. 'Marco, it's Lucie Montgomery. May I come in?'

A lengthy pause before he said, 'Ah, Lucie. Yes, please do.'

I had not seen Marco Rossi since his daughter's funeral six weeks ago at St Michael the Archangel, when the bishop had come out to Middleburg to say the Mass. Today he looked diminished, a crumpled shadow of the robust, energetic man I'd known for years. A wheelchair I hadn't seen him use before was pulled up next to his recliner. I hesitated in mid-step, wondering if I should have come to see him, if there wasn't someone else I could ask to find out what I needed to know about Eleanor Blake. But there wasn't anyone and that's why I was here.

After my mother died, someone told me I would get through the grief that threatened to swallow me whole, but I would not get over it. Whoever said that had been right. Getting through it had been a hellish journey after a wrenching Year of Firsts without her. First birthday. First Mother's Day. First Christmas. First so-many-things.

Marco looked as if he might not even get *through* his grief.

I pasted a smile on my face and held up the carrier case. 'I understand you like my Viognier. I brought you a couple of bottles. One of them is already chilled.'

As if I had conjured her, Giulia stood in the doorway to the study holding a tray with wine glasses and plates, along with a small loaf of bread, a dish of olives, and a plate of salami, prosciutto, and an assortment of cheeses. A corkscrew lay on the tray next to a small silver bucket filled with ice to keep a bottle of wine chilled.

Marco nodded at Giulia, but the smile on his gaunt face was pale and his dark, hooded eyes looked haunted. 'Then we must have a glass of your Viognier, Lucie, especially if you have gone to the trouble to bring me a bottle that is already chilled. Grazie, Giulia. You can leave the tray on the coffee table.' To me he added, 'Would you mind opening the wine, cara? My arthritis . . .'

'Of course.' I cut him off, so he didn't have to explain any further, and picked up the corkscrew. When I had poured our wine and fixed two plates of food, I sat down across from him and raised my glass.

'To . . .' I stopped, then said what we always say in French when we remember the dead. 'To les absents.'

'No.' He shook his head. 'To i nostri.'

To ours.

Violet. Paul. My mother. But also, to everyone.

'I nostri,' I said and we touched glasses.

After we drank, he set down his glass, folded his hands, and tented his fingers. 'So, cattle?' he said. 'Really, Lucie? Are you and Quinn serious about this?'

He smiled as if I'd just landed in a spider web he'd spun especially for me. My face grew hot. So much for thinking I could dance past him and get away with a made-up excuse for my visit.

I started to stammer. 'Well . . . we were thinking about it.'

He flapped a hand, dismissing my little white lie. 'Why are you really here? What do you want from me? Chiara told me about Paul Merchant. I'm so sorry, cara mia. I know you and Francesca, his wife, were the ones who found him. I also know Chiara told you she doesn't believe her mother's death was an accident, nor Paul's. Neither do I. What happened to them has something to do with the work they were doing to keep the roads unpaved out here.'

At least we weren't going to have an awkward conversation about raising cattle at Highland Farm. He wanted to get right down to it.

I set my glass next to his. 'I want to know about Eleanor Blake. And Lorenzo Rossi.'

He drew his head back as if he were avoiding a blow he hadn't seen coming. 'Why do you want to know about *her*? I thought this conversation was going to be about Violet. About what happened to my daughter.'

His tone was harsh. Accusing. *Angry.*

'It is. I mean, it might be.'

'What does that mean?'

I was going to have to go slowly with him. Earn his trust after my inept fumble.

I picked up my wine glass and drank, a bit of fortification

and a small delay to get my thoughts in order. 'I think Violet found out something about Eleanor Blake and the fire that killed her eighty years ago. Whatever it was, she might have used it to blackmail Nash. It was enough of a threat that he backed off from agreeing to buy Grayson Vaughn's land so he could build three hundred and fifteen homes on it.'

Marco picked up his own wine glass. 'What does this have to do with Lorenzo?'

'Were he and Eleanor lovers?'

'From what my father said, every man she met was one of Eleanor's lovers.'

'Why did Lorenzo leave Atoka and go back to Italy?'

'You ask a lot of questions.'

'I know.' Thelma had said Lorenzo didn't go. He was *sent*.

'He left to run our farm there. My grandfather's health was failing and my grandmother couldn't manage the place on her own. My father was in charge of Serenità. It didn't make sense for him to leave when our business was just getting started, so Lorenzo went instead.'

'When was that?'

He frowned, tapping his fingers together. 'Just after the Christmas holidays. It must have been January 1938. Before the war started in Europe.'

'I heard Gianni ordered Lorenzo to leave because he didn't like – or approve of – his relationship with Eleanor.'

'And where did you hear that?'

When I didn't answer, he made a face as if he'd just taken a bite from a particularly sour lemon. 'Of course. Thelma Johnson.'

'Is it true?'

'Does it matter?'

'Do you know what Violet found out about Eleanor – what she learned that might have been information she could blackmail Nash with?'

'There was talk Redmond paid off a few people to stop the investigation into the fire and Eleanor's death.'

'I heard that as well. It doesn't make any difference one way or the other, at least not now – it's water under the bridge,' I said. 'What about Lorenzo?'

'What about him?' His demeanor had shifted and there was a placid, bovine expression on his face. He was done giving up any more information about his family. 'What you said about the fire *does* make a difference if Redmond had something to do with Eleanor's death.'

'Do you think Violet found proof that he did?'

'I don't know. Do you?'

My questions weren't getting me anywhere.

'Do you know what a Claddagh ring is?'

His eyes darted away from mine. Bingo. The answer was yes.

'Eleanor owned one. And so did Lorenzo,' I said. 'Nash just gave Eleanor's to his fiancée as her engagement ring. Do you know what happened to Lorenzo's?'

His wine glass was empty. I refilled it and he drank. 'I found it in his dresser when I was in Italy for his funeral. My aunt – his wife – didn't want it.'

'So you have it?'

'I do.'

'Did Eleanor give it to him?'

'I don't know.'

'Did you know she owned one as well?'

'Yes.'

'How did you know that?'

He closed his eyes. 'There were photographs. And letters. Love letters.'

'Do you have them?'

'Not any more.'

Damn. 'Their relationship was more than Eleanor flirting or having a fling, like she apparently did with a lot of men. Am I right?'

'She was trouble. She was a married woman. Lorenzo . . . had his whole life ahead of him. Our family – we are Catholic – didn't want or need a scandal like that, especially in those days when it was a very big deal.'

'So Gianni ordered Lorenzo to go to Italy.'

'Yes.'

'Against his will?'

'Gianni persuaded Lorenzo that his affair would ruin our

family's reputation when we were just getting started with Serenità, especially because of who Eleanor was. Even if she divorced Redmond, Lorenzo would be excommunicated if he married her since she was also Catholic. That would be a huge scandal. A disgrace.'

'Which Gianni couldn't allow to happen?'

'I don't expect you to understand, but yes.'

'I do understand, Marco. Really.' I leaned over and laid my hand over his. 'Did you know Violet had information she could use to keep Nash Blake from buying Grayson's land?'

'I knew she was working on something to try to stop Nash from putting up three hundred or so eyesore palaces on his land. She didn't tell me what it was.'

'Was Violet in love with Grayson?'

'You'll have to ask him.'

I looked him in the eye, kept my voice level. 'Right now, I'm asking you.'

He crossed one leg over the other. For a long time he didn't speak. I waited again.

'Yes,' he said finally. 'She was.'

'Was it serious? Was he in love with her?'

He nodded. 'She was happy. For the first time in a long time.'

'Do you think she confided in Grayson whatever it was she found out about Nash Blake?'

'I don't know.' He finished off his glass of wine and set it down with an air of finality that our visit was over. He was tired. He wasn't going to answer any more questions. He'd said enough.

Then he added once again, 'You'll have to ask him.'

SEVENTEEN

Grayson Vaughn.

Eli's brother-in-law. He had been in love with Violet Rossi and had agreed not to sell his land to Nash Blake because she asked him not to. After she died, he'd immediately walked straight into Nash's arms, so to speak, and agreed to sell. To do precisely what he promised Violet he would *not* do.

Was it because the roads would finally get paved if Blake Construction came in with their bulldozers and earthmovers and put up a big-ass housing development on what had been pristine farmland? Or was it something else?

Finally, would Grayson sell his land to Nash if he believed, as Marco and Chiara did, that Violet's death wasn't really an accident? And that of all the people who had the most to gain with Violet out of the picture, Nash Blake was at the top of the list?

Go ask Grayson, Marco had said as his parting shot.

But if I did that, would my curiosity and questions make their way from Grayson's lips to Nash's ear? Let Nash know that whatever Violet – and probably Paul – had discovered about Eleanor and the fire, now I was aware of it as well? Wasn't I just painting a target on my back if I did that? Something I had promised Eli and David – not to mention my husband – I would not do?

What did Violet know? How had she discovered whatever it was, some forgotten piece of Blake family history, that the present generation wanted – needed – to stay buried?

If I could find the answers to those questions, I wouldn't need to talk to Grayson.

I might know why Paul and Violet had been murdered. *If* they had been I was pretty certain the answer was yes to both.

I might even know who had done it.

* * *

Quinn had asked me to leave the investigation into Paul's death – and Violet's death as well – to Bobby Noland. But Bobby didn't think Eleanor's death and the fire had anything to do with the two present-day deaths and he had no plans to dig up ancient history. If Violet had learned that Redmond Blake had somehow been responsible for his wife's death and gotten away with making it look like an accident, that would certainly get Nash's attention. But it now seemed to me that she must have learned something else that Nash had a very strong interest in making sure didn't get known.

After seeing Marco this afternoon and looking at Thelma's remembrance book again earlier today, I started wondering if, whatever *it* was, Lorenzo Rossi was also involved.

Over a candlelit dinner in the kitchen – Persia's boeuf bourguignon, which she enjoyed making because it called for an entire bottle of Pinot Noir to be added to the simmering stew – I brought up the subject with Quinn. Who was anything but happy to find out I'd talked to Marco.

'I thought we agreed you were going to let this go,' he said.

'I was until I saw Zoey's engagement ring today and found out it had belonged to Eleanor.'

I told him about Thelma's remembrance book and the photo of a man's arm around Eleanor, his face hidden but wearing a nearly identical Claddagh ring, except without the diamond. 'I think Lorenzo was the person in that picture with Eleanor,' I said. 'Marco said he found Lorenzo's ring in his dresser when he went back to Italy for the funeral. He also said Lorenzo and Eleanor were lovers.'

'You told me Thelma said her mother claimed every man Eleanor met became one of her lovers.'

'OK, she was a flirt. But I think it was serious with Lorenzo.'

'Who hightailed it off to Italy when his brother ordered him to leave. End of story. End of affair.'

'Marco said Gianni didn't want a family scandal. That's why he sent Lorenzo away. Because of Eleanor.'

'So what would constitute a family scandal?' he asked.

'Eleanor divorcing Redmond and marrying Lorenzo?'

'In a devoutly Catholic Italian family in the nineteen forties, that would be a huge scandal, you know that. Divorced Catholics can't remarry, and if they do, they're excommunicated. Or they were back then.'

'You don't need to tell me. My mother went to Mass every day of her life. She never remarried after my father walked out on us. It would have killed her if the Church excommunicated her.' Quinn took a piece of baguette from the breadbasket and mopped up the sauce from his boeuf bourguignon with it. 'Anyway, there wasn't a family scandal involving Lorenzo and Eleanor, because nothing ever happened between them.'

'Well, then, it's something else.' My phone was across the room on the kitchen counter next to Quinn's because we had a no-phones-at-the-table rule, plus we silenced them. 'I need to check something,' I said and got up to get it.

'What?'

'Wikipedia. Font of all knowledge.'

'What are you looking for?' He picked up the bottle of Saint-Estèphe he had opened to go with the boeuf bourguignon and refilled our glasses.

'This,' I said. 'A biography of Wyatt Blake.'

'What about him?'

'Birthday August sixteenth, 1938.'

'So what?'

'Lorenzo Rossi left for Italy in January 1938. Marco remembered clearly because it was right after the Christmas and New Year holidays.'

'And that's significant because . . .?'

'Wyatt Blake was born eight months later. What if he was Lorenzo and Eleanor's son? That's why Lorenzo had to leave Atoka. *That* was the scandal. Gianni found out about it, so he made his brother leave before the news got out.'

'I wonder if Lorenzo told Gianni or somehow he put two and two together. It's also possible Lorenzo never knew about the baby and Gianni just wanted his brother to be far, far away from Eleanor,' Quinn said.

I traced circles on the kitchen table with the base of my wine glass and considered that possibility.

'You could be right that he didn't know. Otherwise, he was walking out on his pregnant girlfriend and his child, abandoning them. Plus, Eleanor could have very easily persuaded Redmond the baby was his, even if she knew – or suspected – it wasn't. Though it doesn't mean Redmond didn't find out the truth. Eventually. Somehow.'

I thought back to Eleanor's obituary notice. 'The fire at the Hollywood Theatre happened in the spring of 1941. By then Wyatt would have been two and a half. So it's possible Redmond didn't find out about the affair – and Wyatt not being his son – right away.'

'OK, but as you said, Lorenzo was gone. No one knew Wyatt wasn't Redmond's biological son except maybe Eleanor and now him. If anything, I'd think Redmond would divorce Eleanor on the grounds of adultery. Not burn her in some awful funeral pyre.'

I shivered. 'It sounds so much more awful when you say it like that. Thelma said her mother said Redmond and Eleanor had a fight the day of the fire. She said it was over a medical test. What if that test was how Redmond found out Wyatt wasn't his son?'

'So then he killed Eleanor in a fit of anger – or arranged to have her killed?'

'And continued to keep it a secret that Wyatt wasn't his biological son.' I nodded. 'Violet could have pieced together that information quite easily. Maybe she found the photos and love letters between Eleanor and Lorenzo before Marco destroyed them. Figured out what had happened – that Wyatt Blake is actually a great-uncle, sort of, and Nash would be a distant cousin.'

Quinn drank some wine. 'That would be a kick in the head. But I still don't get why Redmond didn't just divorce Eleanor. She's the scarlet woman. He's the wronged husband. Everyone's sympathy would be with him.'

'Because when she died, he stood to inherit *all* of her money. Thelma told me Eleanor discovered Redmond wasn't as rich as she originally thought he was. She ended up bankrolling his business, supporting him. Paying off the bills he had run up at Connemara, all the debts. He wouldn't get all her money if he divorced her. Which gives him a very good motivation for murder, especially the kind of money he stood to inherit.'

'True.'

'OK, maybe we're right about this, but there's something else.'

'Now what?' he asked, frowning.

'We haven't got a single way to prove any of it.'

There is a saying around here that Gettysburg had four very bad days during the Civil War, but the Commonwealth of Virginia had four very bad years. Richmond had been the capital of the Confederacy and most of the war was hard fought here in the Old Dominion. When it was all over and done with, our state lay in ruins. Middleburg and Atoka were no exception – impoverished, beat down, and struggling. By 1900, Middleburg's population had fallen to a mere four hundred residents and in Atoka you could count our numbers on the fingers of both hands and maybe one sock off and that included my family.

But in the early decades of the twentieth century, wealthy investors from other parts of the country – specifically the north, east, and midwest – discovered our region and began relocating here, scooping up antebellum mansions for a song and bringing with them a love of horses and fox hunting. As they began investing in our corner of Loudoun County, it didn't take long before we became known as an international breeding, showing, and racing center thanks to our climate, location, and its suitability for horses. Or, as we are known now, the heart of Virginia horse and hunt country.

The oldest hunt in the United States – Piedmont Fox Hounds – had already been established in 1840 in a part of Loudoun County that included Middleburg and Upperville, but in the early twentieth century, with an influx of so many people who were passionate about equestrian sports, more hunts sprang up. Among them was the Goose Creek Hunt, which my family had allowed to ride through our farm as part of their fox hunting territory for more than a century.

By way of thanks to us and the other landowning families whose farms comprised their territory, each spring the members of the hunt hosted an elegant – and opulent – black tie dinner. In addition we were invited guests at the fall and spring races that took place at Glenwood Park, a one hundred and twelve acre park with a world-class steeplechase course – including a

traditional timber and hurdle course and a fieldstone grandstand
– with breathtaking views of the lush Virginia countryside.

The Goose Creek Hunt fall point-to-point always occurred
on the first Saturday in October. Everyone knew the date
and made their plans around it. Though Quinn and I always went
to the spring races, the fall races were more complicated if we
were still in the middle of harvest and couldn't afford the time
off. But this year, since most of the grapes had already been
brought in, I had RSVPed 'yes' to Sam Constantine's tailgate
invitation the week before last. Sam, our family lawyer and
someone I'd known since he could bounce me on his knee,
hosted what everyone in the local hunting and racing world
agreed was the best and most elegant tailgate at Glenwood. Part
of the reason was its coveted location in front of the finish line
where the judging stand was located, but there was also the
excellent food and copious amounts of alcohol served, along
with the extravagant table decorations. An elaborate floral
arrangement, a silver candelabra, statues of horses, foxes, and
hounds scattered everywhere, a sly-looking papier-mâché fox
reclining in the middle of the table and dressed in formal hunting
attire – all presided over by a rainbow-striped horse that had
once graced a carnival merry-go-round and now stood guard
next to the main buffet table.

But Saturday morning when I woke up, I took one look at
my husband's face – he was already pulling on a pair of jeans
and a sweatshirt with our logo on it – and said, 'You don't want
to go to the point-to-point with me today, do you?'

Even after living here for the last five years, Quinn still hadn't
gotten used to what he called the 'horsey ways' of the fox
hunting crowd who lived and breathed horses, hounds, hunting,
and riding. I knew, also, that part of him still occasionally pined
for the romanticized Beach Boys land of endless California
sunshine where the surfing lifestyle was the dream.

His guilty look just now said everything. So much still to do
in the barrel room, racking over the Cab Sauv, sterilizing the
new oak barrels . . . the list went on.

'Do you mind?' he asked.

In a way the answer was no. Everyone showed up at Sam's
tailgate, invited or not. Eventually. Grayson Vaughn had horses

in a couple of races. Zoey Ainsworth taught horseback riding and she would almost certainly be there if she didn't have to work at the hospital. Maybe with Nash Blake. Quinn wouldn't be happy if he knew I intended to use the opportunity to see them in a relaxed, social setting – perhaps lubricated by a couple of drinks from Sam's well-stocked bar – and ask a few questions. See if anybody took the bait.

'No,' I said and then asked, as if it were an afterthought, 'You don't mind if I go – do you?'

He gave me a puzzled look and said, 'No. Not at all.'

'Well, then, I'd better shower and get ready,' I said. 'You know the unwritten rules at Sam's tailgate. Everyone's expected to dress.'

This is Glenwood Park on race day, on a perfect early-autumn afternoon as if it had been ordered up: sharp golden sunshine, a lacquered blue sky, drifts of white cotton ball clouds, a fringe of trees framing fields so intensely green you need to shade your eyes to look at them. Horse trailers, stable boys, grooms, whip-thin jockeys wearing the silks of their owners, the Goose Creek Huntsman – a British heartthrob – riding up and down the length of the split-rail fence greeting friends at each of the tailgates, resplendent in the formal pinks that were the colors of their hunt – scarlet jacket, olive green trim – and everywhere people streaming toward the racecourse. Families with children; women dressed as if they were going to a cocktail party, wearing pretty dresses and heels that were going to sink into the soft, still-damp ground, and hats they would need to clutch when the breeze riffed the brims; men in sport jackets with sharp-edged pocket squares, dress shirts, hunt-themed ties, hunt-themed belts, hunt-themed belt buckles, maybe a straw boater or a Stetson. Other men and women in riding attire as if they'd just been out for the morning hack. Dogs on leashes wherever you looked: Jack Russell terriers, American fox hounds, a couple of Great Danes. Later there would be an award for best hat (women), best tie, best tailgate – Sam would win best tailgate as he always did, because he'd gone all out to decorate.

Sam's tailgate was already in full swing when I got there shortly before the first race started at one. Piper, his fourteen-year-old granddaughter, greeted me and handed me a program as I stepped into the enclosure where a large crowd had already gathered around the food table. There would be the usual abundant fare: quiche, platters of sliced roast beef, ham, and turkey, finger sandwiches, a chafing dish keeping spicy meatballs warm, salads, deviled eggs, a crudité platter, hummus, several kinds of dip. The back of Sam's Range Rover, which served as the bar, would be well stocked with bottles of top-shelf alcohol and his regular bartender would be busy pouring wine and champagne and making cocktails for the usual scrum of people hovering nearby and waiting to give their drinks orders.

I found Sam first, since he was my host, and got swept into a fierce one-armed hug followed by a scratchy kiss on my cheek. The older he got the more I thought he looked like the highly stylized version of Colonel Sanders on the KFC logo. Snow-white Van Dyke mustache and goatee, blue eyes that twinkled like Santa Claus's behind round gold wire-rimmed glasses, the kind smile of an indulgent grandfather, all belying a razor-sharp legal mind, memory for detail, and formidable oratory skills – all of which added up to an almost perfect record for winning his cases.

'How are you, darlin'? Did you get something to eat? A glass of champagne?'

'I'm fine, thanks. Not yet. I will. How are you, Sam?'

'Doing all right,' he said. 'Considering.'

He was the Merchants' family lawyer. Actually, he was everyone's lawyer.

'Frankie said you'd been helping her with Paul's will and that she's beginning to deal with his estate matters.'

Which he wasn't at liberty to discuss with me.

He nodded. 'That's right.'

'You'll be at the funeral?'

'Oh, you bet. And the wake.'

I laid my hand on the sleeve of his tweed blazer. 'Sam,' I said, dropping my voice so no one around us could hear me. 'There's something I'd like to discuss with you. Can I come by your office to talk about it?'

'Sure. Call Jolene and set up a time. I'm a bit booked up at the moment, so if it can wait . . .'

'It's important.'

He seemed surprised by the push back. 'Are you in trouble?'

'No, nothing like that.' I lowered my voice and murmured in his ear. 'I don't think Paul Merchant's death was an accident.'

He drew his head back so he could look me directly in the eye. 'Can you prove that?' His question like the crack of a whip, but also a note of hope in it.

'No. I can't. I'm sorry. But I still think I'm right.'

He looked the way he did when a client let him down by not coming clean until they were in the courtroom standing in front of the judge. I'd seen that look. Disappointment mixed with frustration and slow-boil anger. 'Thinking you're right is not the same as *being* right. And without proof?' He shrugged. 'You got nothing, sugar. The official cause of death is accidental drug overdose and drowning. I think that's gonna stand.'

'And I think calling it an accidental death was to avoid saying it was suicide, which would be so much harder for Frankie and the children.'

'You're still basing that statement on no knowledge or proof.'

My face grew hot at the rebuke, but I wasn't going to back down. Not when I had his undivided attention. 'Did you handle the estate settlement for Redmond Blake?'

He frowned as if he were trying to figure out the free association that had shifted our conversation from Paul Merchant to Redmond Blake. 'That was quite a while ago. Even if I did, I couldn't talk about it. You know that. What makes you ask about it? Now?'

'I heard Redmond didn't have a will.'

He folded his arms across his chest. 'Did you, now? Where are you going with this, Lucie?'

Neither confirming nor denying. 'If someone dies and there is no will, what happens to the estate?' I asked.

'When someone dies intestate – without a will – everything goes to the next of kin. It's about blood.' I got the legal answer. 'That's why you should have a will. So you have complete authority over who gets what after you're gone.' He looked at me over the top of his glasses. 'Do you know how many people in this country *don't* have wills?'

Based on his tone of voice and the look on his face, I took a guess and said, 'Not many?'

'*Two-thirds*. Two out of every three people don't have wills, even though most folks believe having one is important.'

'That probably included Redmond Blake, who didn't have one,' I said. 'Which meant everything went to Wyatt, his son and only heir. Eleanor was dead and there were no other children. Is that what happened?'

His arms were still folded. He wasn't going to make this easy, give up anything. 'Blake Construction is a privately held, family-owned business. Wyatt stepped down from running things day to day some years ago and Nash took over. So he's in charge now. That's common knowledge.'

'In other words, yes.'

'Why are you asking about this all of a sudden?' He repeated his question, this time in his no-nonsense courtroom voice, but we were still speaking quietly.

I lifted my head and stuck out my chin. Hoped he would take me seriously now. 'I'm trying to figure out if Redmond's will – or lack of one – might be related to Paul Merchant's death. And Violet Rossi's.'

Sam reached for my elbow and steered me over to the hood of the Range Rover where, for the moment, no one else was nearby. 'You think Paul's death – *and* Violet's death – have something to do with Redmond's estate?'

'I do.'

He worried his lower lip for a moment and I could almost hear the gears working in his brain. 'All right, let's do this. Why don't you come by my office on Tuesday and we can talk about this some more?'

This time he didn't shoot me down. Tell me I was way off base with my theory. So maybe he thought there could be something . . .

'Paul's funeral is on Tuesday,' I said. 'How about Monday?'

'I've got to be in court on Monday. The funeral is at eleven on Tuesday. Come Tuesday afternoon around three. You're right. We shouldn't talk about this here.'

By three o'clock the funeral luncheon would be over and done with. Frankie would want some folks to come back to her house, but I could beg off so I could see Sam – especially considering the subject of our conversation – and then stop by later.

Sam nodded in the direction of the split-rail fence where his guests were seated on lawn chairs while they waited for the horses and their riders to show up for the first race. I followed his gaze. A Who's Who of everyone I was hoping to see and talk to today: Nash Blake, Zoey Ainsworth, Grayson Vaughn and, as a bonus, Zoey's father, Dallas, who sat near his daughter and his business partner completely absorbed in scrolling on an iPad, occasionally poking at the screen with a finger. Nash and Zoey, heads bent together, holding flutes of champagne – him deeply tanned and silver haired, looking like an aging matinee idol; her with that flaming red hair you couldn't miss in a crowd. Only Grayson was alone, standing at the fence and peering at the racecourse through binoculars, his head turning back and forth as though he was looking for something or someone.

I turned back to Sam. 'I'll see you Tuesday at three.'

Bobby didn't believe me. Maybe Sam would.

'Good. In the meantime, get yourself a glass of champagne and a plate of food. Enjoy the races.'

'Thank you, though first I want to congratulate Nash on his engagement to Zoey.'

He shot me a skeptical look. 'Keep this conversation between us, all right? Don't discuss it with anyone else between now and Tuesday.'

'Don't worry, I won't say anything to anyone. I promise.'

'Good,' he said. 'Because I mean it.'

Zoey Ainsworth saw me before any of the men did. The look that flashed across her face vanished so quickly I wondered if I had imagined it. Apprehension? Uneasiness? Wariness? None of the above? Did it have to do with Nash being here and the universally known fact that I was in the Don't Pave Paradise camp, just like Paul and Violet had been? Was she worried Nash and I would have words, an argument, like he and Paul did the day he died? Did she *know* about Nash's argument with Paul? Did Nash confide in her about his business matters?

Somehow, I doubted it.

By the time I reached her, there was a polite but cool smile on her face as she casually inserted herself between Nash and me.

'Lucie, how are you? How is Mr Ortiz doing at rehab? I meant to call one of my friends over there and check on him, but it's been so busy at Lansdowne.'

Nice diversion.

'That's kind of you. Benny's doing all right, though he can't wait to get out of there, which probably doesn't surprise you. I'll tell him you were asking about him. He'll be pleased.'

Nash stepped forward and slipped his arm around his fiancée. 'Lucie,' he said. 'It's been a while. How are you?'

I felt his eyes travel up and down me, assessing me as if I were one of the horses running in today's races and he needed to decide if I was worth betting on.

'It's been a hard couple of days, Nash. The death of Paul Merchant has been a blow for all of us at the vineyard,' I said and met his bold stare.

His eyelids flickered. 'Yes. I was so sorry to hear about that. He was a good man.'

Not a word about being with Paul hours before his death. And, of course, nothing about the argument Paul had recounted to Frankie.

'He was.' I gave him a cool look. 'I also wanted to say congratulations on your engagement. Quinn and I saw Zoey when we were at the hospital yesterday visiting one of our workers, so we got to congratulate her already. Her ring is beautiful – she told us it's a family heirloom that belonged to your grandmother.'

Automatically Zoey held out her left hand, flashing the ring. 'It is beautiful, isn't it? I just love it.'

'Yes,' I said. 'Especially because it must have so much history, so many memories for you, Nash.'

Seeing Zoey and Nash together like this, it was hard not to wonder what they had in common – other than the obvious. She was marrying money. He was marrying a much younger woman and theirs was a May–December relationship, which might have been enough for him. A decoration on his arm who made him feel young and virile again. She was attractive, even beautiful, in a pretty, flirty minidress. He was good-looking in the handsome, chiseled way of older men that still turned female heads, but his face, tanned and weathered by years working construction outdoors, said he had lived hard and played hard. He also dressed older: navy blazer, pressed khakis, open-neck dress shirt, paisley ascot and Lucchese cowboy boots that had set him back four, maybe five figures. If you didn't know better, Nash Blake and Zoey Ainsworth could have passed for father and daughter. She could have been Hunter's older sister.

Nash smiled at me, acknowledging my compliment about the ring, but the fact that I'd brought up Eleanor, however obliquely, seemed to surprise him and not in a good way. He recovered quickly enough, ready to spar with me. 'It's an Irish Claddagh ring,' he said. 'After my grandfather died, I found it in the attic in a jewelry box that had belonged to my grandmother. I figured his memories of her must have been too painful for him, so he kept her things there. He loved her so much.'

Or maybe his grandfather just wanted everything out of his sight and couldn't bring himself to get rid of his dead wife's jewelry – either donating it or selling it. If Violet had learned something about Eleanor's death – like perhaps that the fire covered up a murder – and Nash knew about it, you'd think he'd want to let sleeping dogs lie. Buy Zoey a brand-new diamond engagement ring that had nothing to do with the past, no ties to Eleanor.

Which brought me full circle. Either Eleanor's death really had been a tragic accident, or Nash hadn't known the fire was set to cover up a murder until Violet brought him proof. But with Violet out of the way and now Paul dead as well, the subject of what really happened in that fire would remain buried and forgotten as it had been for the last eighty years.

Except Nash didn't intend to let the past stay in the past, because he was planning to rebuild the Hollywood Theatre. That didn't seem to make sense, either. Surely he recognized the risk of dredging up ancient history in a small town like ours where people had long memories and, if they didn't remember, they embellished what their parents or grandparents had told them. That there would be talk once again around the coffee pot in the General Store about what *really* happened to Eleanor in that fire.

'Then it's really quite special that you gave that ring to Zoey as a way to honor your grandmother,' I said. 'I also heard a rumor you're planning to rebuild the Hollywood Theatre, also to honor her.'

'The rumor is true.' His smile didn't make it all the way to his eyes. 'My grandmother opened that theater during the Depression because she wanted to give people something to lift their spirits – movies that would distract them when the bottom had just fallen out of their lives after the stock market crashed and so many people lost their jobs and their life savings.'

It sounded as if he was lecturing me.

'Yes, I'm aware of that . . .'

He held up his hand. 'I'm not finished.'

Zoey, who had vanished briefly, showed up with a beer that she handed to Nash, who held his hand out and took it without saying a word. Playing the peacemaker, calming him down, probably because she recognized the telltale signs of his notoriously quick temper flaring and the subsequent fallout.

'Now that Middleburg has an annual film festival and it's getting a reputation as the east coast version of the Sundance Festival in Utah, I think it's a huge omission for us not to have a movie theater,' he went on. 'Nor have we had one since my grandmother's theater burned down. In its heyday, the Hollywood Theatre attracted all the big movie stars of that era who came here when their films were being shown because they were all friends of Eleanor Blake's. Restoring the Hollywood Theatre, which will be called the Blake Theatre, and turning it into the main venue for the film festival, would be my gift to Middleburg. It would also honor my grandmother's philanthropy.'

It was a *take that* rebuke and just about the last thing I expected him to say. Of course he would want the theater to have the Blake name linked to what was becoming an extraordinarily successful and well-attended film festival. He would risk the gossip about what happened to Eleanor starting up again, but figure it would be outweighed – buried, even – by his gift of the theater to the town of Middleburg: The Blake Theatre.

'That's very generous of you,' I said and wondered if I was completely, absolutely, totally wrong about everything – and everyone – I'd suspected up to now.

Beginning with Nash Blake.

'It's almost time for the first race. Y'all haven't placed your bets yet.' Piper, Sam's granddaughter who had handed me the program when I walked in, joined our group. She held a fistful of dollar bills in one hand and an open program in the other.

One of the traditions – in fact, expectations – at Sam's tailgate was that everyone had to bet on each of the races. Usually one of his grandchildren was the race-day bookie and the rule was that you bet a dollar on the horse you thought would win. The winners split the pot – or winner take all if there was just one – but if no one had picked the winning horse, the money was donated to the therapeutic riding school for special needs kids where one of Sam's daughters-in-law was an instructor.

I reached into my shoulder bag and pulled out the wad of one dollar bills I'd brought with me for betting. 'What's this race?' I asked.

'Novice rider flat,' she said. 'Four-year-olds and up.'

Why I asked, I have no idea. Even after all these years, the world of steeplechase racing was still a mystery to me. I picked winners based on whichever horse name appealed to me. Occasionally, if I knew the owner or the rider, I picked their horse. I opened my program. Eeny, meeny, miney, moe.

'A dollar for Lover Boy,' I said, handing her a bill. 'He looks good.'

Nash and Zoey picked their horses and Nash handed Piper two dollars.

'You just like the name, Lucie,' Piper said, grinning. 'That's why you picked Lover Boy.'

'Shhh.' I laid my finger over my lips. 'Don't tell anyone my system.'

'What system would that be?'

I turned around. Dallas Ainsworth stood behind me holding his iPad in one hand, an amused look on his face.

'How I pick my horses,' I said.

'And how *do* you pick your horses?' he asked.

'It's very scientific. I pick a name I like.'

He laughed and asked, 'Do you ever win?'

'Daddy, stop,' Zoey said. To me she said, 'My father takes this way too seriously. He's such a computer geek he thinks he knows how to figure out just about anything. He spent half a day inputting every horse that's riding today and any information he could find about their record and their history. Once he does that, his computer program calculates which horse it thinks is going to win.'

'Which horse it *knows* is going to win.' Dallas smiled at his daughter and flashed his iPad at us. 'I wrote the software program. It's not hard to do. And I do my homework.'

'That sounds very scientific,' I said. 'For real.'

'It's data,' he said. 'And algorithms. Dead easy once you know what to do and how to do it.'

'Is it always right? I mean, horse races can be sort of capricious. A lot of unpredictable things can happen. A fall, a stumble over a fence.'

'True, but I very rarely lose.'

'So which horse are you putting your money on to win?'

He consulted his iPad. 'This race? Gone With the Whinny.'

'Like I said, my father thinks you can solve any problem with computers,' Zoey said, squeezing his arm affectionately. 'AI has only made it easier. And him even more impossible.' She leaned over and kissed his ruddy cheek.

'OK, betting is finished,' Piper said in a firm voice. 'They just called the riders.'

We drifted over to the fence to watch the race, which had already begun on the far side of the field. In the distance the horses and their jockeys looked so tiny they could have been toys in a child's game as they galloped around the track, flying toward us. I went over and stood next to Grayson Vaughn who continued looking at the race through his binoculars, ignoring me.

I figured I'd try anyway. 'Nice to see you, Grayson. It's been a while.'

'That's probably because I haven't been around.'

OK, gloves off. He wasn't going to bother being polite.

'Look, can I just say that Sasha and Eli are pretty torn up about . . . everything? I know they miss you.'

He turned and faced me. 'Don't get in the middle of this, Lucie. It's none of your business and you don't know what you're talking about.'

'That's not true. I *do* know. You, of all people, with horses racing here today, should at least be able to see things from the viewpoint of people who don't want our dirt and gravel roads paved. It's better for the horses, traffic is slower. It's part of our way of life. You know that. Putting up hundreds of houses on beautiful farmland is going to change everything so many people love about living out here.'

'I don't need you giving me grief about this along with my sister and your brother, so please just *stop*.' His voice hardened. 'I know what I'm doing. I get where the Don't Pave Paradise committee was coming from, but I know things now that I wasn't aware of before. Paving some of the roads in Loudoun makes sense. It's way overdue. And we're done here, OK?'

'It's *not* over or finished, Grayson. Just because Paul and Violet are gone, there are still people who are going to carry on, pick up where they left off. You used to be . . . on their side. On Violet's side.'

He gave me a look that was a mixture of pain and anger. 'Don't.'

I hadn't meant to hurt him, but I couldn't see how he could have turned his back on what he'd promised her. Especially after her death.

'Is this conversation about paving the roads in Loudoun? Is that what you two are talking about?' Nash stood at Grayson's elbow. 'Again? Still?'

'*We* aren't. *She* is.' Grayson hooked a thumb in my direction.

'You people,' Nash said and the way he said *you people* sounded as if he were talking about something that needed to be scraped off the bottom of his shoe, 'need to understand that we're not the enemy – *builders* are not the enemy. Your brother, Lucie, is an architect, for God's sake. If your gang of so-called conservationists puts a stop to new construction out here, what's Eli going to do? I don't understand why you want to keep this region in the dark ages. Look at Rappahannock County. Their board of supervisors dug in their heels against any kind of development and as a result their population hasn't grown since

2000. Actually, it hasn't grown since 1920. And because they're totally anti-development, their budget is so meager that all they can afford are bare-bones services for the people who live there. If we go that route, we'll stop thriving. Come on, you're a business owner. Is that what you want for us?'

He stepped toward me, towering over me. He meant to intimidate me – physically and mentally. I took a small step back and regretted it immediately because I was letting him win.

'I read about that, and I agree it's an extreme decision – except that's how they want it in that part of Virginia,' I said. 'I don't think putting up three hundred and fifteen houses on pristine farmland in Loudoun County is progress and that we're going to be better off for it.' I turned to Grayson. 'Do you? Because if that's what you let happen, it's going to destroy what makes us unique. Why this region is so desirable.'

The first horses came thundering by and I heard Dallas crow, 'And look who's first. Gone With the Whinny.'

'Lucie.'

I turned around. My half-brother David Phelps stood there, a tripod with a camera mounted on it in one hand and a half-open camera bag slung over the other shoulder.

'I could use your help with my gear and some photos I need to take,' he said to me in a tight, firm voice. 'Right now, if you don't mind.'

He took hold of my arm and said to Nash, Dallas, and Grayson, 'Do you mind if I borrow her? I'm almost finished taking the final pictures of the point-to-point, so you'll have everything for the hunt's updated website. Grayson, I'll get them to you within the week.'

'She's all yours,' Grayson said. 'And thanks.'

He probably meant me leaving, not the photos.

'Before you go, Lucie,' Nash said. 'I hope you'll think about this, reconsider your position. You can't stop progress forever. Sooner or later, we're going to win. People need places to live.'

'We'll see about that,' I said, my anger getting the better of me at being bullied. 'Paul and Violet left behind maps and diagrams and notes, so we're going ahead with filing the petition with the National Trust for Historic Preservation to get some of these roads named as historic sites.'

'Lucie.' David tugged my arm so hard I had to use my cane to keep from stumbling. 'Let's. Go.'

He pulled me away and I followed him through the crush of people still crowded around the buffet table and the tailgate bar. As soon as we were out of earshot of the others, he said to me, 'What the hell were you thinking? Why did you get mixed up in an argument with Grayson and Nash over paving the roads? And Grayson's decision to sell some of his land to Nash? Two people are *dead*, Lucie.'

'I know. But Nash was just so damn arrogant and smug, confident he's going to win. You heard him. As if Paul and Violet's deaths meant there was an end to any effort to stop them from building out here and paving over paradise.'

'So you let your temper get the best of you?' He was still angry. 'That was dumb. Really dumb.'

'Someone has to fight back,' I said, snapping at him. 'We can't roll over and play dead, just because Violet and Paul are gone.'

'It didn't have to be you.' Stabbing his finger at my chest. Belligerent.

'Well, who else was going to do it?' Damn. Why were we having this argument? We were on the same side.

'Lucie,' he said, and now I saw the worry, concern, and even fear in his troubled eyes, 'you just painted a target on your back by announcing you've got Violet and Paul's notes. That was exactly what we agreed the other day that you *weren't* going to do.'

I gave him a weary look. He was right. 'They're going to find out sooner or later. We can't keep it a secret forever.'

'Better later than sooner.'

'I think I know what Violet might have found out about Eleanor Blake and that it was probably enough of a motive for Redmond to arrange for her death in the Hollywood Theatre fire. She was out of his life, and he also inherited her entire estate, all her money. Unfortunately, I can't prove it. Yet. But I also think whatever it was still matters now and Nash wants to keep it from being known.'

'Come on,' he said. 'We can't talk here. There are too many people. What I said to Grayson was legit about getting some final photos here today for their website. Come with me while I finish up and then we can go somewhere with some privacy.'

'What pictures do you need to take?'

'The photographic equivalent of video camera B roll. Scenery photos. The stable hands leading the horses out to the racetrack. The jockeys saddling up. General stuff. I've got enough of the races.'

I followed him down to the stables behind a stand of shade trees at the bottom of a hill and surrounded by cars and pickups with horse trailers. It was purposely set apart from the race-course, a peaceful spot for the horses that was off-limits to the public so the animals could be kept calm before the excitement of the race.

'Here.' David handed me his phone. 'I told them I needed you to be my assistant. Hold this while I set up.'

'That's the help you needed? Holding your phone?'

'What I *needed* was to get you away from Nash and Grayson. So, hold the damn phone.'

I looked down at the screen at a 3D image of his Nikon mirrorless camera with the lens. It was facing me. There was also a drop-down menu with *auto link* set to 'on' selected.

'What's this?' I pointed to his phone screen.

'Nikon's remote-control program,' he said. 'It uses Bluetooth. I can take pictures with my phone instead of pressing the button on the camera or even using a cable. That way I don't have to worry about camera shake, especially with long exposures. I can also download my photos right away. It's a great little program.'

I stared at his phone. 'You can control your camera with your phone?'

'Yup. That's what I just said. Why?'

'Just thinking. You can probably control just about any piece of equipment with remote control these days,' I said, 'can't you?'

'Uh-huh.' He was concentrating on adjusting the legs of his tripod on the uneven ground so his camera would be level.

'What about a car?'

He glanced up. 'Sure, cars, too. Ever since 1997, cars have

been controlled by ECUs. The technology's been around for a while.'

'What's an ECU?'

'Electronic controlled unit. Cars have more than one, especially new cars. They're nothing but electronics now. ECUs control everything – engine, power train, transmission, brakes. Everything. You can think of them together as your car's computer brain.'

'Could you . . . interfere with one of those ECU systems?'

'If you knew what you were doing, you could.'

'Say you did know. How would you do it?'

'For some of the basic stuff – the really easy stuff – you can just buy the software online. I've done it.' He stopped fiddling with his tripod to stare at me, as if he was trying to figure out where I was going with this.

'You *have*?'

'Sure,' he said. 'I changed one of the commands to "off" so that I don't get that annoying "you are responsible for the safe operation of your vehicle" message on the screen every time I start my engine.'

'What about some of the less easy stuff? How would you do that?'

'Well, if you had access to the car, you could install software that would allow you to have control over it. If you wanted to be nefarious about it, you could install malware. Load a program that would hide itself, make itself invisible so the owner of the car wouldn't know it was there.'

'What kind of control and how would you get access to the car to begin with?'

'If it's at an auto body shop or a repair shop, you could get access there. But it's also as easy as finding the car unlocked. If you're a gearhead, you know how to access the CPU. Install the software and then after that you can connect to the car remotely.'

'What's a gearhead?' Though I had a pretty good idea what he was going to say.

'A person who's interested in mechanical or technical things.'

'Like cars,' I said in a flat voice. 'And computers.'

'Someone like that.'

'And that gearhead could, say, remotely control a car so maybe the brakes wouldn't work? If, say, he or she wanted to be nefarious, as you said.'

'Lucie . . .'

'I need to make a call,' I said. 'Can you finish taking your photos without me?'

'Of course. Who are you going to call?' But his eyes flashed and I knew he'd put two and two together as well.

And came up with the same answer I had.

Someone had manipulated Violet Rossi's car. That's why she'd had no control when it sped over the hill at First Bridge and careened off the narrow road, plunging into Goose Creek where she ultimately drowned, pinned to her seat with her seatbelt still on. She hadn't even tried to escape. Her death hadn't been due to driver error. Someone who knew computers quite well had sped up her car and cut her brakes when she needed them.

She'd been murdered.

Remotely.

EIGHTEEN

Dallas Ainsworth.

Dallas Ainsworth, who created a software program into which he could input data so he could bet on the horses at the Goose Creek Hunt point-to-point and win. Who, according to his daughter, used computers to do just about anything and everything.

Did Dallas load malware into the computer system of Violet Rossi's car so he knew where she was, knew how to control her car? Made her car speed up on Crenshaw Road and then cut her brakes so the car was out of control as it went over First Bridge and careened into Goose Creek?

He worked for Nash. He was loyal to the Blake family; his daughter was *marrying* Nash, for God's sake. Of course he wouldn't want Violet to reveal anything that might damage Nash and Blake Construction in any way. He would have known if she got Grayson to change his mind about selling his land to Nash. If she threatened Nash or blackmailed him. He might have gotten angry about it, maybe decided he wanted to do something to shut Violet up.

Unless it had been Nash. Unless Nash had asked Dallas to take care of Violet, knowing he could tamper with her car. Knowing what he was capable of doing. And what about Paul? Was Dallas the guest who had come by the Merchants' home, spiking Paul's drink with enough lorazepam to make him so dizzy and confused that he tumbled into his swimming pool and drowned?

'Lucie,' David said. 'Talk to me. What's going on?'

'You know what's going on.'

'You think someone messed with Violet's car remotely?'

'Not just someone. Dallas.'

'Jesus. Seriously? That's . . . murder. Are you sure?'

'I think it's possible. I think it makes sense, don't you? What are the three things you need to commit a crime?' I ticked them off on my fingers. 'Motive. Means. Opportunity.'

'And you think he had them?'

'I do.' I wiggled my fingers. 'First, motive. Shutting Violet up, keeping her from talking about whatever she'd found out that Nash wanted kept quiet. Two, means. Dallas knows computers, he knows how to write software programs – we just found that out. So, means – check. Three, opportunity.' That was the one that I had no way of knowing one way or the other. 'If all Dallas needed was to find Violet's car unlocked in order to load the malware onto its computer system, how hard would that be?'

My brother had not taken his eyes off me the entire time I'd been talking. 'Not too hard,' he said. 'What do you want to do now?'

'Call Bobby,' I said. 'What do you bet the Loudoun County Sheriff's Office didn't examine every one of the ECUs in Violet's car because nobody was considering the possibility of it being remotely controlled?'

'I bet you're probably right. What you've got to hope, though, is that the electronics didn't get destroyed in the crash so it's still possible to retrieve that data.'

'That's why I want to call Bobby,' I said. 'The Sheriff's Office has a depot where all the wrecked cars, trucks, and motorcycles are towed in case they're needed by insurance companies or in a court case if someone's suing. Stuff like that.'

'How do you know about this place?'

'I've been there. Every year during prom season and just before graduation the Sheriff's Office tows smashed-up cars – the worst ones possible – and leaves them parked on the front lawns of all the local high schools as a reminder of what can happen if you drink and drive. When Mia was in high school and she hung out with a hard-partying crowd, we used to talk about those cars when she was around and hope she was paying attention.'

'Was she?'

'Nope. She got in a lot of trouble. Almost got blamed for a fatal accident when someone else was behind the wheel and she was too drunk to remember if she'd been driving or not.'

'I didn't know about that.'

'It was a while ago. Fortunately, what almost happened scared her so badly she took off to New York for a couple of years and got her life back together.'

'Where is this wrecked car depot?'

'Leesburg. I'm going to see if Bobby will meet us there.'

'Now?'

'Yup, now.'

'All right,' he said. 'I'll finish up here and then let's go.'

It was a harder sell than I expected to get Bobby to even consider the idea that Violet's car might have been remotely controlled and that's how it had crashed into Goose Creek the day of her accident.

'I don't know, Lucie,' he'd said. 'That theory seems pretty far-fetched. Remote control? And Dallas Ainsworth, of all people? You're pushing hard on this.'

'What if I'm right? Can't your people at least check whether one or more of the electronic controlled units didn't function as it was supposed to? That the commands that should have been there might have been reversed or eliminated?'

'All right, I'll talk to our crash unit and get them to take a look at the computer system in her car on Monday. The car was pretty smashed up, especially the front end, so I can't say for sure whether we'll have access to it, or it won't be damaged.'

'What if we meet you at the crash depot in, say, forty-five minutes and you, David, and I can see whether the computer system is salvageable?'

Silence from him. I could almost hear him digging in. He didn't want to do this. He thought it was a half-cocked idea.

'Bobby, *please*?'

'You can be like a dog with a bone, you know that, Lucie?'

As far as I was concerned that meant 'yes.'

'Thank you. I mean it. *Thank you.* We'll see you in three-quarters of an hour at the depot,' I said and disconnected before he could catch his breath and say *forget it* or *absolutely not*.

I still heard him mutter, 'Jesus H. Christ, she's impossible,' before the phone went dead.

But I knew he'd meet us as I'd asked. Because as far-fetched as my theory was, it was also possible I was right, that Violet had been murdered by a very clever killer.

And Bobby was too good a detective – once he started considering the situation from an angle he had not previously thought about – not to pursue any possibility, however wacko or out-in-left-field it seemed.

David and I had driven to the point-to-point in separate cars, so he followed my Jeep on the back roads from Middleburg to Leesburg. Surprisingly, we arrived before Bobby did – he didn't have that far to drive from either the Sheriff's Office or his home, so I wondered what was up. Hopefully he hadn't changed his mind.

'It's locked,' David said as we stood in front of a chain link fence and a gate with a heavy padlock wound through it. 'I guess we have to wait for Bobby.'

'The *gate* is locked,' I said. 'I know how to get in, though. The fence isn't entirely secure all the way around the perimeter. Come on. I'll show you.'

'Maybe we should just wait for Bobby. He'll be here any minute.'

'Yes, and he'll find us checking out Violet's car, which is where we agreed to meet.'

'Isn't that technically breaking and entering – on Loudoun County Sheriff's Office property?'

'Well, if you want to be technical about it.'

'Or legal.'

'I'd rather ask forgiveness than permission. Bobby'll know where to find us.'

He threw up his hands. 'I give up. Let's go find this hole in your fence. Which I bet will get fixed once Bobby finds out about it.'

It was easier to find the hole in the fence than it was to locate Violet Rossi's car.

'My God,' David said as we walked down aisle after aisle of wrecked, smashed-up vehicles. 'You wonder if anyone could have walked away from some of these – or at least survived their injuries.'

'Violet didn't.'

'I know. Do you know what kind of car she was driving?'

'Only because I did a search of the newspaper story about her accident just now. It was a neon green Jeep Wrangler. Different model from mine. It should be here somewhere.'

'How about that one?' He pointed to a car that looked as if a giant with big strong hands had taken it and crushed it like an empty soda can. 'That's a bright green Jeep. Or was. No wonder she didn't walk away from that.'

She had been found with her seatbelt still attached, drowned in the shallow waters of Goose Creek. I closed my eyes, remembering the Jaws of Life extricating me from my boyfriend's car after he smashed into the front pillar at the entrance to the vineyard. So much intense pain, blood – *my* blood – spattered all over the dashboard and windshield like a giant Rorschach test. The emergency vehicles, sirens screaming as they raced to the scene of our crash.

'Lucie.' David shook my arm gently. 'Are you all right? You've gone completely pale.'

'I . . . no. I mean, yes. I'll be OK. I *am* OK.'

'We don't have to do this,' he said, still holding onto me as if I might pass out. '*You* don't have to do this. I can take a quick look at the car and see if it looks like the CPU is salvageable. We can let Bobby handle it from here. Which is what we should probably do anyway.'

'No,' I said. 'I want to see her car for myself. I'm fine. I'll be fine.'

I needed to see her car. Needed to get over this wave of nausea. Needed to be OK. Finally.

I heard the crunch of boots on the gravel path between the rows of cars before Bobby came into view. When he did, he looked pissed off.

'Lucie. David. How in the hell did you get in here?'

'There's a small opening in the fence,' I said. 'Don't tell me you don't know about it. You can squeeze through it if you shimmy.'

He looked up at the sky and shook his head. 'Goddamn.'

'That's her car over there, right?' I pointed to the mangled Jeep.

'Yup.'

The three of us walked over to it in grim, respectful silence.

I tried not to think about Violet sitting in the driver's seat as they'd found her. The first responders had to cut through her seatbelt in order to extricate her and now I could see the severed shoulder strap dangling like a noose from the roof of the car.

'I know how to extract the CPU,' David said as we stood there staring at the wreck. 'I've got some experience with stuff like this. I worked on cars in my dad's autobody shop when I was growing up.'

It took me a moment to realize he was talking about the man who'd adopted him and became the father he'd known and loved until his death a few years ago. Not Leland, his biological father. And mine.

Bobby shook his head. 'Are you kidding me? No dice. It's evidence tampering if you touch it. We'll take care of it.'

'But you *will* remove it and examine it to see if any of the commands have been turned off or reversed, won't you?' I asked.

'Yes. I promise.' He folded his arms across his chest. 'Where'd you get the idea that Dallas Ainsworth might be behind this, anyway?'

I told him.

'You just saw him?'

'At the point-to-point this afternoon.'

'Does he have any clue you've made some kind of connection between him and . . . this?' He nodded in the direction of the car.

'No. Of course not. We're not dumb.'

'Keep it that way.'

'We will,' I said. 'Though you could give me credit for figuring out that the car might have been remotely controlled – after watching David do the same thing with his camera and an app on his phone.'

Bobby gave me a somewhat grudging nod. 'Credit where it's due. But let's not get ahead of ourselves, shall we?'

'Don't worry,' David said. 'The last thing we want to do is stir up a hornet's nest.'

'Good.'

Except we already had, or *I* already had. Bobby didn't know about it, but David did and I could feel the tension coming off him in waves. I'd provoked Nash and Grayson by telling them we were carrying on with Violet and Paul's work, specifically that they'd left notes behind for us to follow.

But what none of us knew as we stood there in the dappled late-afternoon sunlight, surrounded by smashed up wrecks that were all that remained of someone's horror-story nightmare, was whether Dallas had tampered with Violet's car. And if he had, whether he had acted on his own or followed orders from his boss.

Nash Blake.

The baptism of Ivy Faith Noland – Faith for Kit's mother, who came to the church in a wheelchair – was going to take place at the nine thirty Mass on Sunday morning at St Michael the Archangel Catholic Church in Middleburg. Father Joe O'Malley would perform the baptism and Ivy would be surrounded by the loving family and friends of her parents. Kit had told me St Mike's didn't do private baptisms; instead, the entire church community would celebrate with them, promising to be there for Ivy and support her for what lay ahead on her life journey.

Two days later we would return here again for Paul's funeral Mass. Another celebration of life but this time a life cut short, so much unfulfilled. The exact opposite of today.

When Quinn and I walked through the main doors of St Mike's, which had been thrown open on another unseasonably warm and sunny day, everything that had happened these last few days and the ceremony we were about to witness felt as if an enormous weight was pressing down on me.

A beginning and an end. Hope and heartbreak. Joy and grief. Birth and death.

And, in the midst of it all, maybe there was a killer among us.

Last night I had told Quinn everything, beginning with the point-to-point, my meet-up with David – who was here today taking photos, his gift to Ivy's parents for her baptism – and finally David and me meeting Bobby at the wrecked car depot to discuss removing the CPU from Violet Rossi's car. The possibility that someone had been remotely controlling it, sending Violet to her death.

Specifically Dallas Ainsworth.

Even if I hadn't said anything to Quinn, he would have figured out something was wrong anyway. The nightmare I used to have after the crash that left me with a permanent disability came roaring back last night for the first time in a long time, waking both of us up when I cried out. Eventually I fell asleep in Quinn's arms and when I woke up as it started to grow light, he was still sitting up in bed in the exact same position, cradling me, his pillow stuffed behind his head, leaning against the wooden headboard, neck bent awkwardly as if he'd had a bad night's sleep in an airplane seat.

As we got dressed to go to church, I said, 'I'm so sorry about last night. I promise it won't happen again.'

'You can't promise that,' he said. 'I hope this thing ends soon and Bobby gets to the bottom of it. Finds out who's responsible before something else happens. Before someone else gets hurt. Or worse.' He sounded irritated and cranky.

'I know. I'm really sorry.'

'Tell me you're done with investigating and this time you mean it.'

'I'm done with investigating and this time I mean it.'

He gave me a severe look. 'You'd better be, Lucie.'

Bobby pulled me aside as soon as Quinn and I walked into the church where the Eastman and Noland families were waiting in the narthex for the Mass to begin. Quinn gave me a warning look, but he didn't say anything.

'A guy from the crime reconstruction unit got the CPU out of Violet's car last night,' Bobby said after we were standing outside the church again. 'They're going to put a rush on analyzing it, see if anyone tampered with the commands.'

'How long will that take?'

'I don't know. First we've got to find someone who can do that. Probably someone who is familiar with the electronic systems in a Jeep. To be honest, I'm not entirely sure – that stuff is way out of my league.'

'Then it could take some time, rush job or not.'

'Maybe. But even if we find out someone messed with the car, we won't be able to determine who it was just based on that information.'

'It was Dallas Ainsworth. I'm telling you.'

'Says you. Look, Lucie, we need to do this right. We'll get whoever did it, don't worry. But these things take time and we need to be patient, okay?'

'I know that. But Bobby, listen to me, when this is over and done with, you'll find out that it was Dallas.'

'Bobby. Lucie. What are you two doing out here?' Kit, in a loose-fitting pale pink dress that forgave the pregnancy weight she was still trying to shed, stood in the church doorway, hands on hips. The expression on her face was a mixture of astonishment and annoyance. 'Father Joe is ready to start Mass. The baby's father and the godmother can't be missing. What's going on that it can't wait? Ivy just woke up . . . I don't know how long we've got before she starts fussing.'

'I'm sorry, babe,' Bobby said. 'Lucie and I were just having a quick chat.'

'About what?' She was still upset.

'Going over what the godmother has to say,' I said, as Bobby said, 'I had a question about the luncheon.'

'Seriously? Neither of you is good at lying, you know that? What's *really* going on?' Her gaze shifted from me to Bobby and back again. Then she shook her head. 'Never mind. I probably don't want to know. At least not now. Come on. Everyone's waiting.'

She turned and marched inside.

'She doesn't know about Violet, does she?' I said to Bobby. 'You didn't say anything?'

'Nope. Why do you think I was late to meet you at the wrecked car depot yesterday? She was already anxious enough about everything going right today – plus she's got some work-related stress coming up. I didn't want to pile on anything else. Does Quinn know?'

Of course. Kit still agonizing over her bosses' edict to make some of her staff redundant just before Christmas. Bobby didn't seem aware she had confided in me.

So many secrets we kept from each other. Little ones that

could be batted away and were confidences for a good reason. Big ones that were dangerous enough to get someone killed. My head hurt trying to keep them all straight.

'Quinn knows about yesterday,' I said to him. 'All of it.'

'How did that go?'

'Not well.'

'Figures,' he said. 'Come on. We'd better get inside. We're in enough trouble already.'

'At least something good is about to happen,' I said as we walked into the church and joined the others who were waiting in front of the baptismal font. 'Your daughter is being baptized. And we'll celebrate after that. It'll be a good day.'

But later at the luncheon, as we were handing out slices of Dominique's chef's lemon lavender cake, which had been covered in baby pink roses and lavender petals, Bobby came over and stood behind my chair.

He leaned down and whispered in my ear, 'There's news.'

'What? Already?'

'We found someone to check out Violet's CPU. You were right,' he said. 'The codes were tampered with so that the car could accelerate unexpectedly without the driver controlling what happened or being able to stop it. Same thing with the brakes.'

I twisted around and stared up at him. He had said it would take a while to figure out if anyone had gained access to the Jeep's computer systems. Instead it had only been a few hours.

I felt like the breath had been punched out of me. I'd been sure I was right, but now confronted with the truth, his news was still a shock.

'So now what?' I asked.

'Well,' he said in a grim voice that was filled with regret and self-blame, 'now we're looking for a murderer responsible for the death of Violet Rossi. Six weeks after we closed the case and told her family it was an accident.'

NINETEEN

B obby called first thing the next morning and said he wanted to come by and talk to Quinn and me in private. Even if I hadn't recognized his I'm-not-messing-around cop voice, it didn't take a genius to figure out why he wanted to see us. Reopening the investigation into Violet Rossi's death was going to be like opening Pandora's box and hoping nobody noticed.

We were in the middle of the morning ritual of pumping over the Cab Sauv in the barrel room when he walked in. I took one look at his face and said, 'Do you want a cup of coffee or do you need something stronger?'

'I need something stronger, but coffee will have to do.'

'Why don't we go over to the Villa?' I said. 'We're closed for another hour so we'll have the place to ourselves and we can talk there.'

'You two go ahead.' Quinn waved us off. 'I'll join you when this is done.'

I glanced over my shoulder on the way out and mouthed *you'd better come* when Bobby wasn't looking. He rolled his eyes but at least he nodded.

Last night the temperature had dipped into the forties for the first time since spring. This morning the courtyard seemed eerily silent as Bobby and I walked under the portico connecting the barrel room and the Villa. A few leaves twirled past us, caught in a light breeze, and floated to the ground.

'The cicadas stopped singing,' I said. 'That's why it's so quiet.'

'What?'

'The cicadas. I heard them yesterday and today they're gone because the temperature dropped so low last night. Fall's coming for sure now.'

He looked at me as if I'd just tried to explain that earth tilting on its axis as it rotated had an impact on the seasons changing instead of saying that a bunch of insects stopped chirping because it got cold so we were done with summer.

'Hey,' I said. 'What's going on? Your mind is a million miles away.'

'Sorry,' he said as we walked up the steps to the Villa. He held the door for me. 'I just came from talking to Marco and Chiara.'

'Let me guess. It didn't go too well.'

'That would be an understatement.'

'Why did *you* have to talk to them? You told me the investigation into Violet's death wasn't yours. One of your colleagues caught that case.'

He followed me through the tasting room into the large, sunny kitchen where the staff prepared sandwiches, paninis, charcuterie boards, an assortment of cheeses.

'It's my investigation now.'

'Coffee? Cappuccino? Latte?'

'Coffee. Black, please.'

'What happened?' I flicked a switch on our large commercial coffee maker and coffee beans dropped from a hopper into the grinder. I got a mug from a cabinet and set it under one of the heads. I did the same for the espressos for two lattes for Quinn and me.

'Would you like something to eat? We've got croissants and muffins.'

'Thanks, no. I'm good. And I think we should wait for Quinn before I tell you everything.'

I got milk out of the refrigerator and steamed it while he stood and watched. When I was done, I said, 'At least tell me how much you told Kit, or what you told her.'

He leaned against the counter, folded his arms across his chest and crossed one long leg over the other. 'I told her everything. Start to finish. She guessed some of it, anyway. She won't say a word, you know her.'

'Of course.' I picked up the espresso shots and dumped them into mugs with the hot milk. 'Forgive me for saying this, but you look like hell. You don't blame yourself for what happened, do you? It wasn't your fault that you didn't think to look for someone tampering remotely with Violet's car.'

'Tell that to Marco and Chiara. Actually, *don't* tell them. They don't know anything. That's what I want to talk to you and Quinn about,' he said. 'Where are we going to do this? Here, give me one of those lattes.'

Considerate of him, since I couldn't carry more than one mug at a time. I picked up mine and reached for my cane with the other hand. 'The terrace. It's cool but it will be nice in the sun. It's a gorgeous day.'

Quinn found us as we were sitting down at a table where we could look out on the dusky Blue Ridge framing the nearly bare vineyard.

'Bobby wants to talk to us about a meeting he just had with Marco and Chiara,' I said as he sat down.

Quinn picked up his latte and blew on it, avoiding my eyes. We had discussed this before Bobby arrived. We already knew what he wanted to talk about.

'How did it go?' Quinn asked him anyway.

'Like I told Lucie, not too good. They're pleased we're reopening the investigation into Violet's death when I told them new evidence had come to light,' he said. 'But they're also angry the case was considered closed and the official reason all this time was that it was an accident due to driver error. That Violet was speeding and lost control of the car.'

'The day she came to help us pick the Cab Sauv, Chiara told me she never believed her mother's death was an accident,' I said. 'They must feel vindicated.'

'Vindicated *and* pissed off.' He drank his coffee. 'They wanted to know what we found out, so guess how happy they were when I said I couldn't disclose any information now that the investigation is ongoing – again? Then they wanted to know how we missed whatever it was we just discovered. I couldn't tell them that, either. The last thing I need is to alert whoever did this that we're aware of him – or her – now.' He pointed a finger at each of us. 'That includes you guys. You can't say anything. I mean it.'

'Which is why you're here,' I said. 'To tell us we need to keep our mouths shut about the compromised computer system. You didn't have to stop by for that, Bobby. Of course we know.

It's a homicide now. You're looking for a murderer. I can call David and tell him all this, but he gets it, too.'

'I'll take care of talking to David. Thanks, anyway.' We were getting the cop voice once again. 'Look, I'm just dotting the i's and crossing the t's talking to you two. Under the circumstances, this needs to be done completely by the book. So you and Quinn do not say anything to *anyone*. Same goes for David.'

'What's the Sheriff's Office official story now?' Quinn asked, changing the subject and shifting the narrative.

'That we're reopening the investigation after finding new evidence. That's it.'

'Are you going to talk to Dallas Ainsworth? Bring him in for questioning?' I asked.

Bobby drained his coffee cup. 'Based on what? That the guy's a computer geek? Big deal.'

'He has a motive.'

'So do a lot of other people who weren't happy about the roads being paved, if that's what this is about. It could also be something completely different.'

'Like what?' I asked. 'What else is there?'

'That's what I intend to find out. Look, we don't know who messed with Violet's computer system and we're going to have to do this the old-fashioned way. Build a case, find out who had a grudge against her, the usual stuff,' he said. 'We'll get the person who did it, Lucie. Don't worry. In the meantime, you stay out of it. You've done enough and we're grateful – we wouldn't be at this stage without what you found out – but we're looking for a killer. Understand?'

'We do.' Quinn nudged my foot under the table with his and gave me a pointed look. 'You have nothing to worry about, Bobby. Right, sweetheart?'

I nodded. 'Absolutely. Right.'

Bobby pushed back his chair and got up. 'Good. In that case, I need to take off. Thanks for the coffee.'

'Will we see you tonight?' I asked. He frowned and I added, 'The wake. Paul's wake.'

'Oh. Of course. We got a babysitter so we'll both be there.'

'What about Paul?' I asked.

He gave me a wary look. 'What about him?'

'Now that you've reopened the investigation into Violet's death, don't you think there might also be a connection to Paul's death?'

He looked like he was mentally counting to ten. 'That thought has actually occurred to a few of us in the Sheriff's Office, Lucie, believe it or not. I appreciate the suggestion, though.'

'Look, I'm not trying to tell you how to do your job, Bobby. But Paul's death wasn't accidental any more than Violet's was – someone *did* leave prints on that drinks glass. And whoever did it was also very clever at making it look as if Paul took an overdose of lorazepam and fell into the pool, too doped up to get out, so he drowned.'

Quinn laid his hand on my arm and gave me an all-too-familiar warning look. 'Lucie.'

'Yeah, well, we're clever, too. You'd be surprised. We'll get whoever it was,' Bobby said.

Then he was gone.

Quinn and I signed the guest book at the entrance to BJ Hunt and Sons Funeral Home when we arrived for Paul Merchant's wake just after five o'clock. A vase of all-white flowers – roses, lilies, mums, snapdragons, alstroemeria, and carnations – sat on the table next to the book.

'Those are pretty,' Quinn said.

I showed him what was written on the card. 'They're from you and me. Nikki also had flowers sent from everyone at the vineyard. They should be here somewhere, too.'

He put an arm around me and hugged me. 'You're so good about things like that.'

I skimmed the list of signatures. Paul's wake was the only one being held here tonight, but the parking lot had been jammed and lights blazed from every window. 'A lot of people are here already. I'm glad for Frankie and the kids.'

In fact, most of Atoka and Middleburg seemed to have come to pay their respects, including Chiara Rossi and, surprisingly, Zoey Ainsworth – but then she had been Lily's riding instructor for many years. No Nash. I wondered if he'd be magnanimous and show up – or not.

The news that the Sheriff's Office had reopened the investigation into Violet Rossi's death apparently had already gone around the funeral home like wildfire. Nobody knew what the reason was or how the Sheriff's Office had learned about the new development, but that didn't stop the speculation. I heard snatches of conversation as Quinn and I snaked our way through the crowded rooms looking for Frankie.

'. . . on her way to meet her lover . . . I heard he was married. The Sheriff's Office finally found out who . . .'

'Someone else was there when her car went into the creek . . . left before the emergency vehicles got there . . . can you imagine?'

I lost Quinn when he stopped to talk to Toby Levine from La Vigne Vineyard.

'I need to find Frankie,' I said to him. 'I'll catch up with you later.'

She was standing next to a screen where a montage of photos of Paul that spanned their thirty-five-year marriage flashed by one by one. I joined her, slid my arm through hers, and we watched together. The song 'Remember When' by Alan Jackson, which played under the photos, had been one of Paul's favorites. He and Frankie had danced to it at their thirty-fifth wedding anniversary party last spring in front of family and friends, an achingly tender, romantic slow dance that made all of us swoon and wish for the kind of love they so obviously shared with each other. My heart broke a little.

'I can tell you chose the music to go with the photos.'

'I chose everything. The funeral home put it all together.'

'It's a lovely tribute.'

'That's Lily,' she murmured as a picture of Paul cradling an infant who was probably minutes old came on the screen. She kept narrating. 'Carving the Thanksgiving turkey, wearing the Santa hat I made him for the tree decorating party, finishing the Cherry Blossom race in D.C. the year it poured, in front of the Matterhorn . . . all of us at the Eiffel Tower on New Year's Eve . . . the Taj Mahal . . . our twenty-fifth anniversary in Venice . . . coaching Yale's soccer team . . . with the kids on safari in Botswana . . . behind the wheel of his beloved red Mustang . . . leaving the church after our wedding . . .'

She stopped talking as more photos appeared and the music changed. 'What a Wonderful World.'

I squeezed her arm. 'He had a remarkable life. You both did.'

'He promised me an adventure,' she said, the sadness seeping into her voice. 'We had one.'

'Oh, Frankie.'

'I heard,' she went on, 'that they're reopening the investigation into Violet's death.'

'I heard that, too.'

'I'm looking for Bobby. Hoping he'll be here. They need to do the same for Paul. Now I'm more certain than ever that his death and Violet's are connected. Neither one was an accident.'

'Bobby . . . is very thorough.'

Her voice and her demeanor changed to steel. 'He'd better be, Lucie. Paul did *not* accidentally overdose on lorazepam.'

'Mom.' Yale Merchant, Frankie's twenty-one-year-old son, stood in front of us. It had been a while since I'd seen him now that he was in college. He had his mother's bright blue eyes, but everything else was his father: tousled straight dark hair, tall and slender, erect posture in a dark suit, black tie, and immaculate white dress shirt, an adult all of a sudden, so much like Paul that it hurt. 'Father Joe just arrived. He's going to say some prayers at Dad's casket but he wants to have a word with you first.'

'Go,' I said to Frankie. 'I'll see you later.'

By the time I finished watching the rest of the photo montage I was blinking hard and my eyes were moist. I found a box of tissues on an end table next to a sofa.

'Are you OK, Lucie?'

Chiara Rossi came up behind me as I was dabbing my eyes. She looked as lovely as ever, though tonight she was dressed completely in black – black silk blouse and black palazzo pants.

'I'm fine. Just sad. Sorry.'

She glanced across the room at the photo display as it showed Paul with Lily and Yale when they were probably six and seven, holding a jack-o'-lantern almost as big as they were. Grins on everyone's faces as wide and smiling as the pumpkin's.

'Don't be sorry,' she said. 'I feel as if I'm at Mom's funeral all over again being here tonight. It's hard.'

'Are *you* OK?'

'Bobby Noland came by to see Nonno Marco and me this morning. Guess what he told us – or do you already know?'

There was no point playing games with her. 'I heard that the investigation into your mother's death has been reopened.'

'Do you know what he found? You two are pretty close. You're his daughter's godmother. He wouldn't say a word to either of us.'

'He wouldn't say anything to me, either. Bobby would never discuss one of his cases or talk about an ongoing investigation just because we're friends.' Which was 100 per cent true.

'So you don't know anything? Really?'

I shrugged and hoped she'd take it as a no. 'What about you? Did he ask you and your grandfather anything?'

'Sure. Whether anyone had a grudge against Mom or was there anything unusual going on right before she died.'

'And?'

'Plenty of people were upset at the Don't Pave Paradise Coalition, you know that. Mom had been gathering information for the maps of the unpaved roads, plus spending a lot of time at the Balch Library researching the history for the petition to the National Trust for Historic Preservation.' She paused, her eyes playing back and forth between the photo montage and me.

'What else?' I asked. Because there *was* something. She'd told Bobby. I hoped she'd tell me, too.

She sighed, resigned. 'She was involved in a lawsuit – or starting to get involved.'

'What lawsuit? Someone was suing her?'

'I have no idea. And, no, it was the other way around. She was the one who was going to court. She let it slip, then she got upset and told me to forget she'd mentioned it. She didn't want anyone knowing about it until she was ready.'

'You don't know what "it" was or how near she was to being "ready."' A statement, not a question.

'No and no.'

'She must have left *something* behind. You don't just conjure a lawsuit out of thin air. Maybe she talked to someone – like Sam Constantine?'

'Nope. Sam didn't know about it, either. As for documents – if there were any, I don't know where she kept them.'

A secret lawsuit. Great, just great.

'Frankie gave me Paul's briefcase with all the information about the petition for the National Trust for Historic Preservation – it looks like some of the papers were your mother's and the rest were Paul's. My brothers are helping out. Eli is working on drawing the maps as he promised and David took some amazing photos, which I saw the other day. I'm going to take care of the paperwork. But I didn't find anything that even hinted at a lawsuit among those papers,' I said.

Although I did find a photo of Eleanor Blake and the article about the Hollywood Theatre fire. Chiara didn't seem to be aware of either of those items.

Was Violet going to court to get the Blakes to reveal information about what really happened to Eleanor? Or maybe to find out whether Wyatt was really Lorenzo and Eleanor's son?

'You're taking over from Mom and Paul? That's fantastic.' She smiled and her voice went up an octave. A few heads turned toward us, curious prying eyes and ears.

I put my finger over my lips and shushed her. 'I'm not exactly taking over. And I'm trying to keep it quiet, at least for now.'

'Sorry. Look, I'll help you.'

'That would be great. Thanks. And if you come across anything about the lawsuit . . .'

'Sure. I gotta go, but I'll see you tomorrow at the funeral.'

'You're leaving now?'

Her cheeks turned pink. 'I'm getting picked up. I'm going to be late. See you, Lucie.'

Of course. Hunter Blake. Still keeping their relationship under the radar.

She left and I stared at Paul's montage, watching the photos flash by for the third time.

What if Violet was going to court to get the documents to prove whether Wyatt Blake was really Redmond's son? What would that mean? Redmond died without a will. His estate – and the family business – had gone to his next of kin as Sam had explained to me. What if Wyatt *wasn't* Redmond's next of kin, and that secret had been covered up all these years?

Would keeping it quiet be worth killing for? Once? Twice?

And who would be most interested in keeping that information from getting out?

None other than Nash Blake.

Whose son was Hunter Blake. Who was involved with Chiara Rossi. Of course Chiara was going to be loyal to her mother, but what if I was right and Violet's lawsuit involved something damaging to her boyfriend and his family? Then what?

Then where would her allegiance lie?

I was still thinking about Chiara when I turned to leave and bumped into Lily Merchant. Literally. 'Lily. I'm so sorry, sweetie. I wasn't paying attention. I didn't see you.'

If Yale was the portrait of Paul, the blonde, fragile, angelic-looking Lily was a younger version of Frankie. Dressed in a black minidress that hugged her slender body, eyes big and red-rimmed, a telltale sign she had been fighting tears. I pulled her into a hug.

'What do you need?' I asked. 'What can I do?'

'Nothing.' Her arms went around me in a stranglehold and her voice wavered. 'Thanks, Lucie. Everybody's being so kind. So many people are here. We're all so . . . grateful.'

'Your dad touched the lives of everyone who met him. That's why we're all here. For you and Yale and your mom.'

She stepped back and fished a crumpled tissue out of her pocket. 'There are people I haven't seen in ages,' she said, wiping her eyes. 'Zoey Ainsworth came – it was so kind of her. I wasn't expecting to see her. It's been so many years.'

I froze. 'Did you say you hadn't seen Zoey in . . . years?'

'Not since I stopped taking riding lessons before I left for college.' She stared at me. 'Is something wrong?'

'Do you know if she's still here?'

'I don't. Why?'

'She was the nurse who was taking care of one of the vineyard workers that fell and ended up in the hospital. I wanted to ask her how he's doing.'

Even though he left Lansdowne Hospital a few days ago.

Lily's face cleared. 'Oh, well, I just saw her downstairs. You might be able to catch her. Although I think Father Joe is going to say some prayers for Dad in a few minutes. Are you coming?'

'I'll be right there,' I said. 'I just need to do something.'

When Quinn and I were visiting Benny the other day, Zoey had mentioned that Paul died of an overdose of lorazepam. When I asked her how she knew that, she said Lily had told her.

And just now Lily said she hadn't seen or spoken to Zoey for years. Until tonight.

There could be only one way Zoey Ainsworth – a skilled nurse who had access to prescription medications – was aware of the drug that Paul had overdosed on.

Because she had been at the Merchants' home that afternoon and had slipped it in Paul's drink herself.

TWENTY

I found Zoey downstairs heading for the coat room.

'Leaving?' I asked.

She turned around and nodded. 'I've got the early shift at work so I won't be able to go to the funeral.'

'It was nice you were able to come to the wake. And I . . .' I stopped talking and put my hand over my mouth and began coughing.

'Lucie? Are you OK?'

I shook my head and doubled over, still coughing. 'Water? Please?'

'Um . . . sure. Give me a minute.'

I was still coughing when she returned and leaned down to hand me a plastic cup.

'Here.' She placed her hand on my back. 'Drink it slowly. Take some sips. You don't want to choke.'

I took the cup and sipped and my cough subsided. 'Thank you for the water. I'm OK now. I don't know what happened. I think I just swallowed the wrong way.'

She reached for her coat. 'It happens,' she said. 'Finish the water, but slowly. Do you need me to stay with you?'

'I'm fine. You take off. Thank you again.'

After she was gone, I held the cup by its lip, taking care not to touch it anywhere she had touched. Bobby said he and Kit were coming to Paul's wake tonight, but so far I hadn't seen him.

I set the cup on the windowsill and pulled out my phone.

When he answered I said, 'Where are you right now?'

'This second? The parking lot at BJ's. Why?'

'I have something for you. Can I meet you there? I'm inside.'

'What is it?'

'Zoey Ainsworth's fingerprints.'

'I'll wait for you,' he said and disconnected.

Kit was with him when I handed over the cup, so I told both

of them what had just happened as we stood in the shadows on the front porch of the funeral home, speaking in urgent whispers.

'I bet her fingerprints are going to match the ones you have on the glass shard I found at the Merchants' home. You said whoever they belonged to wasn't in your database. What are the odds that she's one of the people whose fingerprints you don't have on file?'

Kit was stunned. 'Zoey? She's such a sweet girl. Why her? You really think she killed Paul? It doesn't make sense.'

'It makes complete sense. I think Paul and Violet found out something that would seriously damage Blake Construction and harm Nash, Zoey's fiancé. Dallas took care of Violet. Zoey took care of Paul. They wanted to protect Blake Construction since they both have personal and financial interests in seeing that nothing adverse happens to that company.'

'Hold your horses,' Bobby said. 'I've seen a lot of investigations go off the rails because someone gets a preconceived notion about what happened and then everyone stops looking at any other possibility. I'll get this cup checked for her prints and have the lab compare them with the ones we found on that piece of glass. They might match. Or they might not.'

'They're going to match,' I said. 'You know it and I know it.'

'I've got an evidence bag in the trunk of my car. Let me put this where it won't get further contaminated.'

Kit held out her hand to her husband. 'Give me the keys. I'll get it. You keep talking to Lucie.'

'I'm done. I've told you everything,' I said. 'Don't you want to get this checked out tonight? You could have answers before Paul's funeral, give Frankie some closure.'

He looked at Kit. 'Change of plans. Let's go over to the criminal investigation unit and see who's working the late shift at the forensics lab.'

Kit nodded. 'I'll call the babysitter and tell her we might be later than we expected to be.'

'Besides,' I said, 'everyone's talking about the Sheriff's Office reopening the investigation into Violet's death. You're going to get bombarded by people who want to know what you found out as soon as you walk through the front door. Also, Frankie told me she plans to buttonhole you as soon as she lays eyes on you and ask you to reconsider Paul's case.'

'Then I guess she won't mind if we don't pay our respects tonight,' Bobby said.

'If your reason is that you've got new evidence that may lead you to find out who really killed Paul, she'd be the first one to tell you to go,' I said.

'In that case,' he said, 'we're outta here.'

Not one peep from Bobby on Tuesday morning, the day of Paul Merchant's funeral. Could I have been so completely wrong or myopic, as he'd implied, that I falsely accused someone of murder when, in fact, she was innocent?

Quinn and I were in our bedroom getting dressed when Nikki called at nine thirty. I was fixing the knot in his black and charcoal gray striped tie when my phone rang on the bedside table. He picked it up and handed it to me.

'Lucie,' Nikki said, 'a florist just dropped off two huge floral arrangements here instead of St Mike's. I tried to tell him to take them to the church but he said his instructions were to bring them here. What should we do? One of them has two ribbons with "Uncle" and "Brother" on it.'

'Those must be from one of Paul's brothers or his sister. They should be at the church. We can drive them over before the Mass starts,' I said. 'I'm sure Frankie would prefer to have all the flowers with Paul's casket rather than here for the lunch, especially an arrangement that came from family.'

'If I lay the seats down, I can fit them in the back of my SUV,' she said. 'I can run them over right now before everyone gets there.'

'Why don't you swing by the house and I'll go with you?' I said. 'Quinn can join me at the church later.'

'Give me ten minutes to load up my car. I'll drop you and the flowers off and then I need to get back here right away. Dominique's staff are bringing the food over at eleven so we'll be set up and ready when folks get here after the service – I'm figuring that would be around twelve or twelve fifteen.'

'Great,' I said. 'See you in ten minutes.'

* * *

The floral arrangements that had been dropped off at the vine-yard by mistake were beautiful and, as Nikki said, filled up the back of her SUV: an enormous spray of gladiolas and lilies in the shape of a cross with two white ribbons draped across them and a large vase filled with two dozen white roses with variegated ivy wound through them. When we pulled up to the entrance to St Michael the Archangel, the hearse from the funeral home was already there. Two black limousines were parked nearby in the parking lot.

I got out of the car and walked over to one of the dark-suited men who was standing next to the hearse. I tried to surreptitiously peer in a side window.

'Where is . . .?'

'The casket is already in the bell tower,' he said. 'Mrs Merchant, the children, and their family members are in the narthex to greet anyone who wasn't able to come to the wake last night and wants to pay their respects before Mass starts.'

'Thank you. Two floral arrangements were sent by accident to where the luncheon is taking place. We brought them here. They're quite large.'

'I'll find the funeral director,' he said. 'Thank you for doing that. We'll take care of setting them up next to the casket.'

One of the main doors to the church opened and Bobby Noland walked out looking grim.

'What are you doing here so early?' I asked. 'Did you find out . . .?'

He came over and took my elbow, steering me away from the hearse so we were standing by ourselves. 'I just spoke to Frankie,' he said. 'Zoey Ainsworth is in custody and she's being charged with the death of Paul Merchant. She broke down and admitted what happened. You were right.'

The breath went out of me for a moment. When I could speak, I said, 'Dallas?'

'Zoey will get a lesser sentence if she cooperates. I think she's ready to talk about her father as well. One of my colleagues is interviewing her now.'

'How did Frankie take the news?'

'She's pretty emotional. Paul's brother brought her into the bride's room where she can have some privacy.'

'I need to talk to her. This has got to be incredibly tough.'

'Lucie?' Nikki stood next to Bobby and me. 'The people from the funeral home took the flowers inside. I'd better go.'

'Great, thanks.'

Nikki's eyes traveled between Bobby and me. 'I couldn't help overhearing,' she said. 'Did you say Zoey Ainsworth was arrested and that she had something to do with Paul's death?'

'That's right,' Bobby said.

'That's weird. Her father came by the winery yesterday. I didn't see him in the tasting room, but I wasn't there all the time. I did notice him in the parking lot.'

I felt the blood leave my face. 'You saw Dallas Ainsworth in our parking lot yesterday?'

'Yes,' she said and now she looked alarmed. 'I just said that. Why? What's wrong?'

'When?' Bobby asked and I knew his mind was racing along the same path mine was.

'Late afternoon.'

Quinn and I had taken the pickup to the wake last night. I'd left the Jeep in the winery parking lot while I was in the tasting room going over arrangements for Paul's luncheon with Dominique and Nikki.

And I'd never seen Dallas.

My heart pounded like war drums. 'Bobby, Quinn's taking the Jeep to get gas in Middleburg before he drives over here. It was down to about an eighth of a tank.'

'Call him,' he said, but I had already pulled out my phone and was frantically punching his name until the display said *Calling Quinn*.

He answered and I said, 'Are you driving yet? Are you in the Jeep?'

'Yes, why?'

'Where are you?'

'I just turned off Atoka Road. I'm on Fifty, going to get gas at the Exxon in Middleburg like we agreed. Lucie, what's going on?'

Heading into town.

My voice cracked. 'Sweetheart, Nikki saw Dallas in the winery parking lot yesterday. You remember I left the Jeep there for the afternoon? Stop the car. Dallas might have . . . done something to it.'

Silence and then he said in a tight, grim voice, 'Too late. The car just started accelerating and I don't have any brakes. They're gone.'

'Quinn, it's Bobby. Can you turn the wheel at least?'

'No.' He sounded as if what was happening was rapidly dawning on him.

'Can you . . . open your door and get out?' Me, trying not to sound panicked. Or desperate. Leaping from a swiftly moving car was already fraught with danger. Asking him to do that . . .

'It's locked,' he said and my heart stopped.

Bobby swore. 'Let's go. Come on. Keep him on the phone.'

We were going to be too late. I knew it. Bobby knew it. I'm sure Quinn knew it, too.

'We're coming,' I told him. 'We'll be right there, my love.'

I climbed into the passenger seat of Bobby's car as we heard his scream and the airbag exploding followed by the grinding of metal on metal.

'Quinn. Quinn. Talk to me. *Please.*'

Nothing but haunting silence.

TWENTY-ONE

The firefighters who arrived as Bobby and I got there were able to extricate Quinn from the Jeep without using the Jaws of Life. He was unconscious and bleeding but at least he squeezed my hand when I leaned down and told him I loved him as they were loading his gurney into the ambulance. Bobby and I followed as it raced to Lansdowne Hospital though I don't remember much about that trip except the slow drip of dread that ratcheted up my panic and the urgent wail of emergency sirens and bleating horns that drowned out all other noise.

Never two deaths without three, Thelma had said, and she'd almost been right. The third death was supposed to be me. Dallas expected me, not Quinn, to be driving the Jeep, which he admitted when Bobby interrogated him after he was brought in and charged with the murder of Violet Rossi and the attempted murder of Quinn Santori.

Quinn's injuries were serious but not life threatening – almost every rib broken or cracked, a partially deflated lung, a fractured tibia, a concussion, a lot of bruising. I slept in the recliner next to his bed the first night after the surgeons worked on him for hours and intended to stay full time until he was well enough to be moved out of intensive care. Frankie, pale and subdued, came by the next day and told me about the funeral as well as thanking me for the vineyard luncheon – all of which seemed like ancient history. Eli, Sasha, Mia, David, Persia, and everyone from the vineyard staff also stopped by, each one offering to take turns being with Quinn so I could go home and get some sleep, a meal, a change of clothes, for however long it took.

Bobby showed up with Kit that evening, bringing a pot of bright yellow autumn mums and news. Both Dallas and Zoey were in jail awaiting bail hearings. Nash, of course, had hired the best Washington lawyers that money could buy.

'I doubt the judge is going to grant either of them bail under the circumstances,' Bobby said. 'And all of Nash's money and his reputation for philanthropy isn't going to cut any ice, either.'

'Did Nash have anything to do with what happened?' I asked. 'Did he give orders . . . was he aware . . .?'

'He says no. He swears Dallas and Zoey acted on their own without telling him anything.'

'His *fiancée*?' Quinn said, his voice still weak and thready after the surgery. 'Are you serious? He knew nothing?'

I picked up the cup of water from his bedside table and held the straw to his lips. He took a few sips and laid back against the pillows. He winced and briefly closed his eyes. For the five hundredth time I thanked God and anything or anyone else I could think of that he had survived that crash, getting off as lightly as he did. The Jeep looked like one of the worst wrecks David and I had seen at the Sheriff's Office depot only a few days ago.

'How could Nash not have wondered, after Violet died when her car went off the road and Paul drowned in his own swimming pool a few weeks later, whether their deaths might be related?' I said. 'The two people responsible for the Don't Pave Paradise Coalition who were directly opposed to the Pro-Loudoun Progressives – and that's his organization. Did he think they were a couple of unfortunate – or fortunate, in his case – coincidences?'

'I'm telling you. He lawyered up and he says no to everything or else he pleads the fifth,' Bobby said. 'Right now there's nothing we can charge him with. He's not an accomplice, didn't pay anyone, didn't do anything. But the stories in the news . . . Blake Construction is taking a massive financial hit because Nash's partner and his fiancée – father and daughter, no less – are charged with the murders of two individuals involved in a campaign that directly affected his business. I don't know if he'll ever recover from that. Stock in his company has tanked. It's down seventy-five per cent since yesterday.'

'Did you find out anything about Violet's lawsuit?' I asked.

'Oh, yes, indeed.' He nodded.

'Well?' I asked when he didn't elaborate.

'It's how she was blackmailing Nash.'

Kit's eyes met mine. 'He's enjoying dragging this out,' she said. 'The drama. He did the same thing to me. Sweetheart, just tell them.'

'Please,' I said.

'OK. Sorry. Violet found some documents among her family's papers that proved Wyatt was the son of Eleanor Blake . . .'

'And Lorenzo Rossi.' I finished his sentence.

'You *knew*?' He threw me an astonished look and then his eyes narrowed. '*How* did you know?'

'Lucky guess. But also, Thelma Johnson keeps a book of death announcements that goes back to before World War Two. I saw a photo of Eleanor and Lorenzo. You could tell by the way they looked at each other that they were crazy in love,' I said. 'How did Dallas find out about them? Nash told him? Or Violet?'

Bobby's face cleared when I mentioned Thelma's name. 'I should have guessed Thelma would be involved. As for how Dallas found out, we're still not sure about that. However it happened, he did know and decided to stop Violet before she could do any damage.'

'I don't get it. Why kill Violet because she found out Nash's grandmother had an affair with Lorenzo Rossi?' Quinn said.

'Because Redmond died without a will,' Bobby said. 'Which meant his estate went to his next of kin, who should have been Wyatt, his only child. Then Violet found documents proving Redmond wasn't Wyatt's biological father – Lorenzo was. So, she decided to file a lawsuit divesting Wyatt – and Nash – from ownership of Blake Construction, claiming neither of them were legitimate heirs. And if they *were* heirs, to prove it by producing Wyatt's birth certificate.'

'Which would stop Nash – or Blake Construction – from buying Grayson Vaughn's land and building hundreds of houses on it,' I said. 'That's brilliant.'

'It wouldn't be as simple as that,' Bobby said, 'but Violet was desperate to stop Nash and the lawsuit was one more way to tie things up for a while. Not to mention the negative publicity. Just the threat of what she planned to do was enough to get Nash to withdraw his offer of buying Grayson's land. Although as soon as Violet died, Nash went to Grayson and asked him to reconsider about selling. You know the rest.'

'But why kill Paul?' Quinn asked. 'What did he do? And why Zoey?'

'The day Paul died, he had a meeting in D.C. with Nash. He let Nash know that Violet had filled him in on everything and he intended to continue pursuing the lawsuit. Nash was furious and told him to back off.'

'Paul told Frankie about that meeting,' I said. 'And then she told me. What Paul didn't tell Frankie was anything to do with the lawsuit.'

'How did Zoey get involved?' Quinn asked again.

'Nash called her and vented as she was leaving work at Lansdowne Hospital. She decided to go over to the Merchants' home and see if she could get Paul to see reason since she knew him from the days when she was Lily Merchant's riding instructor. Zoey claims that drugging Paul's drink was never her plan – it just happened when she saw the pills in the kitchen after he told her he wasn't backing down. She was frustrated. Upset. But nothing she did was premeditated, so she claims it wasn't first-degree murder.'

'Do you believe her?' Quinn asked.

'What matters is whether a jury believes her. This is going to trial.'

'I wonder how – or if – Wyatt knows about Lorenzo. Or Nash does. You'd think that skeleton wouldn't stay in the family closet too long.'

'That,' Bobby said, 'remains another mystery we've yet to solve.'

It was Chiara Rossi and Hunter Blake who solved it. The two of them showed up not long after Bobby and Kit left, their under-the-radar romance obviously no longer a secret. The way they looked at each other, that expression of unmistakable love and longing, reminded me of the photo of Eleanor and Lorenzo.

'We came by so I could say thank you,' Chiara said. 'Bobby Noland told my grandfather and me what you did, Lucie. I'm so grateful.' Her eyes strayed to Quinn. 'Except I wish Dallas had been caught sooner after what he did to my mother's car. I'm sorry about what happened to you.'

'It's not your fault,' Quinn said. 'You didn't know. No one did.'

'On the subject of knowing things,' I said to Hunter, 'did your father and grandfather know about the affair between your great-grandmother and Chiara's great-uncle?'

By this time, I figured no subject was too touchy, too personal, too off-limits. Besides, I wanted to know.

He nodded.

'Do you mind saying how they found out?'

'It was the skiing accident that killed my great-grandfather. He, my grandfather, and my dad were skiing in Colorado one year. I was at vet school so I wasn't with them,' he said. 'Redmond – my great-grandfather – lost control of his skis and plowed into a stand of trees when the three of them were skiing off piste. When they got to the hospital – it was just a small rural hospital, not much more than a clinic – my father over-heard one of the techs telling a nurse that neither my grandfather nor my father could be donors for a transfusion since neither one had blood that was compatible with Redmond's. He was type A. My grandfather was B and so was my dad.'

'I don't understand,' I said.

'Wyatt, my grandfather, had papers belonging to Eleanor, his mother, including some medical documents, so he'd found out her blood was type O. If Redmond was A and Eleanor was O, there was no way he could be type B. He figured out then that his biological father was either type B or else AB. But *not* A. So not Redmond.'

'Did Redmond know your grandfather realized they weren't biologically related?' I asked.

'I don't know. He died a couple of days later and my dad and my grandfather decided to keep what they'd learned a secret because my great-grandfather also died without leaving a will, which meant everything was supposed to pass to his next of kin, and my grandfather technically wasn't the next of kin,' he said. 'It wasn't supposed to make any difference. Who would care?'

'Eleanor's family would care,' I said and he nodded, surprised and unhappy. 'She financed Blake Construction when it was just getting started.'

'Their family lawyer has already been in touch.' He looked away. 'There's something else.'

The elephant in the room. 'You mean the fire and Eleanor's death?'

'You know about that, too?' Now he looked me right in the eye.

'Just what I read in a newspaper account that was among Paul and Violet's maps and notes about the unpaved roads. Does anybody know how she died or what happened?'

'Her family thought – still thinks – Redmond had something to do with it and that he was angry because of her affair. That he was somehow responsible for the fire and her death.'

'Was he?'

'You tell me. I have no idea.'

If he didn't know – and I believed him – then no one knew. For sure.

'Maybe you have a suspicion?'

He folded his arms across his chest. 'A suspicion is just that. It doesn't count or matter.'

'Fair enough.'

We were done.

After they left, I went over and sat on the edge of Quinn's bed. 'I have something for you.' I picked up his left hand, which was ringless since the hospital staff had given me all his personal items to take home for safekeeping before his surgery.

'What is it?'

I slipped something out of my pocket and opened my palm so he could see what it was. 'This.'

'My wedding ring. Where . . . wait, did you . . . move the Cab Sauv out of the tank already? Lucie, it's too early . . .'

I smiled. 'Nothing like that. Antonio found your ring. It didn't fall into the tank. You were mistaken. It landed on the floor next to it. He spotted it and gave it to me when he was here earlier.'

I took his hand and slid his wedding ring on his finger. 'Will you marry me all over again?'

He cupped my face with his hands. 'You know I will. As soon as I get out of here and it doesn't hurt like hell every time I take a breath, I'll prove how much I love you.' He lifted up his sheet. 'Lie down with me.'

'You have so many tubes and wires . . .'

'It's OK.'

I slipped into bed with him. 'We're going to scandalize the hospital staff if anyone comes in and finds us like this.'

'That's OK, too. We'll just tell whoever it is that it's part of my therapy to get well faster.'

'I like that.'

He pulled me closer and kissed me. 'So do I.'

Acknowledgements

The idea for *Deeds Left Undone* came from a February 7, 2024 front-page article in *The Washington Post* entitled 'A Radical Plan to Save a Rural Oasis: Don't Pave the Roads.' The idea to have many of the rural roads in Loudoun County, Virginia, listed on the National Register of Historic Places is based on a real plan; it is also highly controversial. The Hollywood Theatre in Middleburg was a real place and no longer exists – although several fires gutted the building over the years, there were no fatalities. As for everything else that happened in this book: I made it up and no one, fortunately, has been murdered over the pave-versus-don't-pave debate, contentious though it may be.

As usual, there are a lot of people to thank for the help, information, and time they shared with me. Also, as usual, if it's right, they said it. If it's wrong, it's on me.

Thank you to Phyllis Hermann who sat me down and talked me through some early plot problems during our getaway week in the Abacos in March 2024 and to her and Dick Hermann for being there for me during a difficult and challenging year when I wondered if I would ever manage to finish this book. Lois Tuohy invited me to the Middleburg Hunt's point-to-point, Twilight Jumpers, and as her guest at the Whitestone Farm cattle auction where she made sure I talked to everyone I needed to meet about the issue of keeping some of Loudoun County's beautiful country roads unpaved. Thanks to Mark Duffell, General Manager at Whitestone Farm in Aldie, Virginia, for the invitation to the auction; I imagined Serenità Farm to look a lot like his magnificent farm. Among the people Lois introduced me to on our many outings were Cynthia Plante, as well as Kim Hurst and Mary Lawlor at the point-to-point and John and Penny Denegre at the cattle auction and at Twilight Jumpers. Penny is a Master of the Middleburg Hunt; John told me about roads being incorrectly being named for horses that race on flats in a region where steeplechasing is dominant. As Lois said to me one spring evening when we were driving out to Great Meadow along a peaceful, serene country road for a tailgate and to watch Twilight Jumpers, 'This region is so beautiful; how could anyone not fall in love with it?'

Rick Tagg – winemaker at Delaplane Cellars in Delaplane, Virginia, and my dear friend and advisor for this series for many years – gave me a terrific vineyard tour and an updated education on Winemaking 101, 2024 Version, as a lot has changed since I first started writing this series more than twenty years ago. Kiernan Slater Patusky and Chris Patusky, husband and wife owners of Slater Run Vineyards in Upperville, Virginia, helped a lot with the story and discussed the complicated politics of paved versus unpaved roads in Loudoun County. Thanks especially to Chris for suggesting I check out Crenshaw Road past First Bridge as a good place for an 'accident' to take place, since it ran right alongside Goose Creek.

Thanks to Dorsey deButts of the Middleburg Museum for making me aware of the existence of the Hollywood Theatre in Middleburg (I had no idea), and to Alexandra Gressitt and Anna Carneal of the Balch Historical Library in Leesburg, Virginia, for pointing me to archives with information on the actual fire(s) that took place at that theater.

Jennifer Crane, Esquire gave me legal help on inheritance laws. MPO Jim Smith of the Fairfax County (Virginia) Police Department helped as usual with my questions relating to police matters and investigating a murder. Lucien Burgert called from Paris to explain how a car could be controlled remotely. George Bosse III explained the procedure a funeral home follows when there is an issue with the medical examiner's investigation. Peter de Nesnera, Rosemarie Forsythe, and Cathy Brannon were valuable sounding boards and offered advice on plot problems. Dr Alex de Nesnera explained blood types and genetics. Dr Wanda Pool, DVM, April Arnold, and Luci Zahray offered advice and information on poisons for an early version of the plot that I ended up revising when I couldn't make it work. Finally, my gratitude to The Russler (therusslertripod.com), a website that lists many hilarious malapropisms that helped me with Thelma's fractured vocabulary.

Thanks and love to my editor, Rachel Slatter at Severn House, for wining and dining me in both Nashville and London last year and for her many compassionate extensions on my deadline. Also at Severn House, thanks to Nick May for designing the gorgeous cover, Claire Ritchie for a terrific job of copyediting and catching numerous errors, and Martin Brown, Senior Brand Manager, and Tina Pietron, Assistant Editor, for everything they do to make this book so much better. Even more thanks and love to Dominick Abel, my agent for nearly twenty years, who called and checked on me almost weekly to make sure I was doing OK.

Last year – 2024 – was a hard Year of Firsts after André de Nesnera, my wonderful and amazing husband of forty-one years, passed away on Christmas Day 2023 from complications of Parkinson's Disease and long-term Guillain-Barré Syndrome. There were plenty of days when I wondered if I could sit down and concentrate on writing, so a special thanks to everyone at the Fox Mill Starbucks in Herndon, Virginia for letting me hang out for hours – and hours – to nurse a cup of tea and get some work done.

I often get asked which of my books is my favorite, and my response up until now has been that it's like asking which of my children is my favorite. But in *Deeds Left Undone*, I think I left a lot of my heart in these pages. And so maybe this book is truly my favorite.